MANSTEALING
FOR FAT GIRLS
Michelle Embree

SOFT SKULL PRESS

© 2005 by Michelle Embree

First Edition

Cover Illustration: Christa Donner
Book Design: Alexandria Escamilla

Distributed by Publishers Group West
1-800-788-3123
www.pgw.com

Published by Soft Skull Press
55 Washington Street, Suite 804
Brooklyn, NY 11202
www.softskull.com

Printed in Canada

Library of Congress Cataloging-in-Publication Data

Embree, Michelle.
   Manstealing for fat girls / Michelle Embree.
      p. cm.
   ISBN 1-933368-02-0 (alk. paper)
   1. Teenage girls—Fiction. 2. Overweight persons—Fiction. I. Title.

PS3606.M47M36 2005
813'.6—dc22

2005012966

This book is dedicated to Carole Embree for everything, everything, and everything.

CHAPTER 1

"What do you think you're doing?" My mom stood in the doorway of her bedroom.

"I have a zit, I wanted to cover it up." I tried to look innocent.

"Oh, no you don't. No make up. Get to school."

She left and I dabbed at the zit with her concealer.

Mom got up with me everyday. Even though she didn't have to be at work until eleven and I was sixteen, she still did it. She made my lunches too. Lunches I rarely ate, anymore. Not that I told her that.

"Angie, take an umbrella. It's going to rain." She slid a peanut butter sandwich into a brown paper bag.

"I'm not carrying a big, stupid, green umbrella, Mom." I could swear, she didn't know anything.

"Fine, be stubborn." She stuck the lunch bag in my hand.

"Hey, Mom, I'm gonna go over to Shelby's tonight. I'll be home late, okay?"

"No. Not tonight. Rudy is coming for dinner. I want us all to eat together."

"Why? That guy is an asshole," I said.

"All children hate their mother's boyfriends," she said, mostly to herself.

"That can't be true, Mom."

"And don't say asshole, Angie."

Of course, she was right about the rain. Halfway to school it started to literally dump. I dunked under the awning over the auto parts store. It wasn't really a canvas awning, just a roof made to look like a canvas awning.

I don't know why I bothered trying to wait the rain out. I was already soaking wet.

"Whattya' doin' just standing around?" Shelby asked, rolling up the passenger window of her mother's car. I gratefully jumped into the backseat.

"Why don't you take the bus when it rains, Angie?" Shelby's mother looked at me in the rearview mirror. She was more annoyed than curious. And with her perfect make up and sculpted red hair, she was the kind of mom that looked most natural when she was annoyed.

"I forgot my umbrella," I lied.

Everybody hated the bus, but I really hated it. In seventh grade Mike Forester leaned over the bus seat in front of me, put a fake microphone up to my lips: So, what's it's like being a lesbian pig? he asked. I didn't want to cry but the tears came anyway. Everyone laughed. I mean everyone. Sweat exploded over my body and all I wanted was death. Just death.

"What did you bring for lunch?" Shelby asked.

"Peanut butter."

"You girls should eat some hot food today," Shelby's mom said, using one perfectly manicured hand to dig some bills out of her purse.

"Thanks, Mom." Shelby took the money and gave me a smile. We would use it to buy cokes or candy bars or play skee ball after school. We definitely would not use it to eat lunch. Neither of us ever went very far into the cafeteria, even when we had the same lunch period.

We ate on the edge of the room. We would sneak just inside the door and take a seat at the table with the kids from remedial everything. The kids who were either functionally retarded or on the verge of climbing a clock tower and picking people off at random.

There should be a horror movie called *Cafeteria*. A hundred teenagers trapped inside with nothing to do. And when the popular kids get tired of being so wonderful and pretty and cool, they start slowly killing the rejects by eating little slices of them. Little raw slices, with sides of powdered mash potatoes and canned green beans.

"Mom, just let us out here," Shelby said as we pulled into the big parking lot.

"Don't be silly. It's pouring rain, Shelby," her mother said.

"C'mon, Mom, just let us out."

"What is wrong with you? You ashamed of me or something?"

"No." Shelby's breath made a hazy spot on the window. If only that had been the problem.

"Good morning, lesbos!" Curtis Alroy threw his hands out to Shelby and me as we got out of the car. There were a couple of snort sounds from the crowd and Shelby slammed the car shut as her mother tried to see who said the lesbo thing. You can try to spare a mother knowledge of how horrible your life is, but they still insist on being a witness.

The first bell rang. We had one minute to get to art class.

"C'mon," Shelby said. Her flannel shirt and hair were damp from the rain, but everything else about her was dry. I wanted to scream. To scream at everyone, including Shelby. Shelby who had to go be a lesbian and make every stupid thing in my life even more difficult.

Shelby threw her flannel shirt over the back of her chair. Her lips pursed, and her eyes went that deep jade they turned when she got upset. She hated her mom knowing that everyone teased her, especially since she figured her mom was just waiting for that shoe to drop—the gay shoe that is—anyway. God, how could I ever want to scream at Shelby? I very nearly asked her why the hell she was my friend, but changed my mind.

Once Shelby sat down I said, "You know flannel is toxic when it's wet, right?"

"What?"

"Yeah. It, like, turns nuclear. That's what they used in Hiroshima. I'm serious."

"Flannel?"

"Yeah, they loaded up all those missiles with wet lesbians and then KABOOM!"

"Shut the fuck up." Shelby smiled. And most of the time that was all I truly cared about.

The whole lesbian thing started back in grade school. Back when Shelby first got her little-boy haircut. She showed up for school and everyone started in immediately. Started calling her a dyke and a lesbo and a tuna hound and anything else they could come up with.

Everyone has hair like this on the coast, Shelby explained to me. It just takes forever for St. Louis to get with the times. You watch, everyone will be doing this soon enough.

Of course, that never happened. The bob came into fashion but that was as short as any of the girls ever went. Shoulder length. And then there was Shelby with her virtual crew cut. Since I was her best friend, I caught shit for it too. Which didn't help at all considering the rate at which I was gaining weight.

Shelby never did let her hair grow much past her ears. She kept it cropped and spiked it up with mousse that her mom sold in her beauty supply store. It looked real cool, but everyone teased her about it anyway. People begin in hell. This is one thing of which I am certain.

I got through that day the way I got through every other day of school: braced. Braced for anything, absolutely anything. An insult, a million insults. Maybe Curtis Alroy would grab me and drag me into a bathroom where Mike Forester and Troy Mulligan would pull my clothes off, laugh at me. They could even fuck me. Fucking a pig isn't so bad! Shelby says my imagination is over-active. But only when it comes to very bad things happening to me.

When the last bell of the day rang I met Shelby in the same place I always did, by the sad little tree on back campus. She was watching a couple people knock a tennis ball around the court.

"Isn't there a tennis court at Covington?" She asked without turning to see who I was.

"I don't know if it can be called a tennis court anymore."

"Why?"

"Hasn't had a net for years, and the ground is coming up out of the court in a couple of places. Oh, and somebody spray painted big pot leaves and OZZY all over it."

We walked along the wide road that served as a midway between strings of strip malls and fast food restaurants.

"Let's get some sodas with the money my mom gave me," Shelby said, putting the dollars in my hand. We swerved toward the liquor store next to the karate shop everyone was always breaking into.

Inez Oliver was outside the liquor store, leaning into a pay phone, talking with her hands.

"I'm not having your rape baby, DAD! You either give me the money for an abortion or I'm gonna have you KILLED!"

Shelby and I shot each other a look.

"Hey you, guys!" Inez hung the phone up immediately when she saw us. There was never anyone on the other end. Inez Oliver used your standard payphone to make artistic statements.

Shelby and I knew Inez from the lunch table, where she fit into the most-likely-to-start-picking-people-off-at-random category.

"What's up, Inez?" Shelby asked.

"Oh, I was just . . ." Inez noticed a man walking out of the store. "I was just on the phone with my grandma, telling her I don't give a fuck HOW sick she is, there's NO WAY I'm gonna SHOOT her! Fuck that!"

"Yeah, fuck that," Shelby said, looking every bit of serious. The man walking by straightened a little but did not look our way.

"So what're you guys doin'?" Inez asked, shifting her weight from foot to foot.

"I'm gonna get us a couple of sodas," I said.

"Try and get some beer," Inez whisper-yelled.

"Hurry up," Shelby told me, and set about rearranging her book bag as if it were terribly important.

When I came out of the store, Shelby was alone.

"Where's Inez?" I asked.

"She got in that pickup over there." Shelby pointed. "Some guy. Rough lookin'. I guess he's got beer or pot or something."

I popped the top on my Coke. "You think she's a hooker?"

"I dunno. Like a beer whore?"

"It's possible." I shrugged.

"Yeah. I guess it is, isn't it?" Shelby looked after the pickup as it pulled out of the parking lot.

"Maybe she knows Karen Dryer," I said.

"Karen wasn't a hooker. That was just some nasty shit those assholes started."

"I know. It was just a joke," I defended.

Shelby shrugged at me and threw her backpack over her shoulder.

"God, I hope Robyn's not home," Shelby said.

"Is your mom home tonight?"

"No. She's at the shop until ten. I think Robyn is supposed to be there too, but she only works when she needs money."

Robyn was twenty-four and lived at home. Her only job was occasionally putting in some hours at her mother's beauty supply shop. Robyn was to be considered dangerous if not, in fact, armed.

"Wanna go to the 7-11 and play some pinball?" I asked.

"Sure."

The 7-11 had an Elvira pinball machine. It was pretty cool. Elvira would say these weird sexy things to you when you did something good like, Oh, that's how I like it or That's it, just like that. The board had a picture of Elvira leaning over and showing that amazing cleavage. Elvira was solely responsible for Shelby getting good at pinball. Even I had to admit, it was exciting to look at when all the lights went up.

We played pinball for a pretty long time on the money we had. But then these guys started to hassle us because they wanted the machine and it threw our games off enough that we ran out of balls and money. It was time to go anyway.

"So, you wanna check the Robyn situation or do something else?" Shelby asked.

"I can't hang out tonight. Rudy is coming over. I get to sit there and eat dinner with him."

"Is that the guy with the sleazy mustache?"

"Yep. That's Rudy. Mom seems pretty into him."

"Gross. He looks at me like he wants to be my pimp," Shelby said.

"He probably wants to pimp us both."

"Robyn has a new boyfriend too."

"Lives with his mom?"

"Worse. Doesn't live anywhere."

"Man, did Robyn take a class on how to pick a real winner? Or did that just come to her naturally?"

"Unlike her hair, I believe it's natural."

Robyn's hair had been a weird, unnatural blond for as long as I could remember. The first time I met her, she was thirteen and I was only five. Her hair was a sharp yellow with visibly dark roots, layered on each side and plastered with so much hairspray she looked like she had shutters.

She was in the passenger seat waiting for her mother to pay for some gas. Shelby and me were in the backseat. I couldn't take my eyes off

Robyn's profile. She seemed so grown up with her blue eye shadow and her bored expression.

"What are you lookin' at?" she turned around and asked me.

"What?"

"WHAT are you LOOKIN' at?" she demanded.

I started to cry.

When their mother got back to the car, she asked me what was wrong, but I just kept crying. Robyn flashed a grin, and told her Shelby pinched me. Shelby protested but I couldn't back her up. I couldn't say anything; I just sat there heaving and crying. Shelby got in trouble and I felt even worse.

I knew Rudy was already in mom's apartment when I got there. I could smell him. Not that he stank in any special way. It was the smell Aunt Jean called man grease. According to her, if you lived with a man you had to get used to not only his stench, but his oils too: You can't get man grease outta yer sheets. You can wash 'em a hundred times, stuff never comes out.

Aside from Rudy's man grease, the apartment also smelled heavily of sauerkraut. It's really no wonder I wound up as fat as I did. Mom only liked pork products. When I smelled the sauerkraut, I knew we'd be having polish sausage and potatoes. Probably a store-bought choco-late cake for dessert too. I took a deep breath.

"Hi, Angie. How are you?" Rudy talked to me like I was stupid.

"Fine." I said as little to him as possible.

"Don't you ever smile, girl?" He asked, sipping off a can of Busch beer.

I gave him a wide ridiculous grin and headed into the kitchen.

"Hi sweetie." Mom was wearing a tight red dress and her face was made up. She looked so pretty. Slender and just pretty.

"You didn't have to get dressed up for me," I teased.

"Funny. Go put on a nice shirt and wash your face, dinner is almost ready."

I felt heavy. I hated walking through any room Rudy was in. I avoided eye contact, but I could hear his head swivel to watch me. I changed out of my favorite Rolling Stones t-shirt with the big red mouth on it. I put on a man's button down shirt because Mom said it made me look thinner.

7

"Angie, baby, will you get three water glasses down and put ice in them. Oh, you look so nice. I think you've lost some more of your baby fat.

"Mom, it's not baby fat anymore," I said, reaching for the big glasses.

I sat at the card table that had functioned as a dining room table since we moved in. Rudy was already smiling sideways at me.

"Do you like surprises, Angie?" he asked. My guts seized up and I took a sip of Mom's always too-sweet tea.

"Not really." I searched my mother's face.

"Let's eat first." Mom smiled, waving away Rudy's impatience.

I kept my mouth shut while Rudy gave us a blow-by-blow account of his day at the Chrysler plant.

". . . well, he's a shit head. They always make the stupidest motherfucker they can find a supervisor. Nobody else would do all that work for the nothin' they pay."

"Did I meet him? Was he at the company picnic?"

"Yeah. That's right, wife's pregnant. You met the big dummy."

I pushed my plate away.

"Oh, now, you gotta eat more than that, Angie," Rudy said. His eyes scrutinized my plate. I looked at the food, then back to Rudy with a shrug.

"Yes, sweetie, I made plenty," mom said. Of course she made plenty. She always did. Mounds of bacon, piles of potatoes, buckets of mac n'cheese, not to mention the never-ending supply of freezer pies.

"I'm fine," I mumbled.

"Don't be silly." Rudy grabbed my plate and loaded it with pieces of sausage, potatoes and sauerkraut. It was a mountain of food I couldn't possibly eat. The plate smacked the table as he handed it back, little squiggly strands of sauerkraut slopped greasy over the side.

"Now, be a good girl and clean your plate. Your mother worked hard on this nice meal for us."

"Oh, no. This is the easiest thing to make. It was no trouble at all." Mom shook her head.

"Rita, a growing girl needs to eat, instead of actin' vain about how she looks."

I stared at the plate of food for a long minute. When I looked up at Rudy he was watching me, fork suspended over his own plate.

"Go on and eat." He waved the fork at me.

"What's the surprise?" I demanded of my mother.

"Let's wait for dessert, baby."

"No. What's the surprise? Tell me now."

"Well, Rudy and I have decided to get married."

"When?"

"In April."

I counted the months in my mind: five months of peace left. I took a deep breath and pushed my plate away, again.

"It'll take some getting used to, I know. But it will work out," Mom said.

"And besides." Rudy broke in. "Until then, I'm moving in here. So you won't have to change schools this year. I'm all packed. I'll start bringing my stuff over tomorrow. Then, over the summer, we'll find a big house to buy."

Five.

Four.

Three.

Two.

One.

Zero.

Peace was a thing of the past.

"You've always wanted to live in a house haven't you, Angie? You used to talk about it all the time when you were a little girl," Mom said.

I nodded slowly, going simultaneously numb and hateful. My mother was selling me out for a house slathered with man grease.

CHAPTER 2

The TV was blaring cartoons. Bacon was frying. I opened my eyes just a little. Rudy was out in the living room. A grown man watching Saturday morning cartoons and letting someone else's mother cook for him. My mother.

I didn't want to move. Getting out of bed meant facing the reality of Rudy as a permanent, beer-drinking, cartoon-watching, pork-eating, motherfucking fixture in my life.

I got dressed, took a deep breath and headed for the living room.

Rudy looked up at me. "I thought your lazy ass might sleep all day." He was sprawled in the recliner chair with a coffee mug in one hand and a remote control in the other.

"Good morning, sweetie. There's bacon and pancakes for breakfast, help yourself." Mom's face was made up like she was on her way to a party and her old green robe with the cigarette burns had been replaced with a cream colored little satin number. The bacon smelled so good. If I took one bite, I'd eat a pound of it. No eating for the day. I was going to fast.

"No, thanks. I'll be at Shelby's if you need me." I grabbed my bag and slammed the door before I could hear anything Rudy might have to say.

Shelby opened the side door, her shorts pulled tight around her skinny hips with a man's belt.

"C'mon." Shelby waved her hand and I followed her to her room.

"What do you think?" Shelby held up a drawing she'd done. A pencil sketch of two girl pirates opening a treasure chest full of dildos. It was beautiful. It was beautiful and silly and scary.

"It's so good," I told Shelby, taking it from her hand.

"Is it funny?" she asked.

"Yeah. It's funny. I mean, it depends on your sense of humor," I said, looking at the wide, delighted eyes of the girl pirates. "It's funny, Shelby, it is."

I flopped into Shelby's bed and told her the news about my mom and Rudy.

"No fucking way." Shelby's eyes shot wide open. "No fucking way is she letting him move in there."

"I think she's goin' crazy. She can't stand livin' without a man anymore. That's the way she is, Shelby. Boyfriend after boyfriend, every one of them a complete piece of shit, you know that firsthand. And she's been complaining lately about gettin' old. Like, she won't ever have a man if she gets old."

"Your mom is thirty-five."

"You'd think she was eighty-five the way she talks about it."

"He's so fucking gross," Shelby said.

"Yeah. And now he's in the house. What is that thing they say about vampires? About inviting them in?"

"First rule, never invite a vampire into your house." Shelby pointed at me.

"You see what I'm up against here."

The front door opened and slammed shut. Shelby's body stiffened. She tucked the pirate sketch under her bed with all her other sketches.

"Let's go," Shelby said. She grabbed her red high tops.

One second later, Robyn's big blond hair poked itself inside the door.

"Hey, whattya' you guys doin'?" She asked, surveying the room.

"We're goin' over to Heather's," Shelby said, giving me a look.

"The kitchen is a fucking mess," Robyn said.

"Yeah. I agree." Shelby threw her arms up. "None of it's mine. You oughta get your fucking boyfriend to do some dishes."

"Hey, Vince don't live here. He's a guest."

"He's not my guest," Shelby said.

"Jesus!" Robyn turned down the hall toward the kitchen. "You are the most ungrateful thing that ever lived, Shelby!"

Shelby finished lacing her shoes and we sped out of the house.

"Leaves are starting to change," Shelby said, once we found our-selves on the street.

"You're the ungrateful one?" I asked.

"Yeah. God, do you smell something funny?" Shelby was done talking about Robyn.

"Are we really going to Heather's?" I asked.

"Yeah. We never see her these days." Shelby said.

I met Heather the summer before Shelby and I started fifth grade. Heather and her mother moved into Covington Manor Apartments, right across the circle from my mom and me.

Shelby was jealous. Up until then she had been my only friend and when she met Heather, who was wearing earrings with Michael Jackson's face on them, Shelby said, "That's so stupid."

To which Heather replied, "Your mom won't let you get your ears pierced will she?"

They managed to become friends anyway. The three of us used to go into one of the Covington Manor laundry rooms and play Strip Club. Me and Heather would pretend to take our clothes off for invisi-ble audiences of adoring men. She was Sheena and I was Cherry. We made up other strippers, too. Strippers with names like Gertrude and Helga. Shelby didn't want to be a stripper so she was the club owner instead and she would always side with Sheena and Cherry against the other girls. Or set us up with the really rich men.

Shelby would say something like, "Hey Sheena, that man says he'll give you a million dollars to have sex with him." And Heather would say something like, "A million dollars? Please. I make that much just walking around!"

Heather liked to stuff her shirt with t-shirts so she'd have this huge chest. She did it even when we weren't playing Strip Club. She insist-ed she was going to have really big tits. Bigger than Dolly Parton's. I mean, BIG ONES, she said.

And she was right. Well, she was sort of right. She did end up with one really big tit. The other one, however, never grew. It had a nipple and all that but it was flatter than a pancake, nothing underneath it. And the one that did grow? Well, it just might have been bigger than Dolly Parton's.

Heather got kicked out of Mehlville our freshman year. That one big tit and that one big mouth did it. She wore a shirt that read "Suck Me." Principal Linden didn't appreciate it and called her to the office. But Heather didn't go. She just kept showing up for her classes and being sent to the office again. She took the hall passes and walked around fucking with people from the doorways of their classrooms. Finally, Linden caught up with her between bells.

"Miss Motts? Can I see you in my office?"

"I don't know, can you? Do people go invisible in your office?"

The hall was full of people and reportedly you could see the veins on Linden's big ol' head.

"Your shirt is inappropriate for school. Not to mention generally inappropriate for someone your age. Tell me, what does it mean to you?"

I can't imagine why Linden thought he could intimidate her in the hall like that, but the way the legend goes; Heather looked down at her shirt and read it as if she had forgotten what was on it.

"Suck me? You know. Like suck my left one." Heather grabbed that one big left tit and the hall erupted into laughter. She'd won and the way it was told to me, principal Linden's face could have rivaled a beet in a red contest.

Heather was expelled and immediately began classes at Hallsey. That was the technical school, generally reserved for the biggest of all fuck-ups. The burner kids envied it because the rumor was the desks had ashtrays built right in. Of course, that wasn't true, but why ruin other people's dreams?

Heather swung the door open and took a big bite out of a slice of cold pizza. It made my mouth water.

Shelby headed off for the kitchen to peruse the Mott's refrigerator, which was always full of stuff even though it was just Heather and her mom. Heather's mom liked to keep things stocked. Ever since she made enough money to move out of Covington Manor and into a house, she never let anything run out.

Heather's mom invented these weird sponge curlers for hair, Twist-a-Curl. The sets came in wacky neon colors and you could just twist them around themselves, no bobby pins or whatever. She managed to get them produced and marketed and made a small fortune. Enough, anyway, to not go without.

"Don't eat that Kentucky Fried Chicken, Shelby. That's mine," Heather called into the kitchen.

"My mother is marrying Rudy." I diverted my attention from the pizza.

"Moustache geek?"

"Yeah."

"Suck. What the hell is wrong with your mom? She should be cool, but she's all fucked up."

"Yeah," Shelby yelled from the kitchen. "You'd think she had Robyn for a sister or something."

"Don't worry, Shelby. There's no way you'll turn out like my mom," I said.

Heather laughed. "No, she won't. She'll have it bad for a sleazy moustache LADY!"

"Shut up Heather. I like straight girls. Where's the soda, anyway?"

"In the crisper, don't ask me why."

"I want a diet one," I called to Shelby.

"How can you drink that stuff?" Heather pulled a small pipe from her pocket.

"I can't tell the difference," I lied.

"You're lying." Heather pointed out, holding a hit of pot in her chest.

"Why would I lie about it?"

"I dunno, Angie. Why ARE you lying about it?"

Shelby came back with two root beers and a diet Coke for me. "Jesus, Heather! Are you, like, a full time pot head now, or what?"

"Oh, chill out Shelby. It's no big deal. Just a little herb. Never hurt nobody."

"You're the last person I expected to turn into a hippie," Shelby said.

"I'm NOT a hippie! Punks smoke pot, too."

"Gimme the remote." I stuck my hand out to Heather. "I'm gonna watch MTV while you two fight."

Heather and Shelby went off to the kitchen to cook. The only thing they liked better than telling each other to shut up, was making weird food. I flopped on the sofa and tried not to think about all the smells they were creating. I turned up the volume on Def Leppard singing that stupid song about sugar and showing off their bulges. I wanted it loud to cover the sound of my belly rumbling. If I could drown it out, I could beat it.

Heather bounded back into the room, her hair tied ridiculously in a kitchen towel. "Turn that shit off! I can't stand those fuckers." She hit the mute button. "How far do you think they can ride the fact the drummer got his arm pulled off? I think it's sick for any of those other fuckers to get money off that one dude's missing arm." She disappeared back into the kitchen and left me with my stomach. A few minutes later Heather returned to the room with a full plate and napkins and more soda.

"What the hell is that?" I pointed to the loaded plate.

"Pizza rolls." Heather shrugged.

"What the fuck did you do to 'em?"

"Put 'em in the waffle iron."

"Aren't you supposed to bake them?"

"I bet these are better," she said.

Shelby brought in a plate of fried leftover spaghetti and saltine crackers with cheese on top baked until it was black. I was hungry enough to eat it all.

"Here." Shelby stuck a fork out to me.

"No thanks. That shit looks all fucked up. I think you're stoned too, Shelby." I grabbed up one of Heather's skate magazines and fell back on the couch looking at the pictures, and not letting drool out of my mouth.

"I'm gonna put everything in the waffle iron from now on. These pizza rolls are fuckin' good," Heather said.

"The crunchy noodles are good too. Try 'em."

"Will you two please stop talking about that puke you're eating? I'm gonna be sick." I flipped a page for emphasis.

"I got somethin' for you to read, Angie." Heather jumped up and disappeared down the hall.

"This sounds interesting," Shelby said and crunched another mouth full of noodles.

"You're totally disgusting."

"Am I?" Shelby opened her mouth and stuck her spaghetti tongue out at me.

"Classy, Shelby. Real classy."

"Check it out!" Heather threw two magazines on my chest. "You're gonna like it too, Shelby. Shit, you'll like it the most."

I picked up the magazines. One was titled *Cheri* and the other was a *Hustler*. "Where'd you get these?" I asked, thumbing through the Hustler.

"From Rex. He keeps them under his mattress!"

"He gave you his beat off books?" Shelby asked.

"Well, not exactly gave . . ."

"You stole them!" Shelby laughed hard enough that I thought waffled pizza rolls might come out of her nose.

"Like, what's he gonna do? 'Hey Heather, you seen my tittie mags?'" Heather did her best deep voice.

"He probably thinks his mom found them!" I said.

"That's cold! That is so cold, Heather!" Shelby pointed at her.

"Look at this, the blonde is gonna stick her stiletto in the red head!" I held the magazine out for both of them to see. Shelby snatched it from my hand.

"Man, the blonde has great boobs. She's not really gonna stick that in there? Well, maybe. You think people do that?"

"You mean, do I think lesbians do that?" Heather asked. "I guess. Shit, if you got 'em, might as well use 'em."

"Heather, why did you take these, anyway?" I asked.

"I got to see what the whole fake tit thing is about. I mean, if I'm gonna have one and stuff, you know?"

"Are you gonna get one?" Shelby was solemn. She had grown rather fond of both oddities and tits.

"I dunno. Here. Check it out." Heather pulled up her shirt and bra letting that one big left tit out of captivity. "Okay, so here's The Big One, and then here's this tit." She held a magazine tit next to her own.

Shelby and I were silent.

"Well?" Heather insisted. "What do you think?"

"I'm not sure, Heather," Shelby said carefully. "What do I think of what?"

"How does it look? Stupid?"

"It looks great. To me." Shelby smirked.

"Oh, fer Christ sake!" Heather threw the magazine at Shelby.

"I can't tell that way, Heather. You have to get pictures of women who have one that's real and one that's fake," Shelby said.

"Oh. Gee, Shelby. I should have thought of that. I'll run right out and pick up a copy of *One-Titted Wonder*s. Dipshit."

"Will the fake one even be like your real one?" Shelby asked.

"No. It will be all perky and weird. When I'm old, only one of my tits will sag," Heather said.

I returned my attention to the *Cheri* magazine. "Look at her, she's all like this," I said, dropping the magazine on the table and propping my leg up on the back of the couch. "Is my back arched enough?" I asked.

Shelby checked the picture in the magazine. "Yeah, your back is fine but you need that look on your face, you know, like you're constipated and happy about it."

"How's this?" I asked, giving the best look I could.

"That's good," Heather said. "What about this?" Heather got on all fours, arched her back, and spread her legs wide.

"Wow," I said. "You really do look happy to be constipated."

"Well thank you." Heather stood and took a bow. "Maybe I should go into porn."

"Look at this, it's a whole story about this monster who kidnaps this lady." I handed the magazine to Shelby.

Shelby flipped through the five page layout of a big hairy monster dragging some naked woman into a big basement. He put her body on a concrete block and tied her hands behind her head. Then he spread her legs in a Y and tied them at the ankles to two long poles on the end of the block. Then he pulled a big fake monster dick out of his fur and stuck it in her.

"That's kinda creepy," Shelby said. "Where're the lesbians with the stilettos? I liked that one."

"When I'm done with these, you can have them," Heather said to Shelby and picked up the plates and napkins.

I glanced at Shelby. She was staring intently at the *Hustler* and chewing at her finger tip. I picked up the empty soda cans and followed Heather into the kitchen.

"Oh. I almost forgot," Heather said. "My mom and her boyfriend are going to Atlanta this weekend."

"So?"

"So, let's have a party."

"Here?"

"Yeah. Why not? We'll have it on Friday, the place will be in great shape by the time she gets back. Besides, we'll have it on the patio mostly."

"Your neighbors won't tell on you?"

"There'll be nothing to tell," Heather said. "Hey, Shelby, you think Robyn would get us some beer?"

"She'd be delighted. She loves corrupting minors," Shelby called into the kitchen.

Heather and Shelby made plans for a party. I looked at the cover of the *Cheri* magazine blankly. I wanted to take one of those magazines. I wanted to study one, alone.

"I'm gonna go, you guys. My mom wants me home for dinner," I lied, again.

"I'm gonna stay here," Shelby said.

I walked slow. I could have taken a bite out of anything. Anything at all. I'd tried to diet since the second grade, but nothing ever came of it. I never managed to stay off food long enough to lose any weight.

When I got home, my mom and Rudy were watching television. The apartment was stuffed with boxes and most of mom's furniture had been replaced. Everything was far too large for the space it occupied.

"Look at this," Mom said, pointing to the huge brown sofa taking up the entire back wall of the living room. "It's a convertible sofa." She flipped the middle cushion forward to reveal a table-like surface with cup holders in it.

I didn't have anything to say about this. The coffee table had never presented me with any particular hassle.

"Isn't that great? And the end seats recline." Mom nodded.

"Yeah. Wow."

CHAPTER 3

Sunday. The second day of Invasion Rudy. I stayed in my room most of the day. Got up only a few times for a glass of water. My new diet: water and diet soda. Plus visualizing myself thin. I'd seen a *Donahue* show featuring this lady who said you had to see what you wanted in order to get it. She said you couldn't be rich if you saw yourself as poor. She said you couldn't be rich if you resented rich people. Why would you become what you hate? I didn't entirely agree with her. I mean, what if you just are what you hate? All the same, her advice didn't seem like it could hurt. So, I saw myself thin, I projected positive thoughts toward thin people. Like they needed it or something.

I spent all day reading a book Heather gave me. It was called *Serial Killers*. White guys who cut people up. Hookers and drifters.

I stopped in the middle of a chapter about the mass grave under John Wayne Gacy's house to get a glass of water. The place already belonged more to Rudy than to me. The hallway was lined with brown boxes and milk crates. I peeked over the edge of an open box. It was full of Matchbox cars and those plastic tracks they run along. I could just see the living room turned into a huge raceway.

"Hey Angie." Rudy came through the front door. "You want to put the little TV in your room?"

"Little TV?" As I asked, I noticed our twenty-inch had been pushed aside in favor of Rudy's big screen TV. "Shit, that thing takes up half the room."

"Yeah. It'll be crowded in here. But it's only for a little while. I'll put the other TV in your room if you want it. Otherwise I'll hook it up in our bedroom."

The words: our bedroom. I almost puked right there, but stopped myself, favoring a close examination of Rudy's horrible little moustache instead.

"I'll have it in my room. Can we get cable?"

Rudy smiled. "Of course, gotta have cable. We can even run it into your room."

For a split second, I felt pleased. But, of course, Rudy came with the cable television, like some huge, unseemly adapter.

I went back to my room and fell asleep.

"Angie, dinner's ready," my mother woke me.

"I'm sleeping," I said, rubbing at my eyes.

"I said, dinner is ready. Now get up and wash your face."

The table was set for three with a skillet of Mexican Hamburger Helper in the middle and a jug of whole milk. I sat at the table and mom called for Rudy out the window. He was working on his truck in the parking lot.

"I heard you the first two times, Rita," he called up.

"Well, c'mon then before it gets cold."

"Just a minute, okay?"

"I don't know what's the matter with him. Go ahead and start."

I put a couple small spoonfuls on my plate and Mom handed me two slices of Bunny Bread slathered with sweet butter. I tried to add all the calories in my mind. The way Mom cooks it's hard to gage it all. The bread is, like, seventy calories a slice. The butter? I just shouldn't even look at butter. And Hamburger Helper?

I considered the whole meal two thousand calories without the milk. At least I hadn't eaten anything for like a day.

Mom sat down and loaded her plate up. "Don't you want any milk, honey?"

"No. Water's fine."

"You like milk, I thought."

"Can we use skim milk, maybe?"

"Oh. That stuff's awful."

I ate slowly, trying to chew everything at least thirty times. I heard it helped digestion. Mom ate and relayed a story about one of the women she waited tables with.

"So, she is definitely pregnant. Got her test back today. But she doesn't know if her husband is the father or not."

"How many candidates are there?"

"Oh Angie, just two!"

Mom was like one of the girls at school talking about other people's troubles. She loved to gossip.

Mom put the last of her bread crust in her mouth just as Rudy came through the door. His hands and shirt were black with grease.

"What, you ate without me?" He threw his arms up.

"I told you it was ready, babe," Mom said.

"Yeah and I told you, I'd be another few minutes. You should have waited." Rudy stomped into the kitchen and washed his hands.

I picked up my plate and glass and took it to the sink. Rudy sat down and looked up at me.

"Hey, you're not going anywhere. Don't be rude. Sit down here while I eat my dinner. You and your mother should have waited, so now you can both keep me company."

I sat down again. Rudy looked at me without saying anything. I barely kept myself from blurting: Mom's friend doesn't know who the father of her baby is!

"Shit!" Rudy threw his fork against his plate. "It's cold!"

"Well, of course it's cold, it took you a half hour to drag your ass in here!"

"Heat it up." He pushed his plate toward my mother

"What?" She asked more about his tone than his meaning.

"Look, I worked all day movin' stuff and changin' that damn oil filter. I want a hot meal."

My mother hesitated slightly, picked up the plate and took it to the kitchen. She slowly took a saucepan from the cabinet and dumped Rudy's Mexican Hamburger Helper in it. "It was hot, a half-hour ago," she mumbled, mostly to the stove.

"What was that Rita? What did you say?"

"Nothing."

"Maybe we can get you fixed up with a nice microwave, huh? Would you like that? Something to make your life a little easier?"

Mom said nothing as she returned the reheated food to Rudy's plate. She poured his milk and buttered three slices of bread for him before pulling a fifth of Seagram's out of the liquor cabinet, along with a single shot glass.

"Make my life a little easier, huh?" She poured herself a shot and sat back down at the table. "I guess we're the last people on earth without a microwave. Aren't we, Angie?"

"I don't know about that," I said.

Mom twirled the liquid around in its tiny glass for a moment, then shot it down in one quick motion. She grimaced and swallowed some of her milk.

"Oh Rita, shit, a milk chaser?" Rudy looked somewhat pained.

"Well, it was here," she said.

CHAPTER 4

The next morning I went straight for the pay phone outside the K-mart and called the school. I wanted to try a new trick.

"Hello? This is Rita Neuweather, Angie is sick today. She won't be in class."

I couldn't believe it worked, but it did.

I sat around the apartment all day watching re-runs of sit-coms and ignoring Rudy's everything, everywhere.

When school was about to let out, I went to Shelby's and sat on her porch.

Persia, Shelby's mom's cat came over and rubbed my leg. That cat had always liked me. Of course, Persia liked Robyn too, so maybe she wasn't exactly particular. I was scratching Persia between the ears when Robyn's baby blue Cutlass turned into the driveway.

"Whatcha' doin' Angie, casin' the place?" Robyn asked, stepping out of the car.

"Just waitin' for Shelby," I said.

Robyn opened the trunk of the car. Mounds of plastic bags and loose laundry stuck up like sharks fins. "Cut school, huh?" Robyn yelled over her shoulder.

"Yeah."

Robyn headed toward me with her arms full. "You gonna help me or what?"

I jumped up and took a couple bags. "What's all this?"

"Stuff for the shop. Shampoo and shit. Here, unlock the door." Robyn handed me her keys along with the hundred key chains that were attached. There was a blue rabbit's foot the color of her car, a few little stuffed bears, pewter unicorns, and one that read "Take me drunk, I'm home."

Inside we dropped all the bags on the kitchen floor. Robyn swung the fridge open, running her hand down it as she crouched. Her nails were painted a rich gold color and her thumbnail had a little gold charm dangling from it. I think the charm was a unicorn too. I remembered Shelby saying, If I ever DID see a unicorn, I'd cut its head off and put it in Robyn's bed!

A Busch beer appeared over the top of the door. "Here Angie, have a beer."

"No thanks."

Robyn stood with a beer in each hand and kicked the fridge shut. "C'mon Angie, have a beer fer Christ sake. You're already cuttin' school like a regular delinquent, what difference does it make?"

Robyn shoved the can into my hand and turned on the radio next to the toaster oven. "I hated school too, all those fucking rules and people tellin' you what to do all the time. Grown men lookin' at yer ass all day. You got to get suspended, then they actually tell you NOT to go to school. That's what I did. Until I dropped out."

"I called myself out."

Robyn's eyes perked up. "What? You pretended to be Rita?"

"Yeah."

Robyn laughed, letting a rare smile spread across her face. She reached over and popped the top on my beer. "That's a good one. That's smart."

Robyn sat at the kitchen table. She looked at me as if I were a study in science. "They tease you, huh?"

I took a hard swallow of beer. My face got red and I couldn't make it stop. "Yeah," I sputtered, taking another pull off the can.

"Well, that's what you get fer hangin' out with my sister, I guess." Robyn laughed without smiling at all. "Hey, I got a bunch of make up from the warehouse today. It'd be a crime not to for how cheap it is." Robyn jumped up and started rummaging through the bags on the floor then upended one of them on the table. Little tubes and glossy pink boxes spilled out with a sweet, powdery smell.

Robyn's squared talons sifted through the pile. I watched closely, taking another drink of beer.

"Looka' this." She fumbled a shiny rose-colored box open. "It's this stay-on-all-day lip gloss. You use this brush to put the powder on, then you go over it with the gloss. Try some. Oh wait, here, Apricot Dawn, that's for you. You're an Autumn," Robyn said.

"A what?" I asked.

"An Autumn, that's your coloring. So like browns and oranges are good on you. Don't you know anything about bein' a girl, Angie?"

Robyn continued to thumb through things on the table while I played at the tiny piece of cellophane tape keeping the Apricot Dawn out of my reach. Robyn finished her beer and fished two more out of the fridge.

"Go on, Angie. Finish your beer. There's nothing like a good beer buzz in the afternoon."

Robyn was a creature from the past, with all her bleach-blonde hair falling away from her face in sprays. Her tits were huge and she always showed them off with just a sprinkle of white glitter down that tanning bed cleavage.

"Here, give me that." She stuck her hand out when she noticed I was still worrying that little piece of cellophane tape. Robyn could do anything with the pads of her fingers. After years of wielding two-inch nails she had become adept. In an instant she handed the box back with its little tape flap sticking up.

I eyed it for a moment. Robyn put a seashell-shaped mirror in my hand. I picked up the tiny sponge wand and applied the powder, then the gloss.

"Yeah." Robyn nodded her head. "That looks real good on you."

"My mom won't let me wear make up."

"You're kidding!" Robyn's head fell back and she laughed, hard. "Rita wears more make up than anyone I know! Shit. That's dumb. Here, try this, it's mascara with glitter in it. It's clear, 'cept for the glitter."

I took the tube and another long drink of beer.

"Let me see you." Robyn popped another beer open and held my chin in her other hand. By then my lids were powdered with Heather Mist and lined in Chocolate Fantasy.

"Damn, you got good cheekbones, girl. You ought to think about cuttin' all that hippie hair off. You look like Cousin It."

I looked at myself in one of the huge mirror.. "Man! I DO look like Cousin It!"

I was giggling with Robyn when Shelby walked in.

"Oh shit," she said. "What are you doing to my friend, Robyn?"

"Something you should try, Shelby. A little girl talk, you know, make up, BOYS."

"Fuck off, Robyn." Shelby dumped her backpack on the counter.

"Do you think I look like Cousin It?" I swung around to Shelby with my hair covering my face.

"Maybe a little." Shelby smiled. "Where were you today?"

I brushed my hair back. "I stayed home."

"Yeah, Shelby . . ." Robyn leaned back, taking in the rest of her beer. "You should have so many guts. Angie pretended to be Rita and called herself out of school."

"You did?"

"Yeah, it was no big deal."

"Don't you think you might get caught?" Shelby was irritated. Being at school without each other always sucked.

"We'll see, I guess."

Robyn stood tossing her hair back as if shaking us off like a colony of fleas. "Angie, take that make up if you want it. I can't use it, I'm a summer." She pulled two more beers out of the fridge. "I'm goin' down stairs, ya fuckin' dykes."

Shelby and I widened our eyes at one another, our traditional Robyn-is-a-freak look.

"And you let her paint you up like one of those mall girls." Shelby pointed at me.

Me, a mall girl. Nursing Cokes at the Seven Kitchens and trying to get boys to ask me out.

"You're drunk," Shelby said.

"I am not. I only had two beers!"

"Don't forget to take that make up off before you leave. Your mom will have a shit fit."

"What exactly is a shit fit?" I asked.

"Well, the word originates from the Greek, shidafetus. Meaning to flail ones arms wildly while yelling at one's offspring."

I did remember to wash my face before I left and I scooped up the make up Robyn said I could have. I took the little mirror, too. Between

Robyn and her mother must have had a hundred mirrors in that house.

When I got home Mom had changed out of her uniform and was rummaging through the freezer. "I'm just gonna heat a couple of burritos tonight. That okay with you?" she asked.

"I'm not hungry," I told her.

"It would be easier to do this with a microwave, I guess," she said, putting a frozen burrito on the top rack of the electric oven.

"Oh, because it's so hard to put it in the oven?" I asked.

"Just takes a long time," she said and went to the living room. She curled up on the couch with one of her paperback mysteries.

"Is Rudy going to be here tonight?" I asked.

"Later on. He's finishing up at his apartment. He'll have it all done tonight."

I went to my room and shut the door with a slow click.

CHAPTER 5

I went to school early the next day to avoid my mother and, especially, Rudy. Besides, I had the make up Robyn gave me. Going early, I could slip into the big bathroom on the first floor and apply it. Lean over the sink and open my eyes wide to get the liner in just the right place, like I saw the other girls doing.

The school building was silent. I could hear my own breathing and a radio playing low in some distant janitor's closet.

In the empty bathroom, I pulled out the make up. War paint, Aunt Jean called it. The mirror over the bathroom sinks was huge; it took up an entire wall. I looked at myself. All I could see was double chin. A big wall of chin.

In fifteen minutes the room would be full of skinny girls in expensive clothes swapping bits of gossip acquired, undoubtedly, from endless telephone conversations the night before. They would all ignore me in some obvious way. Cast glances at each other in the mirror, sharing the exhilaration of calling me Lezzylard in their minds. That was the name someone gave me in the seventh grade and it just stuck. I wasn't sure who made it up, though I suspected Mike Forester. The fact that Shelby came out as a bona fide lesbian sealed the name Lezzylard like a coat of shellac.

I went a little lighter with the make up than Robyn. No matter what I did, someone had something nasty to say about it, so I tried my best not to give them any fire power.

I met up with Shelby outside our first hour art class.

"Whoa. I didn't think you were going to take Robyn up on her offer for the make up. Actually, it looks good. Better than when she did it yesterday. I guess you have the face for it."

First hour bell rang. Shelby and I sat down at the back table, waiting to find out what unimaginative thing we'd be working on.

"Pssss," Troy Mulligan spat in my ear. "Special delivery," he said, dropping a sheet of notebook paper in front of me. It was a drawing of a really fat naked girl sitting on top of a really skinny naked girl with a caption that read: I love you Lezzylard, please don't kill me!

Shelby grabbed it and stuffed it in her pocket. Troy and the kids at his table were laughing into their hands, pointing at me and Shelby.

"Don't even look at them," Shelby said.

Mrs. Irwin passed around pieces of square, white poster board and charcoal pencils. She looked hung over, as always. Mrs. Irwin was nice enough, but she didn't give a damn about art. The room was lined with a row of floor-to-ceiling wooden cabinets. They were probably filled with paint and brushes and all sorts of things, but I wasn't sure because I had never seen the inside of one.

"For the next two days, we're going to work on album covers. You can do the cover of some of that stuff you have at home, or make something up. Use your imagination," She said and sat back at her desk where she would read from a book with a croqueted jacket around it. She never wanted us to know what she was reading.

Shelby went to work on a drawing of Curtis Alroy fucking Troy Mulligan up the ass with a big candy cane.

"Merry Christmas," I said.

At lunch I hoisted myself up on a row of bathroom sinks and read from the *Serial Killers* book. Richard Speck killed eight nursing students. Eight of them in one house. He told them he wasn't going to hurt them. He tied their hands and feet and sat them in a semi circle, then he took them out of the room one at a time and killed them. Horribly. Torture and rape and mutilation. One of the cops said the blood in the carpet was so deep it came up over the sole of his shoe and splashed on top of it.

And one woman survived by hiding under a bed and watching. What the hell must life be like for her?

After school I followed Shelby home, where we retreated to her room.

"What do you want to hear?" Shelby flipped through her crate of records.

"I dunno. Something, like, super rock-n-roll."

"Oh. Thanks. You're a big help. Hey, check out that nail polish on my night table. My mom brought me some new colors."

"Well, you know, nail polish will make you straight, Shelby."

"I know. That's why I'm going to paint your nails instead of mine."

Shelby dropped the needle on Ozzy singing "Crazy Train." I took off my boots and socks.

"I like this dark purple," I said.

Shelby took the polish out of my hand with a smile that suggested she knew purple would be my choice. Then she set about painting my toenails. I just listened to the music and faded away for awhile. Shelby wasn't finished painting when the record stopped and she didn't bother getting up to put anything else on.

"All done," she finally said.

"Oh, it's great," I said, sitting up to blow on them.

When we heard Robyn's foot falls in the kitchen, Shelby looked at me with those raised eyebrows.

Robyn's raspy call shot up through the floor. "Shelby, where the fuck are you?"

"Shit," Shelby breathed. She stood up and headed for the door. "What, Robyn?"

I was trying to blow my toe nails dry and reach for my boots at the same time.

"That shitty piece of shit dog next door won't quit fuckin' barkin'," Robyn told Shelby in a low growl. I could tell she was right beyond the door. I stuffed my socks in my boots, ready to leave barefoot.

"What do you want me to do about it?" Shelby's back was framed in the doorway.

"Don't be smart, Shelby! Vince got a new job and he worked it all night, gotta go back tonight."

"Okay." Shelby threw her arms up in the air.

"Stop bein' a bitch!" Robyn came closer to Shelby. I could see the blond ends of her feathered hair. "You wouldn't know SHIT about having to work. And that fucking dog! I hate dogs. Piece of shit."

"Do you want me to tell the Bradleys to put Thor inside so your drug-addict boyfriend can get a nap in?" Sometimes, Shelby couldn't seem to resist provoking Robyn.

"YOU!" Robyn punctuated the word by pushing Shelby against the door frame with a good thump. "You don't know DICK, Shelby." Robyn's tone was vicious but she'd amused herself with the idea that Shelby didn't know dick. Robyn laughed, "Shelby don't know dick. Not one. Not even a little one!" Robyn backed up from Shelby and laughed all the way down the hall.

The refrigerator opened. We held our breath until we heard the door that led to the basement slam shut.

"We gotta get outta here. Things are only gonna get worse." Shelby shook her head and went for her high tops.

"You piece of shit!" I could hear Robyn yelling out the back door. "I'm gonna feed you anti-freeze. You barking piece of SHIT!"

"C'mon," Shelby said.

I had my boots in my hand. I hit the street, barefoot and squinting.

"The sun is so bright," Shelby said, holding her hand against it.

"Where should we go?" I wanted to know. I was careful to step over the lines of melting tar that appeared to keep the streets together.

"I don't know," Shelby said. "Why are you barefoot?"

"I didn't want to ruin my polish."

"Isn't the street hot?" Shelby asked.

"No. Well, yes, actually. It's stupidly hot," I admitted.

Shelby laughed out loud.

"Oh, good. I'm glad it's funny."

"C'mon, let's sit over here." Shelby pointed at a big tree just up ahead of us.

"Isn't that someone's yard?"

"I guess. Everywhere belongs to someone, right?"

We sat down and Shelby inspected my toe nails.

"Baked on," she said, nodding.

"What?"

"You baked it on with that hot street walk."

I reached down and touched a toenail. She was right, not only was the polish dry, it was baked on. I put my socks on as quickly as I could.

I was sure someone was about to come out of the house and yell at us for being on their lawn.

"Let's just walk around for the day," Shelby said. "We used to do that all the time."

Once my boots were secure, she and I started off in the direction of the whole world and nothing in particular, the way we had always done.

The houses in the subdivisions we walked through were so much nicer than anything we ever expected for ourselves. Monroe Street was especially nice. All the houses were deep red brick, two stories, surrounded by big trees and green, green lawn.

"Okay," Shelby said. "What if there's a girl standing on her head and the other girl is eating her out?"

"The Y Not," I said.

Shelby shook her head. "Dinner at the Bonanza."

This was Shelby's favorite game and even though the names she gave any given sex act never made any sense, they always stuck.

"Okay," I said. "What if you sit on a guys dick and turn yourself all the way around in a complete three-sixty?"

"Yard Darts," Shelby said with an authoritative nod.

"You must be so weird to have sex with, Shelby."

"Let's hope so. And let's hope I find out soon."

Monroe Street was also fond of lawn ornaments. Deer or gnomes or kissing frogs. Almost every house had something on its front lawn.

"What are people thinking when they buy this stuff?" I asked, motioning toward a concrete bunny the size of a cocker spaniel.

"I think it's how these people communicate with one another. Like, if the gnome is to the left of the kissing frogs it means they're having pork roast for dinner. But, if the deer is to the right of the Virgin Mary it means don't knock, we're fuckin'."

We kept along the big hill that led to the Monroe Street cut off. At one time, where Monroe curved, there was a fence we could climb that took us to a pond. But the pond had long since been filled in with dirt and a new sub division was built up over it. Newer, smaller houses with vinyl siding and tiny sod yards almost completely devoid of trees. Since then, the families that live near the curve have built up their bushes to keep the new houses out of sight.

We were walking up on the big curve, in the middle of the row of bushes, when Shelby stopped.

"Shush." She held a hand up to me.

I listened carefully and heard a female voice say: "Brandon, just stop. Okay?"

"I can't help it," a male voice said.

I gave a wrinkled lip to Shelby, who was pulling back branches with her arms.

"Come look," She said. "It's Carrie Shuren and Brandon Harris."

"What?" I ducked in to look. This was a treasure. Those two kids were so popular it was ridiculous. I peeked through the branches, Carrie and Brandon were out in the yard sitting in the incredibly green grass.

"Let's just go to your room," Brandon said.

"Stop, it's the middle of the day!"

"He's pawing her like a dog," Shelby said.

"C'mon," Brandon said. "Let's just go. Your parents aren't home."

"Lupe is in there, cleaning."

"She doesn't even speak English!" Brandon threw his hands up into the air.

Shelby curled up her face and stuck her tongue out. "The Shurens have a Mexican maid, how gross is that?"

I shrugged.

"Still," Carrie said. "She'll tell. I can't have people in the house, Brandon. You know that. So, just stop. Let's go shopping or something."

"Shopping? We haven't fucked in, like, a week and you want to go shopping?"

"I don't feel like fucking and anyway, you can't come in."

"Fine, I'll see you later," Brandon said and stood from the grass.

"What? I thought we were going to do something today," Carrie said with her palms turned up.

"Yeah, so did I," Brandon said.

Carrie didn't move. Her absent-minded fingers pulled up tufts of grass.

"Are you SURE you're straight, Angie? There's still time to make a better decision," Shelby said.

I stepped back from the bushes. "C'mon, let's cut over to the park."

"She's crying," Shelby said, still peering at Carrie through the branches.

"Oh yeah? What are you gonna do, take her for Dinner at the Bonanza and make it all better?"

Shelby dropped the branches and turned to me with her world-famous grin. "Maybe I will."

"Well, maybe you should."

"Wouldn't that be something? That girl is so hot. If she turns out gay, I'll be totally vindicated."

"Vindicated? Where'd you be learnin' all them big words?"

"Wouldn't you like to know?"

Our consolation prize for losing the pond was a tiny un-thought-out, unkempt park they called Long Run. It contained a dirty sandbox, a rusted slide, and a lopsided hopscotch drawing.

"And in the Long Run," Shelby yelled as she jumped into the sandbox. "There's always break dancing!"

At this point Shelby busted out her very bad, always so bad, dysfunctional robot break dance. I sat on the end of the rusted slide and laughed.

"I just added that part where I punch myself in the head. You like it?" Shelby asked.

"How could I NOT like it, Shelby? You are a genius of the dance wasting away here in nowhereville."

"I sense some sarcasm, Angie," Shelby said, stepping out of the sand box with her finger pointed at me.

"Who? Me? Sarcasm? Whatever, watch this," I said, jumping into the sand box.

I made up a robot dance that included me having a dick, jerking it off, and eating the come.

"What's that called?" Shelby asked when I finished.

"Banana Crème Makeover."

"You're getting better."

On my way home, I thought about Carrie Shuren. About her sitting in her yard and crying. Brandon Harris was a notorious asshole, but he was cute and his family was pretty rich. Rich enough anyway.

He drove a shiny new car I didn't know the name of and wore shiny new clothes. Carrie and Brandon together gave off a glare, like sun hitting snow.

I climbed the stairs toward our apartment. The sweet smell of pot filled the air. In fact, the second floor landing was saturated with the smell of it. One of our trashy neighbors was having a pot party. Then, it hit me: it was my mom and Rudy. Inside, too fucked up to realize the cops were, surely, on their way. Maybe the cops would come. Maybe Rudy would have some crazy big record and they would put him in jail for life and I would be saved.

I pulled my key out of my pocket and just stood at the door. I couldn't bring myself to open it. The Eagles were playing Take It Easy and Rudy was singing along. Badly, drunkenly singing along. I suddenly understood why my mother was an atheist.

I could hear other voices beyond the door. How many people were in there? And what the fuck were they doing? As I tried to decipher what was being said and by whom, Caroline, our across the hall neighbor, opened her door. "Hi, Angie. Whattcha' doin' out here?"

"Workin' up the stomach to go inside," I told her.

"Sounds like they're havin' a pretty good time."

"Yeah."

"Angie, you should go in and tell Rita to put a towel along the bottom of the door. Even my place is startin' to smell like weed. I don't care, but someone else might. You know?"

"Yeah. Thanks, Caroline."

I put my key in the door and hoped the building would blow-up before I actually opened it.

"Heeeey, Angie!" Rudy swung his arm out to me. "Glad you're here! We ain't tryin' to have a party without 'cha or nothin'."

"You guys, the whole building smells like pot."

"What?" My mothers red eyes got big. "You're kidding?"

"No, Mom, I'm not kidding. Caroline says it's startin' to smell up her place, even. Say's you should put a towel along the bottom of the door."

"Shit," Mom said and scurried down the hall to her bedroom.

"You want a beer Angie?" Rudy asked.

"Rudy, in case my mom hasn't told you, I'm sixteen."

"Shit. I know that, girl. It's just beer though. Hey, these are my friends, Kathy and Tim. They helped me with the last of my stuff."

"Hi," I said flatly to the other two stoned-out, drunk people in the room. "Looks like a storage shed in here."

Mom came back down the hall with a wet towel in one hand, a can of potpourri air freshener in the other, and a package of cherry incense between her teeth. She flung the door open and started spraying air freshener furiously in the hall. I poked my head out and watched her, then I laughed. I'd never seen my mother act so funny in all my life.

Rudy stepped up behind me and laughed.

"Said she ain't been stoned since you was just a baby."

"It shows."

"Okay," Mom finally said with her eyes still wide. "How's that?"

"Fine, Mom. Now it smells like pot and air freshener."

"Okay, good." She breathed a sigh of relief and stepped back into the apartment.

She coaxed Rudy and Tim and Kathy into helping her light an entire package of cherry incense. I went to my room quickly before it, too, would smell like a marijuana sno-cone.

Ted Bundy. The charming killer, that's what the serial killer book said about him. I'd be stuck in my room until morning so I read slowly.

They executed Bundy on January 24, 1989. He really had been a good looking man. I would have fallen for it. For his trick with the broken arm. I would have tried to help him. I stared at the pictures of the women. At their young faces and styled hair. Eyes that never could have guessed what fate they would come to. Those last few moments. The hatred, the absolute fear. The feeling of stupidity for having tried to help that monster with his stupid fucking boat or whatever he needed help with.

"Were gonna hafta switch to Go Fish." I heard my mother in the hall, slipping into her rural Missouri accent. The one she had worked so hard to lose. "I'm too drunk fer anymore poker."

"Well, in that case, I reckon' it's time for some strip poker!" I heard Rudy call from the living room.

"Oh! Rudy! Yer so bad!" My mother sang back as the bathroom door closed behind her.

I could tell another joint had been lit, the smell was starting to come into my room. I grabbed my Who t-shirt, rolled it up and stuck it along the bottom of my bedroom door. Caroline had taught me a new trick.

"Okay, who's up for Go Fish, I'll kick yer asses!" Mom said walking back down the hall to the dinning room table.

I visualized that monster with his big veiny monster dick stuck in that woman tied to the concrete block. I put my book on the night stand and snapped off the light.

My thoughts were detailed. Each foot lassoed to a pole at either end of that concrete block, her hands forced back, strapped down. I slid my hand into my shorts. She was begging him not to. The monster breathed hard, grunted. Then he stepped back to look at her. Her legs struggled against the ropes that tied them. The monster fumbled her cunt open. It was wet. He breathed harder, grunted more. She begged him not to. Please.

I tucked a pillow up between my legs, rolled over on it. I humped at it breathing into my mattress. The monster stuck his big fake dick into her. She said no, no, no as her back arched and she tried not to come. But, she did. And so did I.

CHAPTER 6

Last summer, Mom finally opened her own checking account. The bank gave her a black bathroom scale as a gift for banking with them. Mom was so excited to have her own bank account, we stopped at Dairy Queen for ice cream cones to celebrate. No more money orders! Mom held her cone up to mine for a toast. The scale, however, was a thing for which she had no use. She dropped it at the bottom of the bathroom closet and probably never thought about it again.

Mom only got weighed on those very rare occasions she went to the doctor. I bet she didn't even pay attention when the nurse announced the number, unlike me. I sweated it. Stepping onto that scale, I'd hold my breath waiting for the nurse to use her loudest voice: 172! That was the last official count.

I didn't hear Mom or Rudy anywhere in the apartment. Everything was quiet, which was strange for a school day. The apartment stank of beer and cigarettes, but nobody was awake.

I dug the bank scale out of bathroom closet and took it back to my room. I tore the plastic and cardboard off, stuck them between my mattress and box springs. Rex gave me the idea. I set the little dial on the scale to zero, then stripped off my big t-shirt and panties. I took a deep breath, reminded myself to let it out, and stepped on: 170. For the first time ever a scale read less than it had before. Of course, it wasn't the same scale. Crappy bank scale was probably off. It was probably one of those thin scales. Like the way Aunt Jean talks about having a thin mirror.

All the same, I did the math in my head. A day of not eating equals two pounds. There are seven days in a week. That's fourteen pounds per week. Which is fifty-six pounds in a month, which meant I could weigh 115 in a month. Could that be right? I had to factor everything else in. The body won't lose if it thinks it's starving, so I'd have to put something in it. Trick it. So maybe, seven pounds a week. That's 115 in under three months. Not including getting bloated by my period and being forced to eat under certain circumstances, it was still possible that I could be at 115 in four months, if I was good.

I dug out a spot in my closet for the scale. I stuck it in an old box that had my trophy and medals from the Academic Olympics. God, how stupid was that? I used to actually write speeches and then stand up in front of everyone and give them. I can't believe they even hold competitions like that. I mean, was I gonna go into politics? I hadn't written anything since those speeches except for what Mrs. Webb used to make us write in eighth-grade English. I don't even know what happened to my kiddie diary. Now we don't do shit in English class.

I pulled the full-length mirror out with me and leaned it against my Aerosmith poster.

Two pounds was just that, two pounds. It wasn't twenty or thirty or the fifty-five I still needed to loose. I laid black stretch pants out on my bed along with my big billowing black cotton shirt with the long sleeves. I even pulled out the black lace bra and panties set Mom had given me for Christmas last year. She won't let me wear make up, but she gives me the kind of lingerie I imagine strippers wear.

After all my clothes were out, I stopped in front of the mirror and looked at it. I looked at my body only, avoiding my face. For a split second, I was just a girl. A girl like any girl. Tits, legs, pubic hair the color of molasses, thighs, belly button. I was just a girl, like any girl. Then reality set in. Stomach hanging out. Tits falling strangely off to the sides of my body leaving a space big enough to settle a loaf of bread. Ass flat with a couple of zits marking the territory. I looked at the hairs crawling away from my cunt toward my belly button. My chances for escape were no better than theirs.

I turned the mirror around to the wall and headed off to the shower. I'd have to get going if I wanted enough time to put on make up at school. I lathered my body and shaved quickly. I shaved off all those stupid hairs they call a treasure trail. I shaved my pits and my legs and around my cunt.

When I turned the water off I pulled a pair of scissors from the drawer to the side of the sink and nipped off bits of pubic hair. I grabbed up tufts of it with my fingers, snipped and dropped the hair into the toilet. I did this until I had gotten all of the hair I could pull up with my fingers. Then I swiped the back of my hand between my cunt lips and sniffed. All that bathing and it still smelled like pussy. I sprayed some of Mom's Sea Breeze body spray on what was left of the hair and rubbed Jergens lotion on my thighs. On my way back to my room I made a mental note to lift some FDS from K-mart the next time I was there.

The apartment was entirely quiet like a scene from *Night of the Comet*. Maybe Mom and Rudy had turned into little piles of white powder. Maybe the whole world had turned to powder. The whole world except for me and Shelby. If it were true, I'd eat everything I laid eyes on. Me and Shelby could take cars and go wherever we wanted eating out of stores lined with piles of white powder and free food. Powder that used to be some random asshole. We could see the Grand Canyon, Mount Rushmore, the Statue of Liberty. We could see everything.

I grabbed two oranges out of a bowl on the breakfast bar. The more I thought about Shelby and me exploring the ruins of human life, the more I liked the idea. I hurried out the door and into the parking lot where I discovered that, unfortunately, humanity had failed to relinquish itself to a comet. People were everywhere.

I walked fast. I was late already, and worried about the girl crowd in the bathroom. I passed the Hardees, the smell of biscuits and hash browns and everything wonderful and greasy making my mouth water and my stomach gurgle.

"Angie." I heard a voice from behind me.

"Oh, hey Inez." I smiled as she caught up with me. Her hands were strangely empty of books or papers or any of the things most people carry to school.

"Why you go so early, Angie?"

Something about her was different. "Inez, you got a Mohawk!"

"Yeah." she smiled running her hand over a wide prickly stripe of dirty-brown hair. "Did it with a razor."

"A razor? Really? On your own head?" I winced.

She nodded with a smirk. "When it grows some, I'm gonna dye it blue."

"That's cool. How you gonna do it?" I asked.

"Dunno. I seen it on people. Magazine people."

"I heard you can do it with Kool-Aid."

"Kool-Aid." Inez repeated.

"Yeah, that blueberry stuff." I said.

"Washes out." She shrugged.

"Yeah, but you can't wear it to school, anyhow."

"Fuck school." Her face twisted up.

"Yeah," I said.

"Smurfs."

"What?"

"Crush up Smurfs and put 'em in my hair. Perfect blue."

I was silent.

"Why you go so early, Angie?"

"I just wake up early is all."

"You're lying." Inez shook her head and made a tsk-tsk sound with her tongue.

I looked at Inez. Why was I such a bad liar? "My mom won't let me wear make up so I put it on at school."

"Your mom's a hippie?"

"No, anything but! She loves her make up. Actually, since her boyfriend moved in, unless she's hung over, she gets up extra early to put her make up on."

"And so do you."

I glanced sideways at Inez. "Yeah, I guess I do."

Inez and I walked in silence except for the sound of asphalt pebbles crunching under our feet.

"Inez, why do you go to school so early?"

"Get high." She shrugged.

We passed the McDonald's in the Venture parking lot. I held my breath and watched the cars whiz by.

"You wanna get high, Angie? I do it behind the dumpster at McDonald's all the time."

"No. Not the McDonald's."

"Angie's on a diet." Inez pointed. "She's wantin' that egg McMuffin!"

"I am. I really am!"

"I'm always on a diet," she said. "Guess I always will be."

I looked Inez over. She was meaty. Big tits and ass all covered in her baggy jeans and denim jacket. I'd never noticed before. Inez was just the crazy girl who got fucked up on drugs all the time and burned star shapes into her forearms with a coat hanger and a cigarette lighter.

"Get high behind the florist? That's a good place too." Inez motioned toward the store.

"No. I don't get high."

Inez laughed a long wheezy kind of laugh. "Angie. She's the only one not stoned."

"Doesn't it make you hungry?"

"Sometimes."

"How do you pay for it anyway?"

"Sell it. Sell it to the people. Stay high."

"Sell it to who?"

"To the people. All stoned, all the time." She waved her hand in front of her.

I thought for a moment. "I guess that's true, isn't it?"

Inez smiled her big stoned smile and we stepped onto campus.

"Nobody here," Inez observed.

"Yeah, but they'll all be here in, like, ten minutes."

"Millions of 'em." She nodded.

"C'mon, I gotta get my face on," I said.

Inez and I used the door near the cafeteria. I could hear the clanking of line trays, the banging of metal on metal.

Inside the big bathroom, I dropped my back pack on the floor and fished the big Zip-Loc bag of make up out.

Inez put a joint to her lips and lit it. She settled herself on the edge of one of the green sinks and smoked while I went through my new ritual.

"You need a haircut," Inez said, holding her hit the way Heather did.

"You're not the first person to say that."

"I'll give you a mohawk."

"That's okay, Inez. Thanks."

"Angie's a pretty girl. No Mohawks for pretty girls," Inez said into the curl of smoke leaving her mouth.

I swiped glitter mascara over the last of my lashes just as the door swung open and Mindy Overton entered. Her disgusted stare fell over

Inez and me. Mindy rolled her eyes, "Oh great, it's Charlie Manson and Lezzylard stoning it up. Just what I need." Mindy stepped all the way into the bathroom and the door made its silent whoosh as it closed behind her.

I turned away and tucked my make up back in my bag. When I looked up, Inez's head was hanging limply against her chest, her eyes watching her feet as they swung beneath her.

I forgot they called Inez Charlie Manson. I'd never thought about Inez on a diet. I'd never thought about the whole Charlie Manson business or the burns on her arms or her relentless pursuit of ever more black eyeliner. I'd never thought about Inez, period. But suddenly I found myself in the girl's bathroom ready to go at it with Mindy Overton for her.

"Whatever, Mindy. Why don't you just throw up your fucking breakfast and eat a bag of shit already?"

"What?" Mindy stood in front of me with her hands on her hips and her perfectly tanned thigh jutting out of her teal mini-dress. "What was that, Lezzylard? Were you talking to me?"

"Of course I'm talking to you Mindy. You fucking moron."

Mindy put her hand up toward me. "Ugh, please, fat ass. I'm sure." And with that she disappeared into a bathroom stall.

"C'mon," I said under my breath to Inez. And we promptly left.

"We were in kindergarten together." Inez motioned toward the closing bathroom door. "I used to think she was pretty."

"Well, she's not. She's ugly and getting uglier all the time," I said.

Inez giggled, her red eyes standing strangely alert beneath their drooping lids.

"You need a mohawk, Angie. You'll change your mind."

The hall was packed with loud boys.

"I have to go to art class," I told Inez.

"Yeah. I gotta go make the people happy."

"Hey, Inez, there's a party at Heather Mott's place this Friday. Her mom is outta town. You should come."

"Come and get the people stoned?"

"If you want, I guess."

I was at the doorway to my art class before I realized Inez thought I was inviting her just so she could sell drugs to everyone.

I spotted Shelby sitting on the floor outside the art room, reading a book. That was Shelby's defense. She could read a book and walk to class at the same time.

I stood at her feet, my toes nearly touching hers and she didn't blink an eye. Didn't look up, just flipped a page.

"Hey, Shelby, I just told Mindy Overton to eat a bag of shit."

"Good. Maybe that will straighten her ass out."

The last bell rang and Shelby and I took our seats at the back table. The only other person who sat at the table with us was Jenny Meyer. Jenny had blonde hair so light it was almost as white as the paper we drew on everyday. Her eyes were huge behind her glasses and I think she used to have a cleft lip or something. I'm not sure what it was, but something about her mouth was all fucked up. She sat way down the other end of the table from me and Shelby. There were, like, four or five empty chairs on either side of the table between her and us. Jenny was the only person I knew who looked more alone than I felt. And she'd sit there and glare at us. Just glare. She didn't even draw.

In the sixth grade Mrs. Plavan put me and Jenny next to each other in class. Mrs. Plavan pulled me aside and impelled me to be nice to Jenny. So, I tried to be. But Jenny hated my guts. She'd pinch me under the desk and tell me to suck off in her low, froggy voice. The year before, our freshman year, some burner boys were giving her trouble in the hall, I told them to back off and as they did, Jenny said the only two words she had spoken to me since high school started: Fucking lesbian. Unfortunately, Jenny and I were doomed to be in each other's space forever.

"I invited Inez Oliver to Heather's party," I told Shelby.

"Wow. This is gonna be a regular dork fest."

"It's not like you had better plans. Or did you?"

"Nope, not a one."

At lunch, I slipped out the back door of stairwell B and sat behind the annex building. If I went anywhere near the cafeteria I ran the risk of something terrible happening. I could lose control once and for all, just eat my way through the line, handful after greasy handful of food. Green Jell-O and lumpy brown gravy running down my front side. If I started eating, I might not ever stop.

I lit up one of the long menthol cigarettes I stole from my mom and studied my fingernails. I still chewed my nails. Nothing more unappealing than a fat girl with short, raggedy nails. I wondered if there were calories in them. The smoke hit my empty stomach and gave me an instant head rush. If a smoked a few, I'd be stoned out of my mind for fifth-hour Spanish class.

"The cafeteria smells like boiled socks," I heard a voice from behind me say.

I turned my head, running my eyes directly into the perfect flatness of Carrie Shuren's stomach, her little-girl plaid skirt falling off her hips.

"I never eat lunch either," she said, sitting on the ground next to me, lighting up a cigarette.

"Yeah," I said, slowly. "I'm never hungry this time of day."

"Oh, I'm hungry all right." Carrie had a dreamy, almost maniacal look on her face. "I'm so fucking hungry I could eat every damn thing in that cafeteria. But I won't. Willpower, that's all there is. You know?"

Carrie Shuren talking to me? Something in the universe had shifted dramatically. Of course, no one could see her out behind the annex. No one could see her sharing a smoke and a chat with Lezzylard.

"Let's play a game," Carrie said, her pretty dark blonde hair swung over her face as she reached for her bag.

"What sort of game?" I asked, wondering if Brandon Harris, Troy Mulligan, and Curtis Alroy weren't just around the corner waiting to get me.

Carrie pulled a pen and a notebook out of her bag. "Let's make a fantasy grocery list. On this list, we can put anything we want. It's what we would eat if there was no such thing as fat. Whatever we want, as much as we want. I'm gonna start with a half-gallon of rocky road ice cream and two dozen Hostess cupcakes. And I'm gonna eat it all so if you want some, we'll have to get more."

By the time fifth period bell rang, Carrie and I had covered a full page with goodies. Fried chicken, brownies, french fries, cookies, pretzels, pizza rolls, cheese whiz, chocolate milk, cherry pie, ice cream bars, boxes of nutty chocolates, and on and on.

"Hey, Angie." Carrie actually knew my real name. "You should take a multi-vitamin, otherwise your skin will get bad. Acne and stuff. That happened to me last year."

I watched Carrie walk away. Just how the hell did she get in my head?

On my way to Spanish, I got the dizzies. A light headedness knocked me back. I leaned on a locker, as the hall went in and out of focus. I felt a pain in my neck. I was so hungry my neck hurt. I ducked into the bathroom and devoured the two oranges I'd brought from home. Was Carrie ever going to talk to me again once she found out I'd told her best friend to eat a bag of shit? Doubtful. I'd never speak to her again if she'd said that to Shelby.

After school, I found Shelby outside by the tree, her head tucked in her book.

"Whatta'ya readin' anyway, Shelby?"

"*The Shining.*"

"Is it good?"

"I dunno, a little too much like life to suit me. You wanna go play some skee ball ball?" she asked.

"No. I'm so hungry, I'm gonna pass out."

"Didn't you eat lunch?"

"No. I'm gonna go home and make some grilled cheese."

"You know what cheese is, don't you?" Shelby asked.

"Yeah. It's old milk."

"That's what they say, but really, it's cow snot."

"Shut up," I said.

"No, I'm serious! Comes straight out of the cow's nose. All they do is add the coloring. Of course, it's already sort of yellow."

"That is so disgusting."

"Still, it's all true, I read . . ."

Just then Curtis Alroy's cherry red Mustang slowed beside us. It was full of boys. Mike Forester leaned out the passenger window and threw a beer can at Shelby's head. Shelby ducked and the can barely missed her.

"Tell your girlfriend to go on a diet," one of them yelled. Then Curtis sped away.

"Why do guys have to have such loud cars, anyway?" Shelby picked up the can and flung it away from us.

"Those guys get whatever they want," I said. I watched the Mustang rush away toward the mall. A sick bubble filled up my gut.

The same feeling I had when Mike Forester called me a lesbian pig. The same feeling I got when Troy Mulligan dropped his drawings in front of me in art class. It was probably him that yelled. I couldn't be sure, all those guys might as well have been one guy. They were exactly the same.

"When they die, it will be horrible, slow, and alone. Trust me," Shelby said.

"If you are devising a murder plan, count me in."

"You wanna come over? Robyn is supposed to be at work."

"No. I gotta go see my mom's friend. She doesn't know who her baby's daddy is and she's kinda freaked out. My mom wants me to check in on her." I lied my ass off.

Shelby narrowed her eyes on me. She tried to figure if I was lying or not.

"Since when you been the counselor?"

"It's just something I said I would do."

CHAPTER 7

I cut over to the K-mart to take care of business.

I only had eight dollars so most of my shopping would be the five-finger discount kind. I grabbed a box of strawberry Slim-Fast. I picked the extra strength formula Dexatrim and stuck it in my stretch pants. One aisle over I found the FDS. I looked at the different scents for awhile. What did I want to smell like? Powder Puff? Daisy Fresh? Summer Breeze? I just wanted to not smell like pussy. I wanted to smell like nothing. Finally, I chose Powder Puff. I liked the pink box. I stuffed it down the back of my pants.

In the same aisle, I grabbed a pack of pink razors and stuck them down the front of my pants. I found the Clearasil and put a tube of it in next to the razors, then headed for the checkout line. I'd been stealing from that K-mart since I was nine years old, but it still made me nervous. Heather had been caught stealing a Bon Jovi cassette.

"Bon Jovi is stupid," Shelby told her.

"He's cute. You just wouldn't know that."

"I know what cute boys look like, Heather. And I can tell you he's not cute, he's stupid."

"Those guards followed me because of my tit."

"What? You were stealing and you got caught." Shelby poked a finger at her, "You can't blame that on your tit."

"They kept looking at it. While they had me in back, waiting for my mom. The security guard, the manager, the real cop they called. All of them were looking at it, staring the whole time. Like, *The Tit Who Stole Manhattan*." Heather looked between my left tit and Shelby's almost non-existent left tit with wide leering eyeballs and made her point.

"That sucks," I breathed, and even Shelby didn't have a smart comment to make about it.

I waited in line hoping the cellophane around the razors wasn't making too loud of a crunch in my pants. The sound was deafening to me. I scanned the covers of all the magazines, acting as casual as possible. *Cosmo* had an article: Lose Ten Pounds in FOUR Days! All it said was to stop eating. Which I had already figured out. It recommended four grapefruits a day and some celery.

I made it through the line paying only for the Slim-Fast. I headed for the doors marked EXIT. Nervous as hell, I stopped at the quarter machines and bought two of those little plastic balls filled with goo. One was orange and the other pink. Shelby loved that goo shit. She just thought it was so gross it was funny. I smiled at the security guard on my way out and finally took a real breath. Some people like the feeling of shoplifting. I hated it.

When I got to the field, I stooped in the tall, brown grass and transferred everything from my pants to my back pack. I was going home to eat. I needed to eat something, but not what I was about to eat, which was anything I could get my hands on.

I didn't even bother dropping my back pack before I swung the fridge door open. I grabbed a single wrapped slice of American cheese, tore the plastic off, and shoved it in my mouth. I turned on the big screen and flipped the channels for a minute. I always thought if we had cable I would never be bored again, but I was wrong. I settled on a *Murder She Wrote* re-run.

Cheese. Butter. Pickles. Bread. Potato chips, Oreos and a can of Coke. I made four gooey cheese sandwiches, the first of which I ate in three bites as I made the second. Tell your girlfriend to go on a diet.

I kicked off my shoes, curled into the couch and ate. I watched Angela Landsbury pretend to be shocked, then indignant, then gracious. Guilt-free eating. The very best kind. But after two more sandwiches I felt full and kept eating anyway. I ate the other sandwich, and the entire bag of greasy off-brand potato chips. By the time I got to the cookies, I was absolutely stuffed. Still, I ate like ten or twelve of them.

I fell back into the crook of the sofa, pulled Mom's fuzzy pink afghan around my stomach and held myself. Over the rubble of the empty chip bag and Coke can on the coffee table, I watched a commercial for Levi button-fly jeans. During a shampoo commercial, I fell asleep.

I woke up almost two hours later, still groggy and full. At least I had time to clean up the coffee table and get safely to my room before Rudy would be home. I crumpled up the chip bag and shoved it to the bottom of the trashcan. I wiped out the skillet I'd used and put it away. I turned the TV off and headed for my room just as Rudy's key hit the lock.

I shut my bedroom door quickly. My book bag was still in the living room, which meant my homework was in there too. I fell back on my bed. What the hell I was gonna do for the next two hours before Mom got home? I closed my eyes, tried to stop myself from thinking.

Rudy was lurking around somewhere, maybe even snooping through my bag. Shit. What if he found that fucking box of FDS? I would die of shame. Absolutely die. I had to go in there. Get in there before a couple of beers made Rudy curious. I pulled in a deep breath, readied myself for the experience. That's when the door swung open.

"Hey, Angie. Whatcha doin' in here all by yourself?"

I sat up. "Don't you knock?"

"Why? You doin' somethin' you don't want me to see?"

"Yeah, I was just getting ready to cook up some smack, Rudy."

I stood as casually as I could. I evaluated how much of the doorway was taken up by his body. All of it. His back leaned into the jam, his arm stretched to the other side of the frame. A Busch beer can dangled from his fingers.

"See, that's why I got to check up on you, girl. Too much freedom will ruin you." He smiled a smile I did not understand.

"I was getting ready to do my homework, actually."

"All work and no play, huh?"

"Yeah. Sure. I guess."

Silence fell between us. Rudy studied the posters on my wall. I steadied a sinking panic against a pound of digesting cheese.

"No way!" Rudy pointed to the corner of my room. "You like The Who?"

"Everybody likes The Who."

"I got some stuff on original vinyl. I mean, from when it came out." His face softened.

"Really?" I acted excited even though I couldn't have given a fuck if my life had depended on it. "Good condition?"

"Oh, yeah! Course." He nodded.

"You got it here?"

"Yeah, come look." Rudy's body left the doorway. His hand motioned for me to follow. I let out a heart-pounding breath and passed through the doorway.

Rudy's beer was set on the corner of the coffee table and he knelt in front of a milk crate flipping through records.

"Here it is, mint condition." He put *Meaty Beaty Big and Bouncy* in my hand. I swear his chest really did puff up.

"Can I take it out of the plastic?" All I wanted was to get away, but for the next few minutes, I praised his record collection instead.

"We can put this Who record on, if you want."

Rudy was in the corner. Not between me and the door.

"No. I got a social studies test tomorrow. I'm going over to Inez's house. She takes better notes than me." I moved toward my bag as I spoke.

"Well, okay." He was disappointed. "You must get all A's, huh? Smart girl?"

"Yeah, mostly. See ya." I slipped out the door and literally ran down the stairs. Outside, I walked. Walked away from the apartment. Moving toward nothing in particular. There wasn't anything in particular to move toward. I didn't think about it.

The sky changed from light blue to purple as I arrived, for whatever reason, among the bushes outside Carrie Shuren's house. It wasn't dark enough to be hidden so I turned the corner and walked it until I hit the service road. The sky changed again from purple to navy black and I went back. Back to the bushes at the end of Monroe Street.

Fake black shutters, drawn ivory curtains. I wanted to knock on the door. I wanted Carrie to be happy to see me and invite me to her room to listen to music. I wanted to tell her everything. The binge, the FDS, Rudy, Curtis Alroy's Mustang, Inez, Aunt Jean, everything.

I wanted to scream and cry it all out to her. I wanted her to nod her head. To understand.

I laid back in the grass. I looked at the stars. Dimmed stars strangled by streetlights and a wall of chain stores hiding just beyond the thin line of trees that separated Carrie Shuren's world from mine.

When I finally got myself home, my mother was parked at the kitchen table. I assumed the drink was her usual 7&7. Her hair was pulled back in one of those horrible bows I always told her went out in like 1985. The bow was the same red as her Red Lobster apron, which she was still wearing.

"Hi, Angie," she said. "You hungry? I could heat up something."

"No, I ate after school."

"Yeah, she did," Rudy said, coming down the hall. "Ate everything in the house. I had a whole bag of chips in there. Did you eat a whole bag of chips today?" Rudy asked, throwing his arms up.

My face went beet red and hot. "Me and Shelby watched some TV."

"That girl can eat at home. I ain't got two kids."

"You ain't got no kids," I said, before I realized I was saying it.

"Not now. Neither of you." Mom waved her cigarette in the direction of Rudy's about-to-say-somethin' mouth. "I had a hard day. Can we all at least pretend to get along?"

Mom, for the first time ever, looked old. Rudy bowed his head a little and stepped behind Mom. He started rubbing' her shoulders.

I sat down at the table next to her. "So, what happened today?"

"Same old shit. Some asshole from the regional office came in today. Happens a couple times a year. Always guaranteed to make for a shit day. I've been there five years, you'd think they'd leave me alone. But no, can't do that. They gotta implement New Procedures. So now we gotta cash everybody through before they pay, like that makes any kind of fuckin' sense. Gotta do all the math for change every time. Slowin' everything down is all their doing. And they want us to give some ridiculous speech when we get to the table and all anybody ever wants to do is order their damn lunch. You'd think these people never ate in a restaurant. God knows they've never had a real job, you know, one where you work?" Mom dumped the rest of her drink down her throat and set the empty glass in front of me. "Angie, would you make me another one?"

Aunt Jean taught me how to make 7&7's at cousin Bev's wedding. I was eight and as far as Aunt Jean was concerned, I was a damn good cocktail waitress. "You want me to make you a bath?" I asked as I delivered her drink.

"Yeah, that sounds good."

I used a couple squirts of a bath oil Mom had gotten from her Secret Santa the previous Christmas. I grabbed her little silk robe off a hook and laid it over the back of the toilet. Under the sink, I found a red candle melted into an old saucer and lit it.

"Okay, Mom. Your bath is ready," I told her as I rounded the corner to find her and Rudy kissing.

"Thanks." She pulled her head back from Rudy.

I left them alone. Went to my own room. Turned to the story of Ed Gein. He was a killer, but he seemed more confused than anything. He gutted some people like deer and hung them in his barn. I felt sorry for him. I don't know why, but I did. Though I don't suppose I would have if I'd been gutted.

My bedroom door swung open again; twice in one day the same uninvited guest.

"Look here, girl." Rudy said. "Don't you EVER upset her like that again. From now on, no more of your friends in the house. And, no more eatin' after school. You can wait for us, so we can all eat like proper people. Any questions?"

"Nope. Not a one," I said.

Rudy shut the door with a hard thump. I went back to my book. Back to Ed Gein's small-town barn.

CHAPTER 8

Fashion Industry Secret: They don't make jeans for girls with big guts and no ass. How many pairs of stretch pants have I worn the crotch out of? Always the first part to wear out. I used to still wear them with a hole or two until I realized I must have looked like a chronic pussy scratcher.

I opened the FDS and stuck the empty carton between my mattress and box springs. I was accumulating quite a collection of contraband under there. That princess with her pea, or whatever, would have broken her back in my bed.

I aimed the aerosol can and gave it a good spray. It definitely smelled like powder. It felt powdery but sticky too. I hid the can under the bed. Mom was sleeping in again, so I took two Dexatrims, mixed a Slim-Fast, drank it and left. I hit the sidewalk and there was no way I was going to school. How the fuck did anyone go to school?

I went straight for the pay phone and called Mrs. Beckham. I told her Angie had allergies. She suggested Tylenol. I was free for the day.

I headed for the Field House, a circle of trees in the middle of the field next to the K-mart. It was like a little island out there. The older guys dragged a couch and coffee table under the trees. Heather said she lost her virginity to Mike Patterson in the field house during our freshman year. She was probably telling the truth, but Shelby liked to accuse her of lying. Shelby told Heather she couldn't have fucked Mike Patterson because if she had she would know he was really a girl. I don't know where she came up with that.

I ducked under the branches to find the familiar couch and makeshift coffee table. The way the sun came through the branches-made the inside circle glow orange. It was almost beautiful, except for the reeking mold.

"Hi," a voice came out of nowhere. I screamed and jumped about ten feet in the air.

"Jesus, God! You scared the fuck out of me!" I said.

A skinny boy with black spiky hair was laughing and pointing.

"I didn't mean to. I swear. I tried to keep my voice down. Are you okay?"

"Yeah. I'm all right."

He laughed some more. "You should have seen your face!"

"Okay, Okay. You scared me. I jumped out of my skin. Let's forget it," I said.

I dumped my backpack onto the couch and sat down. We looked at each other for a long minute before he asked, "What's in the bag?"

"School books, stuff." I shrugged.

"You're a strange one."

"Why's that?"

"You come out here to study?"

"No. I had to leave the house like I was goin' to school. I had to look like I planned on goin' to school, you know?"

"I guess. You go to Mehlville?"

"Yeah. Where you go? I haven't seen you before."

"I don't."

"You don't what?"

"I don't go to school, at all."

"Really?"

"Yeah. My mom moved us up here from Tulsa a few weeks ago. She registered me at that Mehlville or whatever, but I never showed up and no one seems to notice. So, I figure, if I just never go, nobody will ever know the difference."

"You don't think your mom will catch on?"

"Probably not."

The whites of his eyes were as pink as strawberry Slim-Fast.

"I'm Pike," he said, sticking his hand out to me.

"Angie."

"So, Angie, what the hell were you gonna do all day?"

"I was gonna read here for awhile and then, I dunno, go watch some cable or something."

"So, you really are going to study?"

I reached into my bag. "I was gonna read this."

"*Serial Killers*, huh? You get into that shit?"

"Sure. It's creepy. And it's real, you know? Like, these guys really do all this stuff to people. Kidnap 'em and cut 'em up and stuff."

"Who's your favorite?" Pike asked.

"Right now, it's Henry Lee Lucas. Him and his friend killed a lot of people. They don't even know how many. Could be as many as three hundred. Henry's mom dressed him like a girl when he was a kid."

"Manson too."

"Oh yeah?"

"Dresses make people crazy. That's what's wrong with women."

"Shut up." I threw the book at his head.

When he leaned over to pick the book up, I studied his profile. He was all acne and thick black eyelashes. He was certainly cute enough though. Small and cute. My imagination spun away from there. I pictured him as my new boyfriend. We were going steady and I lost my virginity with him and he got a cool car and we got married right after high school and he got me sardines and ice cream while I was pregnant.

By the time he handed the book back to me, we were getting a divorce.

"Well, don't worry, you look like the cross-dresser type anyway. Which is lucky for you, considering the alternative," Pike said.

"Might be too late. My mom put me in dresses when I was a kid."

"Oh, no! Just like Lucas and Manson! You could be ten seconds away from your first meltdown."

"Why do you think I followed you out here?" I opened my eyes wide and tried to affect a glazed look.

"That's fucked up. But, can you do this?" Pike moved his eyebrows so that one was up while the other was down.

"Yeah, I can do that." I mirrored his movements, keeping the wide-eyed thing going.

"All right. Okay. That actually is a little scary."

I fell into the couch. Pike was pretty funny, but I didn't want to have a crush on him.

"Were you just going to sit here and get high all day?" I asked.

"Yeah, pretty much. I ain't got nothin' else to do. No school, no friends, no money."

"But you have weed? How do you have weed if you don't have any money?"

"Oh, I brought this stuff with me. I used to sell it back in Tulsa. Stayed high that way."

I nodded. That seemed to be the basic equation: Sell + Weed = Stay High.

"You can come over to my house. My mom leaves for work pretty soon, then we can watch TV until school lets out."

"TV? Wow. Is that what people do for fun around here?"

"Yep. Get used to it."

I settled in, putting my legs up on the wobbly table and opening my book. Pike pulled a little notebook out of his pocket and started doodling in it. I tried to keep my mind focused on a chapter called The Mind of a Serial Killer, but I kept wondering what Pike was working on. After reading a few sentences I peeked over at him, but I couldn't see the picture he was making.

"It says here that serial killers hear voices telling them to do it," I said. I wanted Pike's attention but I didn't want him to know that I wanted it.

"Yeah, like I hear voices telling me to smoke weed and you hear voices telling you to lift stuff from the K-mart."

"What?"

"Oh, c'mon, Angie. I saw you over there. Taking stuff out of your clothes and putting it in your bag. You must be pretty slick." Pike looked over the edge of his little notebook and raised an eyebrow.

"I dunno, maybe," I said, looking over to where I had transferred the goods. My face flushed. Could Pike have seen that bright pink box of FDS? I'd have been less concerned about Rudy or Pike or anyone else in the world catching me carting around a dead body.

"Maybe you can show me how it's done. In that store, I mean. You know, where the cameras are and stuff," Pike said.

"You just got to watch out for security, is all. It's easy because they all strut around. You can spot 'em a mile away."

"Do they have guns?"

"I don't know. Doubt it."

"Comic books?"

"Yeah. A few. Lots of magazines, though."

"Well, you can still show me around."

"Yeah. Maybe some time." I motioned for Pike to follow me out under the tree branches. I wasn't going think about whether or not he might have seen the FDS. If I let myself wonder, I'd get totally obsessed with it.

"My mom should be gone by now," I told Pike.

A car went by on Sunworth Road. It stopped and backed up. I took in a sharp breath. Whatever was about to happen would be some kind of horrible embarrassment. As far as I was concerned, Pike could live the rest of his life without hearing the word Lezzylard.

"Angie, what the fuck are you doing?" It was Robyn's baby-blue Cutlass full of all that peroxide blonde hair and sweet perfume.

"Just goin' to my house, Robyn."

"Cut school again? Get in."

"No. We don't need a ride."

"Don't be stubborn, Angie. You'll get picked up out here in the open. Then you'll never be able to cut again." Robyn pushed the passenger door open. Pike shrugged and climbed in the back, I sat in the front. Pike did not realize his doom was imminent.

"Who are you?" Robyn looked at Pike in the rearview mirror with its little smelly pine tree dancing back and forth.

"I'm Pike. I just moved here."

"What the hell kind of name is Pike?"

"What the hell kind of name is Robyn?"

"Is it short for something? Smartass. You know, like Dick is short for Richard?"

"Funny you should ask because, Richard, actually, is short for Pike. So you can call me Rich, Ritchie, Dick, Dickie. The options are endless."

"Okay, Dick. You fucking smart-assed brat. You'll be lucky if I don't drop you off at that school and let you get caught cuttin'. I asked you a simple question and you gotta give me a bunch of lip and here I am doing you a favor and everything."

"How about you don't do me any favors, Robyn? I mean, a minute ago I was having a perfectly nice day and now I'm here with some obviously psychotic woman insulting my name."

"That's it!" Robyn pointed her finger at him in the rearview mirror. "You're going to school." Robyn made a quick, gravel sputtering turn onto Meadow Brook Lane. She smiled the way she did when she was about to hurt someone. "This street will take us right past the tennis courts, to the front door, Dick. How you like that?"

"I don't like it or dislike it, Robyn. I feel utterly neutral about this whole thing."

"Robyn." I broke in. "Can you please just let us out? There's no point in dropping him off, he doesn't even go to Mehlville."

Robyn stomped the brakes and we all lurched forward.

"Robyn," I said. "I don't need whiplash over this. Okay? We're just going to get out and go to my house." I pulled the door handle and heard it click before Robyn sped off again. "Robyn, C'mon. The door is open. You're going to end up getting me killed."

"Stop whining, Angie. For fuck's sake. I'll take you and Dickass here to your house. Dickass, is that short for Pike, too?"

"As a matter of fact, Robyn, it is. Some of my best friends call me Dickass," Pike said coolly.

"Well, we ain't friends, Dickass." Robyn pointed one of those nails at his reflection.

"I won't argue with you there, Robyn."

"Good." Robyn calmed as quickly as she had angered.

I let out a breath, if we could just get out of the car and away from it before she went crazy and ran us over, we'd live another day.

"Hey." Robyn turned to me. "This party tomorrow? I gotta get money from you guys before I go to the liquor store."

"Okay. I'll talk to Heather and call you tonight. Maybe she can bring it by or something."

"Yeah. Somebody get me some money and then me and Vince will be there about seven or so tomorrow."

"Or we could get it from your house so you guys wouldn't have to go out of your way."

"Nice try, Angie. There's no way I'm gonna let you kids hang out and get drunk without any grown-ups around. Me and Vince are gonna chaperone that shit."

"What?"

"You heard me."

I didn't say anything else. There was no point arguing with her. The more resistance she sensed the more she'd have to squash it. Besides, I was still stuck in her stupid car with the door barely latched. Robyn could go racing onto the highway and I'd fly out at eighty miles an hour into four lanes of traffic.

"How in the world do you know that woman?" Pike asked as I unlocked the apartment door.

"She's my best friend's sister. I've known her most of my life."

"Oh. I'm sorry to hear that."

"You really pissed her off."

"Seems easy to do."

"Yeah, nothing's easier. Didn't you have crazy people in Tulsa?" I went instinctively to the refrigerator. I wasn't specifically hungry. That's just what fat people do. Gravitate to refrigerators.

"Crazy people are everywhere. I just haven't been in a car with one since my dad died."

I rummaged around the top shelf of the refrigerator. "Oh, was your dad nuts?" I'd never met anyone my age with a dead parent. I wasn't sure what to say.

"He was officially nuts. Papers and all. And he liked us to know he could kill us if he wanted to."

"That's exactly how Robyn is." No one had ever said it that simply.

"That's how crazy people are. What's this about a party tomorrow?"

I didn't want to talk about the party. It was sure to be a dork-fest as Shelby had described it. With, of course, Robyn and Vince harassing us.

"Oh, my friend's mom is out of town and she's gonna have some people over. It'll be lame."

"Is it like a slumber party? Like girls-only kind of thing?"

"No. I just don't know how many people will be there. They have a pretty nice house and everything."

"Oh." Pike flopped down on the couch, obviously hoping to be invited.

"You can come, if you want. I don't know how much fun it will be. Especially with Robyn and Vince there. But, Heather and Inez smoke plenty of weed. And, I dunno, if you want to come, you can. I'm just not promising it will be cool or anything."

"I'm anti-cool anyway," Pike said, and turned on the TV.

We watched one of those ads you had to watch all the way through to find out what was being sold because it didn't make any sense.

"Does this actually make women buy perfume?" Pike threw a hand into the air.

"I guess. Why else would it be on?"

"It doesn't make any sense."

"Maybe it comes back like one of those voices killers hear." I got on my knees next to him and whispered in his ear, "Buy Obsession, kill your neighbor. Pike, kill your neighbor."

Pike chuckled, pushing me off. "Don't you think if you heard a voice like that you'd, like, do something about it? I mean, if I really heard a voice say that, I'd tell someone."

I was still whispering, "Not if you'd already killed your neighbor, Pike. Kill your neighbor."

"That's twisted. I don't even know my neighbor."

"Hasn't stopped anyone else."

I flipped through the TV channels trying not to stop on food commercials. But, that's all there ever was, really. Food and boobs.

"You're going too fast," Pike said.

"There's nothing on. Trust me." I put the remote in his hand and went to the refrigerator, again. The Dexatrim was wearing off.

"Pike, you hungry?"

"I'm always hungry."

I grabbed a can of Coke for him and looked around for something Rudy wouldn't notice missing. There was a box of off-brand cream-filled cupcakes at the bottom of the freezer. It had probably been there since before Mom even met Rudy. She had gone through some kind of half psychotic obsession with those cupcakes, once. She bought a whole shit load of them and refused to eat anything else for like two weeks. I grabbed the box and hit it against the counter to break apart the layer of ice formed on top of it.

"Here." I handed Pike the Coke and the box of cupcakes.

"These are frozen solid," he said.

"They'll thaw," I said. My stomach rumbled.

Pike threw the cupcakes on the coffee table with an icy thump.

"I guess I'll have a couple sometime tomorrow. Hey, can we get high in here?"

"You can smoke some out my bedroom window." I pointed Pike down the short hall as if he couldn't have found his way to the west wing without a very specific map.

In the bathroom, I swallowed two more Dexatrims. I had to make it to our stupid family dinner without eating. I pulled my stretch pants down and sat on the toilet for a piss. I thought I'd lose my mind when the smell hit me: Powder Puff FDS and pussy. That was it. Like Mom's cherry marijuana night. Like that pine tree over the rearview mirror in Robyn's car, which always reeked of White Castle hamburgers and cigarettes with just a hint of pine. Tons of worry about being caught with the stuff and all just to still smell like pussy.

I found Pike leaning out the window in my bedroom. I don't think it ever had a screen in it. I remember my mother saying, what do we need screens for? We have air-conditioning! She was so excited about that when we moved in. She'd never lived anywhere with any kind of air-conditioning, much less central air.

"Here." Pike stuck the joint out to me.

"No thanks. I don't get high."

Pike shrugged and returned his attention to the browning grass landscape outside the window. I popped a Velvet Underground tape in and pushed play.

"You like this shit?" Pike's face twisted around the words.

"No. I just put it on to bother myself," I said, pulling a shoebox from under my bed.

"Oh, good. Sarcasm."

"Now, THAT was sarcasm."

Pike turned his head to look at me. "Touché."

"What does that mean? Touché? I've heard it before. What does it mean?" I was digging through the bottles of nail polish I kept in the shoebox.

"I don't know what it means. It's French. It could mean anything."

"You done with that joint? I want to paint your nails."

Pike took a long hit then slowly crushed the roach out on the windowsill. He was neat and focused about the whole action, slipping the roach into a little cellophane baggie, like the ones that come around a pack of cigarettes. He let the smoke curl slowly out of his nose and gently shut the window. When he finally turned to me, his face was a wreck of drooping eyelids and a sloppy smile.

"Jesus," I said. "Get wasted often?"

"I'm always wasted. You got black polish?"

"Yeah, but I want to paint your nails fuchsia. No, wait. Cotton Candy Pearl. It's so you."

"Okay." He moved from the window and sat next to me on the floor.

"Okay? You're gonna let me paint your nails pink? Aren't the guys gonna make fun of you?"

"What guys, Angie? I don't know anyone here besides you. And even though you're a cross-dresser, and there's nothing wrong with that, you appear to be all girl. Besides, fuck anyone who doesn't have a sense of humor. In fact, fuck a lot of people who do. I mean . . ."

"Okay, okay, give me your hand." I yanked his arm my direction. "Your nails are filthy!"

"Isn't that what the polish is for? To cover up the dirt?"

"NO!"

"Oh. I thought that was how girls got away with being dirty. Polish and paint and perfume."

"You did not. Go wash your hands and under the sink is some incense, bring it in here."

Pike pulled himself up slowly and wandered into the hall. He was a really dirty boy. But he didn't stink in any particular way. I picked through the box, putting aside bottles I planned to throw out. Some of them were six or eight years old. I didn't want to wind up like my mother, who had boxes of decaying make up at the bottom of her closet and under her bed, some of it probably twenty years old. Aunt Jean says we should call the fucking Smithsonian.

Pike finally returned to the room with most of a cupcake sticking out of his mouth. "Good, frozen," I think he said.

"Do you have chocolate all over your hands now?"

Pike looked at his hands, shook his head and gave both paws a hard wipe down the front of his black denim pants. The rest of the cupcake was swept up by his tongue and loaded into his cheeks. He looked like a dirty punk rock chipmunk.

Pike sat next to me on the floor while I shook the bottle of nail polish.

"Where's the incense?"

"Huh? Oh. I forgot. I'll get it."

"No never mind. That pot smells like incense anyway."

"Opium," he said, smiling at the bottle in my hand.

"What?"

"Opium. It smells sweet like incense. Tastes sweet, too."

"Opium? Isn't that like heroin?"

"No. Actually, heroin . . ." Pike raised his index finger and looked at me. ". . . is heroin and opium is opium. Don't ever forget that."

"I won't," I said with mock seriousness and began painting his square, dirty nails.

"This is going to take a couple of coats," I informed him.

"Well, we have plenty of time, don't we? Just tell me we can lose the Nico." Pike pointed to the stereo. "That right there, THAT is heroin."

"If you'll quit complaining, I'll turn it off," I said, and I did it.

"Put on something else. God, you have tons of records."

"Yeah. I like music."

"I see that Circle Jerks, put that on."

I was applying the third coat of paint to Pike's nails when he asked, "Can you put black lighting bolts on them?"

"Maybe on your thumbs. The rest are too small. I could put dots on those."

"No. They have to be the same. Put dots on all of them."

"Alright. Dots it is. Then we go to Heather's. I gotta break the Robyn news to her."

CHAPTER 9

Heather was barefoot on her front porch sharing a cigarette with Rex. Her eyes lit on us and her back straightened when she saw Pike.

"Shit." Pike breathed. "She isn't gonna, like, kick my ass or anything is she?"

"No. I only know one Robyn."

"And that's one too many."

"What? You didn't go to school today either?" Heather asked.

"No. I had a previous engagement," I told her.

I introduced everyone. Rex gave Pike a shake and Heather wiggled her fingers, then swung her head my way, her eyes squinting against the sun. "What are you guys doin'? Just walking around aimlessly?"

"No," I said. "We've been sitting around aimlessly. What are you guys doin'? Studying for a cancer research group?"

"Something like that. Waitin' around for a bag."

"I've got some smoke if you want, while you're waiting." Pike offered.

"I still got a little. Wanna match?" Heather asked.

"Sure. My kinda girl," Pike said and Rex gave him a look.

"Sorry, man," Pike said, showing his palms.

"It's cool, just don't let it happen again." Rex winked.

"Shut up, Rex. You don't own me!" Heather swung the door open and jutted that one big tit out. "You are NOT my boyfriend."

"Oh, so, like, if I was your boyfriend, I'd own you?"

"No, stupid. You sounded like my boyfriend and you're not, okay?"

"Okay," Rex said, showing his palms this time.

We all flopped down in the living room. Dotting the chairs like so many black spots on Pike's pink nails.

Rex, Heather, and Pike got to the business of smoking weed. And that was a serious business. Everyone knew how it was done, even me. I knew Heather was pulling her tray out because it clanked with the sounds of her tools. Like a surgeon's tray. It even had a pair of hemostat on it. An object I knew the name and use of only because of Heather. So it really was like a surgeon's tray and should any of us, for whatever reason, need an artery clamped shut, Heather would be ready.

I looked around at the stacks of beauty magazines Heather's mom collected. All shit. I wanted to see those porn mags again.

"Hey, Heather, where are those . . ." My eyes fell on Rex. "Nevermind."

Rex might have actually needed an artery clamped shut if I'd said what I almost did.

I studied Rex for a moment. He had seen the monster porn. Did he enjoy it? Did it hang in his mind the way it did in mine? I imagined Rex lying on his bed. His dick in his hand. The magazine propped up on his chest. I could see his hand moving up and down. Rex breathing heavy, staring at the picture of that woman with her legs lassoed, wanting a monster she didn't want to want.

I pictured Rex's face going flaccid, giving in. Did guys like to watch themselves jerk off? Did they like to look at their cocks while they handled them? If so then maybe he'd prop the magazine up on his thighs. Come right on that woman in her monster's dungeon.

Rex took the joint from Heather and settled back into one of Heather's mother's straight-backed chairs. He closed his eyes and took a long hit into his throat and lungs. Rex with his Fuck Everything t-shirt, his dirty-brown devil-lock hair cut. His monster porn. Was he the monster fucking that woman? Damn. Rex was hot. Way hotter than I had ever noticed before. Rex—and that woman and that monster and that magazine and his dick in his hand—was just hot.

Rex leaned forward as he handed the joint over to Pike, stomping his boots on the floor and coughing out his hit. Pike took the joint from him but not before he gave me a raise-eyebrow look. I was absolutely busted staring at Rex. A hot blush came over my face. I lunged for a *Cosmopolitan* stacked neatly under the coffee table. I opened it quickly and held it in front of my face. It was a Guess model bent over the trunk of a sporty red car. Her back was arched. A man stood behind her looking at her ass and clutching a gas pump. I wondered if it was illegal to fuck a woman with a gas pump, and decided it probably wasn't.

When my blush finally faded, I threw the magazine on the floor and sat up straight. "So Heather, about the beer situation for tomorrow night?"

"Yeah. I heard Robyn was gonna do it. That she was gonna buy it for us."

"Yeah, she is." I paused.

"There's a catch, though," Pike said, handing the smoking joint to Heather.

"A catch? What catch?"

"A catch 22 even," Pike said.

"A what?" Heather asked.

"She's going to chaperone," I said quickly.

Heather snapped her head back in my direction and spit out her hit. "She's what?"

"Okay." Rex stood. "Let's not waste the goods there, dear." He took the joint from Heather's fingers.

"Chaperone? Robyn?" Heather asked, without expecting a reply.

I raised my eyebrow and held a finger up, "With Vince, no less."

"Vince? Who's Vince?"

"Her boyfriend," I said.

"Well, they can't," Heather said, as if it were that simple. Then she looked around at Rex and stuck her arm out. "Give me that, you fucking junkie." Heather took a long drag then spoke softly to the joint, "She can't. That's all. End of story."

Pike looked over at me. "Can you get beer from someone else?"

"No. Not me. Heather, can you get beer from someone else?"

"We could steal it." Heather's eyes lit up.

"Oh sure. Let's just steal it. That's great Heather. Should we get all fucked up on pot first or just try it straight?"

"Oh, good. More sarcasm." Pike pointed at me.

"Well, that's not really practical is it? Stealing beer. I mean, we could steal somebody's parent's supply, maybe. But just walk into a store and take it? Are you nuts? Where would we put it?"

"Why don't we all just drop some acid instead?" Rex said. "I've got fifty hits in the freezer at home."

"Well." Heather leaned toward me. "What about Inez?"

"What about her?" I shrugged.

"That girl has such a big ass," Rex said to Pike.

"Well, doesn't she know that guy?" Heather asked. "Randy or whatever? That weirdo with the pickup? I think she sells him pot or something."

"Who is this Inez?" Pike asked.

"She's crazy," Rex said. "She cuts up her arms and talks to herself and she's got this big ass and . . ."

"Rex!" Heather interrupted. "Let's stick to business here."

"Sorry, dear."

Heather put her hand up like she was about to read Rex the riot act, but stopped when she looked toward the picture window, where a face impressed itself onto the glass. The face blew its cheeks out, making a ring of fog around its head.

"It's Alien," Rex informed us with a grin.

Alien's name was a reference to how completely weird looking he was. He had big bulging blue eyes and an oblong shaped head that seemed strangely big for his body. Alien was always hitting on me. Staring at my tits, sitting close to me and using old pick up clichés with a snigger. Come here often, baby? That kind of thing. I understood it. Ugly guy. Fat girl. Alien figured if he ever had a chance at getting laid it was with me. I guess.

"Fuck off!" Heather yelled and smacked the glass with the palm of her hand. That's the way people treated Alien. He was ugly and he knew it and he'd impose himself on people. Make people pay attention to him. Sometimes, I wished I was more like him. Just walk into a room like, I'm fat and I'm here to make you miserable. But most of the time I just told him to fuck off.

Heather swung the front door open. "Get in here asshole. We have a problem."

"Problem? Drug problem? Can't help you there. But you certainly have a need-a-tittie problem and I'm available for that. Since no one needs a tittie more than me."

"That doesn't even make any sense, Alien!" Heather threw her shoulders backward.

"Hey, Alien." Rex squinted his eyes. "Have you actually gotten uglier?"

"Oh, like that's possible. But you, stud boy, could suffer." Alien threw the weight of his body into Rex, the chair tilting back toward the wall as Alien landed.

Rex rolled him to the floor and jumped on top of him. "Now you die, you little troll!"

"Enough, you guys! You're gonna break something!" Heather pounded on Rex's back. Rex stopped, rolled off Alien, leaving him on the floor in front of me. "Hi Angie." He smiled and gave me a little air smooch. I gave him the finger.

"Rex is the only one who profits from this Buddy System," Alien said.

"You came up with that, and I never agreed!" I said.

The Buddy System was Alien's brain-child. The idea was that all of us would pair off into friendly couples that had sex. Not boyfriend and girlfriend, just friends who did it when they weren't busy doing someone else. Rex and Heather already had this down, and Alien wanted to extend its benefits to himself with me as his Buddy.

"Man," Alien said as he stood. "If it weren't for all the love in this room, I'd find new friends. Speaking of which, who the fuck are you?"

"I'm Pike."

"Pike? That's a name?"

"No."

"No?"

"No." Pike shook his head. There was silence as they looked at one another for a beat or two.

"So, what's this problem anyway?" Alien flopped on the couch next to Heather.

"We need someone to buy beer for tomorrow night," Heather said.

"I thought lesbo's sister was gonna do it."

"She will. And she wants to chaperone," Heather told Alien.

"Oh. Oh no. I get laid tomorrow night. No chaperones. Absolutely not."

"Lesbo's sister is fuckin' crazy, man," Rex explained to Alien. "Wait until you see her fuckin' hair. Dude, it's so disco!"

Alien looked at Rex. "I heard lesbo's sister is a secret military weapon. When they need to kick some horny guy's ass they send her in and . . ."

"It's true, lesbo's sister is, like, totally . . ."

"Stop calling her that!" Heather yelled. "Jesus, you guys suck total ass."

"Better than being a half-ass sucker!" Alien said.

I went to the kitchen to call Shelby. While I listened to the rings, I also checked out the fridge. It was beautifully full of beautiful food. I was hoping Robyn would not be the one to answer, but of course she was.

"Hey Robyn, let me talk to Shelby." I surveyed the neat row of cheese and lunch meat that lined the top shelf of the refrigerator.

"Angie? Are you on top of this money thing? I'm not gonna do this just whenever you all get your shit together. I'm gonna work it into my schedule, not yours."

"I'm on it, Robyn. We'll get you some money tonight, okay?" I said.

Robyn let the phone drop to the floor and screamed for Shelby.

"Hey," Shelby said. "What the hell are you doing? You're not at school and when I get home Robyn is having a fucking fit about beer money and some kid named Dickass and you trying to jump out of a moving car."

"Well, she's exaggerating a bit. Just come over to Heather's."

"For what?"

"Like you don't want to get away from Robyn?"

"I'll be there in ten." Shelby hung up.

I closed the refrigerator, then filled a glass with water to wash the saliva out of my mouth. I was hungry enough to actually begin drooling.

"We got an idea," Heather told me as I returned to the living room. "Luann's parents." Heather had that spark in her eye again.

"Luann Bartel?" I asked knowing perfectly well there was only one Luann in the world.

"Oh, sweet Luann," Alien whistled.

If Carrie Shuren was the most beautiful girl among the popular people, Luann was the most beautiful among the party kids. Luann had long black hair that curled all over her head. She wore red lipstick and little black dresses all the time. She had a perfectly beautiful face and when she was stoned, which she always was, she just looked sexy. But Luann was much cooler than us. As far as I knew she dated grown men and hung out at bars and rode around in cool old muscle cars. And when she was home, she smoked pot and got drunk with her parents and their friends. That was the rumor anyway and I thought it was unmanageably glamorous. I knew Rex HAD to be hot for her and I wasn't sure who to hate. Her, him or me.

"I don't know her parents," I said.

"Not you, dummy." Alien pointed. "Rex, he lives a couple of doors down from her. The lucky bastard."

"Okay, big guy. Get on it," I said to Rex.

"Well, I'm not sure if . . ."

"Do you actually know her parents, Rex? Or are you just showing off for Alien here?" I asked.

"Whoa," Pike breathed and navigated his way out of the living room.

"I don't know if they're home, Angie. What's up your ass?"

"Couple Twinkies shy of a good day?" Alien said.

"Shut up a-hole. Let's just get the money together. Shelby is on her way over here. I guess she has something to throw in."

"I ain't got money," Rex said. "But since I'll be doing the work, I guess it's a trade."

"My mom's boyfriend left me fifty bucks for the weekend," Heather said.

I felt horrible. Hungry and horrible. I grabbed my book bag and went to the kitchen. I filled a water glass, did not cry, and took three more Dexatrims. I didn't care if my heart exploded.

"What's up carpet muncher?" I heard Alien say.

"Oh, don't I wish I had a carpet to munch," Shelby said. She and Alien got on pretty well with each other for reasons I never cared to question.

"Your fucking sister wants to chaperone!" Heather yelled.

"Yeah, I heard," Shelby was saying as I came back to the room.

"But we got a better plan," Heather told Shelby.

I smirked at Rex, as he tried to melt into his chair. I knew I was right about Rex not really knowing Luann or her parents well enough to call in this favor.

"Well, what's the plan then? We certainly can't have Robyn over here," Shelby said.

"Rex is pretty tight with the Bartels. He's gonna have them pick it up," I said.

Rex shot me a hard glance. "If they're even home. If they don't mind. It's not for sure."

I opened my mouth to be a smartass, but was cut off by Shelby addressing Pike as he came back into the room.

"You must be Dickass."

"Indeed. And you must be that psycho's sister. It's a pleasure." Pike stuck his hand out to Shelby.

When no one else could see, Shelby sparked her eyebrows up at me. Pike was pretty cute, as far as boys went. I rolled my eyes back at her.

CHAPTER 10

Friday morning. Party morning. The only thing worse than school day was a school day with a fucking party to follow it. It's not open-heart surgery dumbass, I consoled myself.

My stomach was fluttery, sick-feeling. Maybe I'd come down with something horrible and not have to go to any party, ever. I managed to get myself up on the scale. My eyes squeezed tight and just stood there for a few seconds before looking down to read the numbers. 167. That was five whole pounds of fat I had managed to get off me. Vanished it into the atmosphere somewhere. Maybe it would circle the school building and attach itself to Mindy Overton's ass.

As pleasing as that thought was, the fat didn't really go anywhere. It just sort of deflated, the fat cells. Like millions of little, sucking mouths trapped inside my skin.

When the lunch bell rang, I slipped out the back door of Stairwell B to the Annex. I really did want a smoke. I was up to nearly a pack a day. I even stole a pack from the Kroger the other night when I went with my mom.

I lit a Kool, dragging the smoke down my throat and into my lungs. It felt fantastic. I was looking at the cigarette, when I heard the rhythmic click of Carrie Shuren's footfalls.

"Hey there," she said, sitting next to me.

"Hey." I blew out a cloud of smoke and tried not to look too excited, not as excited as I actually was anyway.

Carries eyes were a little glazed. Maybe she was on one of those new anti-depressant drugs all the rich kids were taking. The rich girls anyway. Like those girls had anything to be depressed about. Fat girls should get free anti-depressants from the government, from a tax pool supported by all the people who torture us. Aunt Jean once said, I'd have a couple of nervous breakdowns if I could afford them.

"What you eat today?" Carrie asked, lighting her own cigarette, a Camel without a filter. This amazed me completely.

"Nothing," I said. I was proud, being able to tell that truth.

"You still doing that Slim-Fast business?" She asked as she exhaled.

"Sometimes," I said, blotting out a crazy image that popped into my mind. An image of Carrie Shuren's legs spread open and my face nuzzled into her pussy. Involuntary evidence of the fact I must, indeed, be a lesbo.

Carrie took another drag, tilted her head my way with a smile, "Heard you told Mindy Overton to eat a bag of shit."

"Oh. Well, I . . ."

"That bitch should eat a bag of shit. A whole bag of it too," Carrie said.

"I thought you two were friends."

"We are. She's a bitch though. The queen and all. You know that. She doesn't treat me any better than she does anyone else."

"But she's your friend?"

"Last year, when my face got all bad? She rescheduled picture day for the hockey cheerleaders and didn't tell me. Everyone was in it except me. My mother was so pissed at me."

"At you? Why?"

"For not being on the ball. That's her favorite expression. She would never believe Mindy would do that on purpose. That any one of those girls would."

"Oh."

"And, before Mindy started going out with Troy, she was so all over Brandon all the time. Seriously, she'd like send him these sexy notes about what she would do to him and everything. They were fucking. I know they were."

"How can she be your friend then?"

"I dunno. Be glad you don't understand."

I didn't know if she was insulting me or not.

"You look good, Angie. You're really taking it off. The weight," Carrie said.

"Am I?" It felt amazing, Carrie Shuren telling me I'm doing good. Another image popped up in my mind; I'm fucking Carrie, like I have a dick or something.

"Yeah, you look like you've lost a good five pounds, at least. A couple more and those cheek bones will come out. How are you doing it?"

"Dexatrim."

Carrie smiled. We both lit cigarettes and sat in silence for a few inhales and exhales.

"Dexatrim? Maybe that's a good idea. I have a plan, see? A seven year plan."

"That's so grown up," I said.

"I know, but check it out. One day a week I fast. I don't eat anything. The other six days I eat, like, salad and juice and stuff, right? I do that for a year. Then, the next year I fast two days a week. Then the next year, three. Right? Until, finally, after seven years I just fucking photosynthesize!"

"You're going to photosynthesize?"

"Sure. Why not? I love to lay out."

"You're a genius." I said. And I meant it.

After lunch, I went to the bathroom, took a couple of Dexatrims and ran into good ol' Mindy herself.

Mindy rolled her eyes. "Jesus, you are, like, in every bathroom all the time."

"And you are, like, totally destined to be fat, Mindy. You've got that face, you know? That born-to-be-fat face."

"Fuck off, Lezzylard. You fucking wish."

"I don't have to wish," I said to Mindy's back as she left the bathroom.

When I met Shelby after school I was thinking about dinner. Well, actually, I'd been thinking about dinner all day. It kind of helped with the Rudy situation. Him making me sit down and eat with him as if we were a family, as if we cared what happened to each other, as if he wanted anything good for me or vice versa. Not eating all day made that horrible situation something to look forward to.

"Are we meeting Charlie?" Shelby asked.

"Don't call Inez that. It's ugly." I wrinkled my face at her.

"Whoa. Got a crush on her or something?"

"Fuck you, dyke. How you like that? You call me Lezzylard when I'm not around?"

"Of course not, Angie. I'd never do that."

Shelby and I headed for the main road silently. I was fuming. I didn't want to have friends like Inez or Shelby. Or myself for that matter.

"Look, I'm sorry about calling Inez Charlie," Shelby finally said.

"Forget it. It doesn't matter. I'm just on a trip is all."

"Okay, so, we're meeting her, right?"

"Yep. Outside the liquor store."

When Shelby and I got to the parking lot of the strip mall where the liquor store and the karate shop were stationed, Inez was on the pay phone making blunt, exacting gestures with her hands. Shelby and I exchanged a look.

"You think cocaine is gonna shut me up? Huh?" Inez was completely filled with the spirit, as religious folks say. "I saw you KILL a man! And you think drugs are going to keep me quiet?"

Inez looked over at me and Shelby with a wink. A woman came out of the liquor store carrying a twelve pack of Heineken. She jumped when she heard Inez. She looked at Inez and made a straight line away from her.

"There aren't enough drugs in the world to keep me quiet. And you can kill me too, but I've told everyone. AND there's a letter in a safe deposit box with everything I know written down. So go ahead, KILL ME. I fucking dare you!" Inez hung up the phone and looked at me and Shelby with her big, beautiful stoned smile.

"So, what's up?" Inez asked.

"Nothin' stoner," Shelby said.

"Tonight, I'm gonna bust out this amazing Thai-stick. You won't believe it."

"You guys hungry?" I asked, looking around at the zillions of restaurants: Dairy Queen, Roman's Pizza, Wendy's, Arby's, Mcdonald's, Hardee's, Kentucky Fried Chicken. And those were just the ones I could see from where we were standing. Beyond them there were more. Many more. Something dangerous was welling up in me. Something two or three or four more Dexatrim would not keep quiet. You can't keep a good man down, were the words that ran through my head.

"I'm, like, starving." Inez grabbed her belly.

"I'm always hungry, Angie. You know that." Shelby licked her lips.

"Let's go over to Billy Bear and eat the pizza people leave," I said.

"Yeah!" Inez's eyes lit up. "People leave crazy pizza layin' around over there. Beer and birthday cake too, sometimes. If my brother's friend is workin' he'll give us cups for soda."

Billy Bear Pizza. An amusement complex a thousand years of evolution in the making. Inside, millions of blinking lights, hundreds of bells and whistles. Balls to roll for prizes and balls to roll yourself around in. Walls of prizes and people in bear suits running around hugging everyone. Pizza and a salad bar longer than the length of my mother's apartment. A big room with long tables where you can eat or have a party while mechanical animals play old rock music.

"But there's no way I'm going in there without getting high," Inez added.

"Let's stop at the Field House then. If I smoked pot I'd definitely want to be high in that place," Shelby said.

The three of us headed across the field, the browning grass coming up over our knees at some points. All I could think about was food. Inez and Shelby were talking about something, but I was miles away. I was eating sausage and onion pizza and french fries and chocolate ice cream. I was eating cheese and crackers and carrot cake. Fig newtons and strawberry milk. I was eating every food there ever was to be eaten.

"So, will you help me, Angie?" Shelby asked.

"What? Help you what?"

"Bring my records over to Heather's, that's what we've been talking about."

"Oh. Sure. But I got to be at dinner tonight. Every night now that Rudy is around. And we eat late cuz mom doesn't get off work until six. So, I don't know."

"I can help you," Inez said.

"Okay. You can come with me after Billy Bear."

Shelby ducked through the circle of tiny trees. "Hey Dickass!"

"Hello, sister-of-the-future-mental-patient. How are you today?"

Inez and I ducked into the trees and we all sat immediately on the couch.

"Holy shit," Inez said, looking at Pike. "You are the stonedest person I have ever seen."

"Thank you." Pike seemed genuinely flattered.

"So, what happened with the beer thing last night?" I asked Pike.

"Total fuckin' weirdness." Pike shook his head. "We go by this house, big place but all run down," Pike began, but was distracted by Inez bouncing up and down on the couch cushion whispering, "Paper, paper, paper, paper."

"You want a rolling paper?"

"Meow!" Inez said.

"You must be Inez," Pike said and fished his wallet out of the same dirty pants he'd been wearing the day before.

"Not only that, I'm a professional skee ball-ball player. And after we smoke this, I'm gonna get me the biggest fucking pink panda bear in the whole world. And you can come if you want, because you're nice."

"The only part of what you just said, that I understood, was smoke."

"Meow!"

"Woof!"

"Meow!"

"Woof!"

"Meow!

"Woof!"

"Stop It!" Shelby said. "You fucks are freaking me out. Just smoke your shit, already. What about the beer?"

"Liquid shit," Inez said, taking the paper from Pike.

"Oh, so we go by this house. There's all this hippie music inside and you can smell weed all the way down the driveway. So Rex knocks on the side door and an old gray haired burn out dude comes to the door and he's like, Did we order a pizza? And Rex is like, No man, is Luann here?"

"Act it out," Inez said.

"What?"

"Act the story out," Inez said, putting the joint in her mouth and lighting it.

"Okay." Pike stood to his feet. "So, the burn-out guy doesn't seem to know the word Luann and he's like, huh?" Pike said, bending over a little. Inez giggled.

"And there's all this music and stuff and the guy turns around and yells into the house, Hey Crystal, like, where's your kid man? So, this lady in this big swirly nightgown comes down the steps with this big dog, and the dog sees us and starts for the door." Pike got down on his knees. "And the burner kinda shuts the door all, like, No Jerry, these are Luann's friends." Pike is acting like a snarling dog and going for Inez's legs. "The Crystal lady says, Luann's out with her boyfriend." Pike stood and acted like an angry lady swishing his hips and pursing his face up.

"That's so good," Inez told him. Shelby nudged me.

"Then the dog finally breaks free of the door and backs Alien up into the trashcans. And Alien is like, nice doggie, nice big doggie. And the dog is goin' crazy and Crystal and the dude are gone but the door is open and the guy finally comes back and he's on his knees going, C'mon Jerry I got a treat for you, I got a nice pop tart for you Jerry. And it's like the fuckin' dog knows the word pop tart and goes running after it and the door swings shut and it's like none of it happened to begin with. Except Alien is like, You fuckers were gonna let Jerry Garcia rip my balls off! That is so NOT PUNK."

We all laughed. Hard.

"So, no beer?" Shelby managed through her laughter.

"Yeah, we got it. We just hung around outside the liquor store until we got someone to buy it for us. It took longer than it should have because Alien had to give a lecture series on the meaning of punk."

"Don't tell me Rex took the beer with him. We'll never see it." I shook my head.

"No way." Pike reached over and swiped a thick piece of pine brush off a stack of five cases of Pabst Blue Ribbon and a fifth of Early Times.

"Meeee-oow!" Inez expressed our sentiments exactly. Pike took a bow and pinched the smoking joint from Inez's fingers. Shelby looked at me and raised her eyebrows. Which meant Pike was definitely pretty cute as far as boys went.

Pike covered the stash of booze over with the brush. We all ducked out of the circle of trees and started across the field. Inez continued on the subject of her coveted pink panda bear.

"Wait till you see it. It has the saddest eyes in the whole world and it's like a million feet tall and just the prettiest pink. Kinda like your nails, actually."

"You like these?" Pike wiggled his nails at Inez. "You don't think the guys are going to make fun of me?" Pike gave me a look.

"What guys?"

"Precisely," Pike said and started across the field. The rest of us followed taking long steps through the tall grass.

I'd never met anyone quite like Pike. If he gave a fuck what anyone in world thought about anything, he didn't show it.

"Should I start smoking pot?" Shelby asked all of us.

"Probably," Pike and Inez said in unison.

"Jinx," they also said simultaneously. I tried to beat down a rising jealousy at what seemed to be a burgeoning romance.

We all headed toward Billy Bear Pizza, which was next to the K-mart. I focused on the sign over the entranceway. The words Billy Bear were scrawled in pink and yellow neon. We made it past the entrance. The weird thing about Billy Bear was that you were supposed to be eighteen to get in without your parents. Which was patently absurd. It was a huge arcade. But we managed to hide out there sometimes when we skipped school because everyone who worked there was either a high school drop out or a pot dealer or both. The day manager was one of Luann's boyfriends, at least that was the rumor, and he was an acid dealer who was always on the look out for unregistered guns.

I went straight at the room with the long dinning tables. I hoped for mounds of cheese and crust. When I turned the corner, the Billy Bear band was playing "Surfin' USA." All their mechanical limbs worked mechanical instruments to provide an entertainment that those of us from St. Louis couldn't really understand. I'd never seen a beach in my life, and didn't ever expect to see one. No one was in the room. I spotted a messed table near the stage and approached it with the hunger of a starving dog.

Once I'd reached the table, the Billy Bear band kicked up with "Leader of the Pack." The table was covered with debris. Crumpled gift-wrap paper and greasy marinara stained napkins. I found a couple of pizza crusts and devoured them. I scooped up a dollop of cake icing and walked back toward the game room.

The salad bar was positioned exactly between the dining room and the game room. My private hell, surrounded by food I couldn't eat. I wanted everything I saw. Potato salad, garbanzo beans, chocolate pudding, cottage cheese. Salad bars are always lit so the food is just the right color. All that shining clean metal and sparkling crushed ice loaded with big bowls of gleaming, perfect food. I was so busy looking down at it all, I ran head first into some skinny stoned-looking boy.

"Oh, sorry," I said, jumping back from the ham cubes and landing next to the melon balls.

"Hey, you're here with Inez, right?"

"Yeah. Who are you?"

"I'm a friend of her brother. You want some game tokens?" His mouth twitched a little.

"Sure," I said, sizing him up. His red Billy Bear polo shirt hung off his shoulders like it was made for someone twice his size.

"Here," he said, handing me a couple dozen tokens. "And you can use this cup for sodas or lemonades or whatever you want. I can't get any plates for the salad bar right now. Not enough people in here."

"Beer?" I asked, as if it were more important than food.

"Yeah, I can see about some beer." He wiped his nose with the back of his hand.

"Cool," I said and nudged past him with my stupid cup. I filled it up with diet Coke and went in search of Shelby. But she was already right behind me.

"There they go," Shelby said, pointing to a group of adults heading toward the dinning room with like a million kids crawling all over them.

"Jesus, they're infested," I said.

"I bet they ordered a lot of pizza, but they're going to fill up on salad and soda and leave everything behind," Shelby said.

Pike came up behind us, talking into his cupped hand like it was a walkie-talkie. "Double nuclear traveling west with multiple pizza tickets, do you copy? Over."

"We should roll 'em," Shelby said.

"God, if those people had any clue about us they'd run screaming," Pike said.

We found Inez playing skee ball ball.

"My panda is still there," Inez informed us, then rolled a perfect fifty.

"She really is a professional skee ball ball player." Shelby shook her head in the direction of Inez's second fifty in a row.

I tried to play a game of skee ball ball with Shelby. Tried to pay attention, I mean. I kept looking over my shoulder at the salad bar, at the skinny stoned kid with the twitchy mouth. I kept waiting for him to turn around with a huge, steamy pizza and a suddenly beautiful face.

"You okay?" Shelby finally asked me.

"Yeah, I'm just thinking about tonight. What should I wear?"

"Wear whatever, Angie. It's just a beer party. You don't even need to change."

"I guess you're right."

"You're not nervous about the party, are you?"

"No. Why would I be?"

"I dunno. You just seem kind of far away."

I shrugged.

Part of me wanted to scream it all out. The truth. The truth about food and me. The truth about the rest of my life. Part of me wanted Shelby to understand all the facts. The fact that I would never have a boyfriend. I'd never have nice clothes. I'd never look good, ever, not once in my life. The fact that I'd die a virgin and worse, I'd die no one. No one at all. I'd wait tables until it killed me, just like my mom only I wouldn't make as much in tips because I'm fat and then the state would pay for me to be cremated. But before that even happened a mortician or somebody would get their last few cruel jokes in about what a big fat thing I had been in life. Okay, maybe my imagination did run away with me sometimes.

Inez tore her long tail of green tickets out of the machine and smiled at them as she carefully folded each one over the next, counting to herself as she went.

"That's another hundred and twenty. I have twelve hundred at home. I only need . . . two thousand one hundred and eighty more," Inez told us.

"

"There's our boy," Pike poked me a little and pointed to Inez's brother's friend. He was holding a big pepperoni pizza and smiling. He jerked his head the direction of the dining room and went toward it himself. My mouth was so full of saliva I thought I might drown. I let everyone go ahead of me. I needed to practice my nonchalance with food.

The Billy Bear band played "The Monster Mash" and the double nuclear with their small army were slumped over plastic plates mounded with salad.

"Mommy, I get in the balls," one of the kids said.

"Yes, honey, in a minute. First we eat some pizza."

"Pizza!"

Pike and Inez laughed into their hands. I compulsively swallowed, watching Shelby absently tear out a slice of pizza. It was slow torture.

"Mommy, I play with my balls," Pike whispered to Inez.

"Yes, honey, but not while you eat your pizza," Inez said.

"Pizza!" Pike finally tore into the pie.

I gratefully followed suit. I had the whole piece down before Pike said, "Mommy, I play with my balls in the pizza!"

"Okay," Shelby said with her mouth full. "That's just weird. Stop it."

"I think Shelby should be the Mommy," Inez said with her eyebrows arched.

"Mommy!" Pike looked at Shelby.

"No." Shelby put her hand up. "Don't even start."

"You're right, Inez," Pike said, dropping the kid routine and working at the pizza like a normal person.

We all ate giggling at the two families. After their pizzas came it was total mayhem. "I don't like onion." "I don't like pepperoni." "I don't like cheese." One little girl kept running in front of the stage trying to take her clothes off to the music.

"Oh, good," Pike said. "Child strippers. Will Billy Bear Pizza stop at nothing to amuse us?"

After we finished eating, Inez announced she was going to play more skee ball ball before we left. Pike and Shelby followed her while I piled all our greasy napkins and empty cups onto the pizza pan. I cast a glance toward the families, who were just finishing up. I wondered if they were going to take what was left. I couldn't help it. I wasn't hungry anymore. I just couldn't help thinking about what might get left behind.

"So, how are we gonna get this beer to Heather's place?" Shelby asked once we were safely back in the circle of trees.

"Alien and Rex and some other guy are meeting me here in a little while. We can drag it over there."

"I gotta go," I said and hurried, figuring I was already late.

Mom and I met in the stairwell. For this I felt lucky. Rudy got mad if I wasn't home at least by the time she was. And since I had no intention of being in the apartment alone with Rudy, I could either stay away until I knew she'd already be home or wait around outside the building until I saw her car pull up.

"How's your week been, baby?" She asked.

"Okay," I said. It was our new communication style. We used words to say nothing. She chalked it up to me being a teenager and I chalked it up to her being hell-bent on marrying a fucking asshole.

"I thought I'd make those crescent dog things for dinner. Won't take long."

"That sounds good."

"You goin' to a sleep-over tonight, right?"

"Yeah."

"Well, you'll have to save room for cake." She smiled a sort of tired smile and I felt real guilty. A sleep-over with cake and movies and nail painting. That's what she thought I was off to do. More like beer and pot and people slipping off to the laundry room to fuck. God, I really did want to just go to a slumber party. But those days were long behind me and whatever the hell was ahead of me seemed dull by comparison.

CHAPTER 11

Dinner went by without much hassle. Mom made hotdogs wrapped in prepackaged crescent roll dough with a lettuce salad on the side. Besides The Who, Rudy and I had crescent dogs in common. We both loved them.

"You need your sleeping bag, Angie?"

"No, Heather has plenty of blankets," I said, somewhat alarmed. What if I had to show up at the party with my fucking Snoopy sleeping bag under my arm?

I slipped into the laundry room one building over. I put my make up on, then made the trek over to Heather's.

The sun was just beginning to set as I approached Heather's house. I could hear music playing. Not super-loud or anything, but I could hear it. Rex was on the front porch drinking beer through a ski mask with a Dead Kennedys patch stitched on the forehead.

"Around back," he said in a deep voice.

"What the fuck are you doing?"

"Trying to scare people into going around back."

"Well, you should use your real face then, huh?"

"No, that pigfucker Alien should be out here," Rex said loudly over his shoulder so his voice could be heard through the house.

"You rang, Monsieur Jizzmouth?" Alien asked as he came through the screen door.

"Yeah, where's my beer?" Rex shrugged his shoulders.

"Oh, so now I'm like your bitch, is that it?"

"Where's Shelby?" I asked.

"Angie, it's a party. Shouldn't you, like, wear a dress or something?" Alien said, smiling a little at his own nastiness.

I opened my mouth to say whatever might drop out, but Rex cut me off. "You're the bitch, Alien. Why don't you slip into something less comfortable while you're in there getting me a beer?"

"You wish, homo," Alien said, disappearing back into the house.

I left Rex on the porch trying to pour beer through his dumb ski mask and went in search of Shelby. I hadn't even made it to the actual party and I was ready to leave.

There were about fifteen or so people on the back porch. Where they all came from I couldn't possibly guess. Shelby was among them but she was busy talking to some girl I'd never seen before. Since Shelby was the person I always talked to, I had nothing to do with myself. I edged closer to the crowd, pretending to dig through my pockets for something.

Heather spotted me and got to her feet. "Angie!" She waved me her way as she walked to the edge of the patio. Heather tilted her head in the direction of Shelby and her companion. "That's Colleen. Luann's cousin. She's totally gay."

My stomach went straight to my throat. Heather pinched my arm and giggled, completely thrilled.Heather had been telling Shelby to Just get some pussy, make sure you really like it, for the last two years. A forced smile held my rising jealousy somewhere below my face. Pushed all the sweaty evil into the fleshy parts of my body. Maybe it would turn into a kidney stone and I could have it removed.

I didn't recognize anyone else except Inez, who smiled and wiggled her fingers at me. Her mohawk was spiked straight up with some kind of goo that made it shine in the yellow porch light. She sat crossed legged on the flagstone next to Pike. The two of them rummaged through a milk crate full of cassette tapes.

"Get a beer." Inez pointed to a big red ice chest near the edge of the patio. I shrugged and went for the chest. A boy about as dirty as Pike was next to it. As I reached for the lid, he grabbed it and lifted it open.

"Allow me." He smiled, then dipped his arm into the ice, pulled out a can, popped the top and handed it to me. "Chivalry is NOT dead," he said.

"Was that chivalry?" I asked, having no idea what to say.

"I'd like to think so." He winked at me.

The urge to say thank you was immediate, but I bit at my lip instead. The boy smiled even wider and he was cute as hell. All messy black hair, smooth skin, and long thin arms.

"I'm Mantis. You're Angie," he said, shaking my hand. "We went to the same junior high."

"Oh, did we have a class together?"

"No. Not really. We had P. E. the same hour in eighth grade."

"Oh." I took a quick drink of beer. P. E. meant he'd seen me in my fucking gym clothes. The boys and girls gym classes were held at the same time, boys on one side of the gymnasium and girls on the other. It was so horribly stupid. What was the point of separating the classes if we were still in the same room? In that big room with all the boys watching all the girls. Heather used to reapply her make up after she got into her gym clothes. And Tiffany Auburn wore her big, heavy hoop earrings through the whole class and then complain about her ears bleeding after we did laps.

"So, how do you know my name?" This question I immediately regretted. I'd been Lezzylard since the seventh grade. Everyone knew me. I was a legend in my own torture.

"Because you won that speech contest. You got the trophy for the school."

"What? Oh yeah." I dropped my head. That silly trophy. Those cheap medals gathering dust in my closet. I guessed it was better than him saying, because you're a big fat lesbian.

"I'm a writer too," Mantis said.

"A writer?"

"Yeah, I write poems."

"Poems?" I said, not knowing why he was telling me this.

"You know, like song lyrics?"

Just then Rex pushed between us with his ski mask still pulled tight over his face.

"Move it. I'm getting drunk off my ass tonight."

Rex pulled two beers out of the ice chest and handed one behind him to Luann. Luann Bartel. He did know her. I took another long drink off my beer and glanced up to see Mantis still looking at me. I was cornered. I shifted my weight back and forth between my feet. It didn't feel right on either one.

"Wow, the sky is really purple," I said stupidly.

Rex squinted at me through his ski mask. "It does that everyday, Angie. It's called sunset. And tomorrow morning there will be an event known as sunrise. You should get comfortable with these concepts." Rex patted my shoulder. Luann actually giggled Luann Bartel with all her glamorous everything. She probably shit confetti. One big, beautiful party coming out of her ass. And Rex standing there making fun of me. Rex with his monster porn under his mattress and his pretty pink dick hanging around my imagination for reasons even I couldn't fathom.

"Shut up. What's with the stupid ski mask, anyway?"

"I'm practicing for the ski vacation me and my extremely wealthy family are planning," Rex said with a kind of Mr. Howell accent on his tongue.

Luann giggled at this, too. I could grant her that Rex was hot, but funny? That was going too far.

My hands found nothing useful to do. My body took up too much space. I dumped beer down my throat, tried to look happy, stepped back a little and snuck a glance at Pike and Inez. Pike's hair was also freshly spiked with shiny goo and he appeared to be wearing eyeliner. Pike and Inez were talking about a cassette tape held in Pike's hand.

Rex followed my gaze and said, "Can't blame the kid for liking a big ass." Rex turned to Luann, obviously expecting her to retreat from the cooler with him.

"Hey Mantis," Luann said, avoiding Rex's body and blinking her eyes.

"Hi Luann. Feeling better?" Mantis gave Luann a mild smile.

"Yeah." Luann wiggled past Rex completely, so she was standing next to Mantis. Her lips were all red and her hair was in a perfect state of chaotic black spiral curls. Most of the girls on the patio seemed to emulate her party-girl style. Of course, no one really got it as right as Luann did.

"I wasn't sick really. Just real hungover, you know?" Luann laughed and Mantis just smiled at her.

"Drunk for life!" Rex yelled holding his beer up. Luann gave a bothered look over her shoulder at Rex. I wanted to punch her. I wanted to punch Rex. But just then a yelp from a now larger crowd overtook everything. It was a group reply to Rex's call to be drunk for life. I gulped down the rest of my beer, grabbed another and pushed my way out of the corner.

I headed for Inez and Pike. Inez hugged me when I flopped down next to her. I hugged back, tight. My shoulders relaxed. I took out my cigarettes, offering one to Inez and Pike, who both turned up their noses as if I'd offered them a piece of road kill.

I popped the top on my fresh beer and looked around. A crowd of kids were drinking beer, flirting, being alternately punk or pretty. A little sweat gathered around my hairline and I inhaled smoke. Inhaled deep and hoped for something, anything, I didn't know what.

"What should it be?" Inez asked holding up a cassette tape. "Day-glo Abortions or Cro-mags?"

"Did you two do each other's hair?" I asked.

"Yeah," Pike and Inez said in unison. I wished they would stop doing that.

"C'mon Angie," Pike goaded. "What should we play next? You're the music lover."

I dipped my head toward my can of Pabst. Since I'd been at the party, people had treated me like someone. Mantis called me a writer. Pike called me a music lover. Heather brought me closer to everyone as if I belonged close to them. I just wanted to leave. I just wanted to go to my mother's apartment. To her apartment the way it was before Rudy, the two of us watching her little twenty-inch TV, laughing and drinking root beer. Or figuring out a jigsaw puzzle on the card table that used to be in the dinning room before Rudy's big-assed thick wood table arrived. I wanted to go away.

"Cro-mags," I told Pike and Inez. I looked around for Shelby. I wanted to take her with me. I spotted her next to the beer cooler with the older girl she'd been talking to. Nothing was safe anymore.

I took in another long drag of beer and wished I'd said Day-glo Abortions.

"Angie." Inez slapped my leg. "We're gonna start a band. What you think of The Cheese Eaters?"

"Well, cheese is good," I said, wishing I had some. Wishing I had a big brick of American cheese and a bag of potato chips. "What about The Cheese Smokers?"

"That's so cheesy," Pike said.

"I'm not gonna laugh at that, Pike. I'm not," I said.

"What would happen if you smoked cheese?" Inez asked.

"It would melt all over your pot," Pike said just as Shelby passed in front of me.

"Shelby!" I said, leaving Pike and Inez to contemplate the wide world of cheese smoking.

"Angie!" Shelby leaned toward me and took my hand in hers. She was a little drunk and very nervous "This is Colleen." Shelby gestured behind her and gave me a wide-eyed look. Colleen was beautiful and fleshy and she looked somehow meaningful.

"Shelby has been talking about you," Colleen said, taking my hand.

"Yeah, she's a bitch like that." It was a dumb, ordinary thing to say. I should have just said, Hi, I'm Angie I'm completely banal. Shelby and Colleen were friendly. Preoccupied, but friendly, as they moved back into the growing party. Shelby turned and gave me a big mimicked gasp. She was happy. Who would expect another lesbian at an event like this? A party where all the songs were guys voices singing about fucking sluts or being cool for fucking ugly girls. Shelby was stuck with us, but Colleen probably knew a million beautiful dykes who threw their own parties and danced to music about life without men. I hoped there was music like that some-where out there.

Inez watched Shelby and Colleen walk away with their fresh beers. "I think an older woman is perfect for Shelby."

"They just met. Maybe we don't need to marry them off right this minute," I said, taking in more beer. When I looked back around at Inez and Pike they were stop-motion staring at me.

"I mean, they might not be each other's type. Do you think gay people just automatically fall in love with all other gay people?"

"Well," Pike began slowly. "They seem to like one another. You know?"

I looked up at Shelby and Colleen. I nodded my head. "Yeah. They do."

Rex was still after Luann's attention. He was talking loudly to Alien, "Man, I got the fuckin' best acid in town! You wanna trip? You'll trip your balls off on this shit!"

Heather looked over at him with her narrow stare. "What about me, Rex? I don't have balls."

"Oh, when you're on acid, everybody has balls."

"Or you can just trip that one tit off," Alien said. "And wake up normal."

"At least I have options," Heather said and walked through the sliding glass door and into the house.

Inez and Pike and me all looked at each other.

"Why's he got to dick out on Heather?" Pike asked.

Without another word the three of us got on our feet and followed Heather. As I passed into the house I noticed Luann's attention shift from Mantis to Rex. "You got acid?"

In the kitchen Heather was opening a huge bag of chips. She looked briefly over her shoulder to find all of us there, awkwardly standing around on the beige tile.

"We smokin' a joint or what?" she asked over her shoulder.

"I thought you'd never ask." Inez laughed and we all followed Heather down the hall to her huge pink, frilly bedroom. Heather averted her eyes from us, until we were inside her bedroom and Pike said, "Wow, it's like going stoner-punk with Barbie."

Heather finally turned around and met our eyes with her usual smile. "You got that right! Hope you're ready."

"Ready? I've been waiting my whole life for this." Pike's sweet smile spread across his face and Inez touched his arm, somewhat unconsciously. Soul mates? That's what Heather would say. True love? That's what Shelby would say. Temporary insanity? That was my guess.

Pike handed Inez a rolling paper and Heather pulled her tray from under the bed. I started looking through Heather's tape collection. I wanted to hear Suicidal Tendencies sing "I Won't Fall in Love Today." Shelby might have a girlfriend. I'd never worried about it before. In fact, I'd sometimes seen myself married and decked out with a big house and all that shit and me sitting at my glass top kitchen table telling Shelby she'd find someone. Good thing I didn't have to be friends with myself.

"I think Mantis likes you," Heather said, just as my shaky, monstrous fingers fell on the tape I was looking for.

"I didn't even know that guy." I pushed the cassette into the jaws of the stereo.

"Well, you know him now," Heather said. I didn't turn around. I fast forwarded the tape, stopped, hit play, fast forwarded, stopped, hit play, fast forwarded, stopped, rewound, then stopped right on the last note of the song before the one I wanted. I leaned myself into one of the big speakers Heather's mom got her after they managed their way out of Covington. I wished my mom could invent something. Maybe, like, one of those boots on a spring like in cartoons. Call it Rid-Ye-Man. She could make commercials featuring Rudy tumbling out the window and into the flatbed of his pickup truck.

"If we're gonna have a band called The Cheese Smokers, we should probably actually smoke some cheese," Inez said.

"Smoke cheese?" Heather was holding her hit. "What do you mean? Like hang it up in the garage and set a fire in there?"

Inez took the joint from Heather. "Could we turn your garage into a smokehouse?"

"I think we should roll some cheddar up with this Thai-stick. Shit, Inez, this pot is awesome," Pike said.

"Why the fuck does Alien have to be so mean?" Heather asked somewhat rhetorically.

"Cuz everyone is mean to him." Inez shrugged.

"I guess in a couple of months I'll be mean too," Heather said.

"He just tries to show off for Rex," Pike said.

The joint was filling the room up with smoke. By the looks of everyone, they were already really stoned but they kept smoking anyway. Drinking when you are already drunk. Smoking when you are already stoned. Eating when you are already full. It's all the same thing. Sickness, revolving itself around all this god-awful meanness.

CHAPTER 12

I stretched out on the floor and then, all hell threatened to break loose.

"Where the fuck is Heather?" A big voice boomed from somewhere in the house.

Heather's eyes got big and she grabbed the joint from Pike, snuffed it out on the edge of her tray, and slid the tray back under her bed.

"It's Robyn!" I said, jumping to my feet. My immediate reaction was to keep Robyn out of Heather's room. But just as I got to the door it swung open, nearly hitting me in the face.

"Hey, watch it!" I yelled.

"Watch it?" Robyn glared at me. "You might want to be the one to watch it there, Angie. Maybe we should call Rita right now and tell her yer drinkin' and gettin' stoned. I bet she'd love that!"

"What are you even doing here?" I wanted to know.

"Lookin' out for you, Angie." Robyn moved closer to me, her finger stuck straight in my face and her cleavage threatening to explode right before my eyes.

"Lookin' out for me by hittin' me in the face with a door? That doesn't make any sense!"

"I'll tell you what makes sense here, Angie. You got that?" Robyn was right up on me then.

"Who do you think you are, anyway?" I asked.

"I'm the one who's gonna keep you out of trouble, maybe even jail for that matter. What you think about that?"

"I think you should calm down. That's what I think."

Robyn slowly pulled her finger back from my face. Her eyes went from narrow to observant.

"That lip gloss looks great," she said. "You put it on good too. Funny how it stays on even though you're suckin' on beers and joints isn't it?"

Before I could say anything, Robyn turned her body, her cleavage and her pointed finger on Heather.

"What the hell are you thinking?" Robyn demanded.

"What do you mean?" Heather asked.

"Smoking up in your mom's house? That's fuckin' stupid. And who's watchin' everyone? You can't just walk away from a party you're not supposed to be havin'. People will steal shit. Then what are you gonna do?"

"Nobody is going to steal anything, Robyn," Heather said, getting to her feet.

"Yeah? That's what you think now. You think that cuz you don't know shit. You don't know shit about how people really are. You're just a kid."

I moved out into the hall where I could see all this bullshit unfold from behind Robyn's hair. I felt someone next to me and looked over to find Vince. I studied the side of his face for a second. His jaw sticking out, tongue working at the back of his lower teeth. His skin was rough, reddish looking. Around his neck, he wore a thick gold chain. I lifted my eyes from his necklace and met his stare. Vince kind of smiled and winked. I slid along the wall behind him and away from Heather's room.

"Well," Pike said, "shouldn't we get back to the party then, and keep an eye on it."

"Shut up, Dickass," Robyn said. I rounded the corner to the kitchen and found Rex with a couple other guys. Rex stood on the counter with a big brown glass bottle in his hand. He brought the bottle up over his head and threw it at the floor with all his strength. It bounced, to a shared groan from the guys, but didn't break.

"What the hell are you doing?" I shouted.

One of the guys grabbed the bottle and handed it back to Rex. "We drank up this schnapps. Heather can tell her mom she broke it on accident," Rex said.

I went for the bottle but couldn't grab it before Robyn turned the corner.

"Get the fuck off there. Who are you?" Robyn had a fist twisted into each hip.

"Why, you keepin' a demerit list?" Rex tried to act cool but he immediately took himself off the counter and sat the bottle down on it carefully. I almost laughed out loud. He was scared of her. And well he should have been.

"This is the shit I'm talking about," Robyn said to Heather. Rex and the other guys went back to the patio. I looked through the glass and saw a bunch of older guys hanging around. Just sort of taking up all the space on the patio.

"Vince, make me a drink," Robyn commanded and shoved her huge purse in a cabinet next to the refrigerator.

"What was that noise?" Pike whispered at me.

"Rex trying to smash a bottle against the floor."

"Why?"

I just shrugged at him.

"C'mon, Heather, you gotta finish introducing me to everyone," Pike said putting his arm out to Heather.

"Yeah," Robyn chimed in. "We wouldn't want a perfectly good dickass going to waste."

I followed the stoners outside. There were plenty of dirty skater boys and pretty burn-out girls around the red cooler, and another cooler had arrived with it's own group of malcontents. These were obviously Robyn's friends. Mean looking older guys with gold chains around their necks. There were four or five of them. They all looked like the same dude.

"Hey." one of them pointed at Inez. "Randy, ain't that your weird little girlfriend."

"What?" The guy who was obviously Randy turned around. "Shit, Inez, you fucked your hair all up."

"It's called a mohawk, Randy," Inez said, ducking her head and focusing on the beer cooler.

"She ain't my girlfriend, man. She's just some little chick-a-dee I know." Randy slapped his friend on the shoulder. They were talking too loud. Loud, like everyone at the party was supposed to listen to them.

Rex came barreling toward the cooler, winding up behind Inez.

"You seen my ski mask?" he asked her.

"Go fuck yourself," Inez said, shouldering him out of her way and grabbing for a beer. Just then I heard a can pop open behind me, and Mantis was there.

"More chivalry?" I asked, taking the can from him.

Mantis smiled and held his own can up. "Those guys are fucked up. They're scaring everyone off." Mantis spoke to only me. The Robyn-friend-guys had made a little private circle around their cooler and shot the shit about hockey.

"What the fuck is up with Inez?" Rex pushed up beside me.

"That guy's being a dick," I explained.

"Randy? Yeah, that guy is friends with my brother. He's a fuckin' moron. But, what does Inez expect, anyway?"

"She gave herself a mohawk, so what?"

"Girls don't get mohawks, Angie. Everyone knows that."

I narrowed my eyes in on Rex. "What does that mean?"

"It's just the truth." Rex shrugged and walked away.

I watched him with the sense I might throw my beer at the back of his head.

"Where you goin' faggot?" One of Robyn's party boys asked as Rex passed by them.

"Takes one to know one, huh buddy?" Rex said and turned the corner of the house. The guy squinted after Rex for a second.

Randy handed the guy another Michelob, "Hey, that's Evan Douglas's little brother. Don't fuck with him too much."

The guy nodded and followed behind Rex.

"Shit," I whispered. As much as I hated Rex at that moment, I wasn't into him gettin' the shit kicked out of him by THAT guy. Robyn maybe, but not her asshole friend.

"Don't worry," Mantis said into my ear. "There's a bunch of people around the side getting stoned. Luann has a big bag and Alien and Tombs are both over there with a couple of other guys. Tombs has his board, too. Good weapon, that is."

Mantis was smiling. I didn't know what to say to him.

"Who's Tombs?" I asked.

"He's another skater. Just built a half pipe in his back yard."

"Oh," I said, scanning the crowd for Shelby. I couldn't see her any-where. Heather was going from one little cluster of kids to the next, talking, laughing, avoiding the weird dude gang.

Inez and Pike were over by the cooler. Inez had her head dipped squarely into her beer can. She was wedged between Pike and the cool-er, while people grabbed beers and ice water leaked out around the cooler. I had been in just that spot earlier. It was the trapped spot. Can't go back, can't go forward, can't be where you are.

I went toward them, Mantis following me.

"Hey you guys, let's go back into the yard and stretch out," I said.

The weird guys were between us and where we were going.

They surveyed me, all of us, with intense eyes and silent mouths. It was like being in a room with five Rudys.

After we passed by them into the darkness beyond the patio lights, one of them said, "That faggot was even wearin' make up."

We went straight to the very back of the yard and threw ourselves in the slightly moist grass. Our position was perfect. We were hidden, but we could see the rest of the party on the patio lit by porch and kitchen light. We could watch the weird guys around their cooler and the other kids pulling away, forming their own groups. I settled myself before I realized I'd been so concerned about our getaway, I'd forgotten something very important.

"Oh, shit," I said, looking back at the party. "I should have grabbed more beer."

"Never fear, your favorite faggot is here," Pike said, pulling out the fifth of whiskey they'd scored the night before. Pike twisted the cap off and took a good slug. I took the bottle next. It was my first taste of whiskey and it was horrible.

"That stuff is awful," I said.

"Here wash it down with some beer." Mantis handed me his can.

"This is like watching TV," Inez said. "Give me a paper, Pike."

The weird guy who followed Rex came back around the corner with a bunch of kids behind him, Rex and Luann included. They all seemed to be getting along just fine.

"See, Luann smoked him out. You can tell," Mantis said.

The music changed from Minor Threat to Fleetwood Mac.

"Why didn't Robyn just have her own party?" I asked.

"Oh my god, my ears are bleeding!" Pike said, falling into the grass. "Where's that whiskey?"

I passed the Early Times happily to Pike. Inez lit a joint and smoked at it for a second.

Robyn came out the sliding glass doors; Vince followed closely behind her. "Robyn, for god's sake, it's forty lousy bucks. Why do you have to give me so much grief about it?"

"How much money do you already owe me, Vince? Huh?" Robyn said without turning around, without putting any real effort into her words at all.

She stood near the group of dudes with a big plastic tumbler in one hand and fished a cigarette out of the pack that jutted from the hip pocket of her jeans with the other. Vince lit it for her. "Robyn, you know I'm good for it," Vince appealed to her.

"No, I don't. Besides, I don't want you hasslin' me tonight. I just want to have some fun."

"If she wants to have fun she should stop hangin' out with those assholes," Inez said through her hit.

I laughed, and took another sip of whiskey, a smaller one. I still shivered though, and handed the bottle to Mantis.

"Robyn, you didn't tell us this was gonna be a faggot party." one of the Michelob-guzzling geniuses said. His voice was so loud we would have heard him whether we'd been eavesdropping or not. Shit, the whole neighborhood probably heard that one.

"I didn't know people like this even existed." Pike threw his hand up to take the bottle from Mantis. Mantis, who'd leaned over me and never completely moved back. Mantis who was now sitting up against me. I wanted a cigarette but I didn't want to move. I liked him sitting against me. I hated it. I didn't want it to stop. I wanted to smoke.

"She only brought guys with her," Mantis said.

"She only hangs out with guys," I said.

"Why?" Mantis was really leaning on me then, getting closer, which didn't seem possible.

"Where'd them girl faggots go?" Randy asked, searching the brightly lit patio for Shelby and Colleen.

"That's my sister, ya fuckin asshole." Robyn pointed one of her crazy long nails at him. It looked absolutely astonishing with back lighting.

"Ain't nothin' wrong with bein' a girl faggot." Randy put his hands up. All the guys seemed to agree and they clanked Michelob bottles in what appeared to be a kind of celebration of girl faggots.

"I fucked that guy," Inez said and passed the joint again. Mantis snapped his head her direction and froze.

"How do you even know him?" Pike asked.

"I don't. I was really drunk down at the river, at Missouri Bottoms. Mantis, you were there. We had a big fire, the night Chuck let the cooler float away and Tombs tried to bust his head with his skate board."

"I remember that. I don't remember that fuckin' moron though."

"He was down there with some people. I went to take a piss and got sick and then he was kissing me."

"After you puked? That's disgusting. Licking the puke out of someone's mouth?" Mantis was making a screwed up face into the joint.

"Vince! I'm fucking serious. I ain't givin' you any money. Now shut up about it." Robyn shrugged Vince off while the other guys watched Luann walk across the patio. Rex, the poor bastard, was still following Luann.

"What do you mean he was kissing you? How'd you start talking to him if you were sick?" I asked.

"I don't know. I don't remember. He was kissing me and everything was spinning and I could see Tombs standing on the bank screaming about something, but I just couldn't get there. I just couldn't balance enough to walk or get up or whatever and I fucked that stupid guy. After that I kinda tried to like him. Got high with him a couple of times but he's really stupid. I don't know why I fucked him."

"Beer goggles," Mantis said. "Happens to everyone."

I took another drink and found out why they call it courage. "Is that a good thing to say right now? I mean you got your hand on my leg."

Pike laughed and pointed. "Dude, she called you!"

"No one could need beer goggles with you, Angie," Mantis said.

"Oh, oh, oh god, that's cheesy!" Pike said. "It's the Fleetwood Mac. We're all being poisoned!"

"I gotta pee," I said. Mantis helped me up off the grass.

I rounded the little metal garden shed that was designed to look like a house even though it just looked like a metal garden shed. There I found Colleen kissing Shelby. Or Shelby kissing Colleen. Either way, they were kissing.

"Hey, I gotta pee," I said.

Shelby started giggling. A good giggle. The way she used to sound. This made me giggle too while I pulled my pants down. Even Colleen started to giggle and I guessed maybe she was cool enough to kiss Shelby.

"Are those guys still out there?" Colleen asked.

"Yeah." I giggled and peed. "If you sit back here with us, it's like fuckin' Robyn TV," I said, then lost my balance and fell backward.

"I just fell in my own pee, you guys!"

"She's funny, Shelby," Colleen said and they both helped me up.

"You been hittin' that beer?" Shelby asked.

"Whiskey."

"Oh shit."

"That Mantis guy wants to touch my boobies." I was dead serious when I said it but somehow the three of us just melted into laughter. Shelby and Colleen let me lean on them on the way back to the whiskey.

"Just so you know," Shelby told Colleen. "Robyn is my sister."

We all flopped into the grass, me next to Mantis. "What happened while I was gone?"

"Well, that Robyn lady is gonna kill her boyfriend and that other guy is following Luann around and pretty much everybody left."

Luann came out of the sliding door in a glamorous whoosh. It was just a way she had. Heather was behind her toting what appeared to be a huge bottle of vodka. Heather handed the bottle to Robyn and as she did one of the weird guys said, "Damn, do you only got one boob? You guys, look at this."

"This is fucking ridiculous. These people are obsessed," Pike said.

"Should we do something?" Inez asked.

"It's a little late to abort them," Pike said and I laughed and laughed against Mantis, who received my body as if he had been expecting it.

"Stop asking me, Vince!" Robyn said through clenched teeth.

"Oh, calm down, bitch!" Vince yelled back.

"Bitch? I'm a bitch, now?" Robyn yelled as she threw the tumbler behind her. It flew in an arch of red liquid, hit a brick wall, and then rolled silently across the patio.

"You want to make somethin' out of nothin'. That's what bitches do, bitch," Vince said, making hand gestures into his chest. Daring Robyn to go for him. Which she did. Robyn threw herself into Vince. He tried to stay standing but after a couple of back steps he was flat on the lawn with Robyn on top of him. She was punching him in the head real good. Sharp whacks.

The weird guys all just stood there looking at the fight. Until one of them said, "C'mon Vince, I didn't come out here to watch you act like a fuckin' pussy."

Vince grabbed Robyn by her hair and rolled her off him into the grass, and she clawed at his face with those nails. He reared back and slammed a good fist into her eye.

"Shit," Shelby said and got on her feet. She ran toward the crowd of weird dudes.

"Oh no."

"Fuck this."

"What's she doing?"

"Should we go over there?"

We said these things to one another without moving from the grass.

Shelby got to the group and kicked Vince in the ribs as hard as she could. "Fucking knock it off!"

"Fuck you, you little dyke!" Vince took one hand out of Robyn's hair, squeezed her neck with the other one, and then swiped at Shelby with the first. This threw Vince's balance off enough that Robyn could get control again. In a spilt second they were back on their feet and throwing punches.

"Will you guys fucking grab them already?" Shelby appealed to the weird dudes who took this as a kind of challenge to their manhood, I guessed anyway, because they immediately took action. One grabbed

Vince and another grabbed Robyn. Robyn managed to get in a pretty nice kick on Vince, right in the balls, as the two were being pulled apart.

"You son of a bitch, you gave me a black eye!" Robyn shouted and tried to spit in Vince's face.

"You deserved it you fucking slut!"

This went on for a few minutes, the two of them threatening and insulting each other as they struggled against their captors. Shelby and Heather and Rex and Luann and Alien and Tombs were the only people left on the patio and they stood in a group together next to Randy and the other weird dude, watching.

"Where's that whiskey, Mantis?" I asked with more of a stammer in my voice than I had expected.

"Right here." He nodded his head toward the bottle neck sticking up from between his legs. He wanted me to grab it from there. From next to his cock. I knew this, I guess, because I was drunk or because sex is a natural instinct or maybe because it was so fucking obvious. Whatever it was, I wanted to do it. I was pretty turned on. Was it the fight? The booze? A combination? God help me.

"Thanks," I said, slipping my hand between his legs and grabbing the base of the bottle instead of the neck. Mantis let out a little breath. I wanted to hear him do more of that. More breathing like that. The night was weird and horrible and violent and drunk and sexy.

I took a drink off the bottle and felt Mantis's hand slide along the top side of my ass and come to a stop on my hip opposite him. Mantis had his arm around me and I really liked it. I got so wrapped up with it that, although I had been staring at Robyn TV, I hadn't really been watching. I missed a couple of important things. Like Robyn and Vince being released and seated in patio chairs on either side of the porch. Like the disappearance of Luann. Rex had just noticed himself and was looking around for her like a lost puppy.

"Luann doesn't like Rex," I said. "You'd think he'd catch on by now."

"She likes him enough if he's got drugs," Mantis said.

"Oh, well, then maybe she does like him. Rex usually has pot and acid and pills and stuff."

"She'd prefer some Coke."

"Oh," I said, stiffening. I hadn't thought about hard drugs. Luann doing coke? She'd end up like Vince. Licking the back of her teeth and wearing bad jewelry. I got a picture of Luann with hair on her chest and a big gold chain draped through it. I giggled and Mantis pinched my hip. Did he think it was my ass? God, does my hip have enough fat on it to make it seem like an ass? Suddenly I felt awful. I had momentarily forgotten about being fat. Mantis following me around all night and everyone being so nice to me and all of us sitting in the grass, I'd forgotten. I guess that's whiskey. I guess that's why people drink it.

I felt very big and very weird and I wanted Mantis to take his hand off me. No, I wanted him to leave it there. I wanted him to touch me, touch me again and again. I wanted him to touch me the way thin girls get touched. I wanted to feel Mantis touching something thin. I wanted to have a surrogate make-out session. This is crazy. This is me. This is my life. I took another drink off the bottle.

Mantis had gone from being a cutie, a new friend, a possible make-out partner to a demon, a danger, a guy with thick beer goggles on. Or worse, maybe I was a joke. Maybe he was gonna kiss me and try and fuck me and all these random people would show up and have a good laugh. Hell, maybe it was even Luann. Maybe this was a game they were playing together. Getting my big fat body out of its clothes. Oh god, things were getting bad. What was I thinking? Fuck. I'm so goddamned stupid.

Luann reappeared from inside the house and Rex seemed relieved. He came to her side and she asked, "Where's Mantis?"

"I dunno, I haven't seen him in a long time. Why?"

"Why what?"

"Why do you want to know where he is?"

"Because, we are like, well, we are kind of dating." Luann shrugged and two million conversations started all at once. A million on Robyn TV and a million on the grass.

"You're dating Luann?" Inez asked, giving his arm around my ass a bad look.

"Damn, you don't even try to hide hittin' on someone else," Pike said. "Pretty low if you ask me."

Inez nodded in agreement.

"I'm not dating Luann," Mantis said, shaking his head and making a whizzing sigh with his tongue.

"Well where'd she get that idea then?" Colleen finally spoke up and we all turned toward her. I'd nearly forgotten she was there.

"Yeah." I turned to Mantis. "Where'd she get that idea?"

I moved away from him just a little but it was enough to insult him and he snapped his arm quickly off my ass/hip and put his hands to his face.

"You're lookin' good tonight," one of the dudes said to Luann.

"Leave her alone already, Mark," Robyn said from her chair.

"Oh, you gonna beat my ass too?" Mark asked Robyn.

"Don't tempt me, you fuckin' pig."

"Oh, now I'm a pig? That's not what you said last summer when we were screwin' in your old man's pool."

"Well, I should have," Robyn quieted herself, I assume, because she knew what was coming.

"You fucked Mark?" Vince asked, standing and kicking the patio chair from under him.

"Mantis?" Luann called into the darkness.

"Are you gonna answer her?" Pike asked.

Mantis rocked his face back and forth in his hands and just groaned.

"I didn't even know you then," Robyn said.

Mark was snickering and opening a new bottle of beer. He was quite proud of the disturbance he'd created. Robyn got on her feet. "You stay back, Vince. Just fucking calm down."

"I ain't gonna calm down, Robyn. You gotta fuck everybody in town?"

"Wow. You and Robyn have a lot in common, Mantis," Pike said.

"Oh, this is the worst party I have ever been to." Mantis looked up again. "No, I'm not going to answer Luann. She's not my girl-friend. It's a long story about Luann, and I'm not gonna tell it right now. And all hell is getting ready to break loose, again, if you haven't noticed."

"Oh shit," I said, looking up to see that Alien and Rex had both grabbed their boards and were standing alongside Tombs in a threatening line up.

"Don't hit her again," Rex said to Vince.

"Rex, don't." Shelby moved closer to him. The fear in her voice was sharp. Sharp enough to get Alien's mind working.

"Heat," Alien said quickly to Tombs and Rex.

"Smart kid, there," Randy said.

"Heat? What does that mean?" Colleen asked.

"Guns," Inez replied flatly.

"What the fuck are we gonna do?" Pike sat bolt up right and looked at the rest of us. None of us were breathing when a group of older, long-haired adults turned the corner of the house. Everyone on the porch seemed to take a breath and hold at least part of it inside their lungs.

"That's Luann's mom," Pike said. "I remember her from the house."

"Hi, Luann. We got here as soon as we could, everything all right?" Luann's mom smiled, looking around at everyone and their tension. "I thought this was supposed to be a party. Actually, I thought this was supposed to be a high school party. You guys show up at kiddy keggers often?" Luann's mom tilted her head. She was giving the men a you-should-be-ashamed-of-yourself look, a look I wanted to remember for future use.

The weird dudes dropped their heads, except for Vince, who was still looking at Robyn like he was gonna kill her. Luann's mom walked toward Robyn. "Well, I guess I know who done this to your face, don't I?"

"This don't concern you, ma'am," Vince said and I suddenly realized what an adult was. It wasn't Robyn and her buddies, they were just kids. Big bully kids, but just kids. The circle of newly arrived hippie grown-ups had, somehow, just taken charge of everything. I could feel Pike and Mantis relax.

"Well, actually, it quite concerns me, young man. A bunch of grown men hangin' out at a party with my sixteen-year-old daughter. That concerns me plenty. And then somebody gave this woman a good shiner. It's fresh, so it musta just happened. Which means it happened in front of my kid, which means it concerns me. Would you care to argue?"

"No, ma'am." Vince finally dropped his head.

"Good. So here's what's gonna happen. You boys are gonna move on, right now, as a matter of fact. I'm gonna put some ice on this woman's face, then Dizzy is gonna drive her home and I'm gonna go in here and watch some TV while these kids finish their party, so don't even think about comin' back. Any questions?"

"I can just get a ride with them, I'm fine, it's okay." Robyn tried to tell Luann's mom.

"No, it's not okay. You get in that car with them and I'll have the police pull you over and charge you all with contributing. And that's just what I know I can do, let's not mention drunk driving, drugs, illegal weapons, and all of what-have-you. Maybe you should humor me."

"Let's go, guys," Mark said, picking up the handle of the cooler they'd brought with them.

"You can leave that," one of the hippie dudes said, and Mark dropped the handle. The guys walked around the house. A couple of the guys with long gray hair and weird-assed sandal shoes followed behind them. Luann's mom and her remaining male friend led Robyn back into the house.

I burst out laughing. "Robyn just got kidnapped by hippies!"

CHAPTER 13

Morning came and I was curled against Mantis on the grass behind the shed. He had one arm slung over my tits and his knees pushed me up into a tight ball. Dew covered everything with tiny crystals. I was freezing. Mantis slept heavily. I laid there for a couple of minutes, shivering, having to pee, hoping I might fall back off to sleep. I didn't want Mantis to wake up. My eyes and mouth were glued shut and I hadn't the faintest understanding of what I was supposed to say or do.

The longer I laid there, the more cold I felt, the more I had to pee, the more my head hurt. And then confusion set in. How did I wind up cuddling with Mantis behind the shed?

I lifted Mantis's arm carefully by the wrist and set it back on his own chest. He stirred and looked at me through slit eyelids. Oh shit, here we go. Wait until Mantis finds out he spent the night with Lezzylard.

"I gotta piss," I said. I got up instantly and made my way back to the house.

As I rounded the shed, I saw a cluster of people sitting on the patio. The stereo was playing low and they all smoked.

Heather's neighbor opened her back door to let her dog out. The little shit went right for the fence and barked. I waved, hoped she would call the dog off. But she stood wide-eyed, staring at me. A report would definitely be given to Heather's mother.

Heather and Rex and Alien and Luann sat cross-legged on the patio. Somehow they remained completely oblivious to the dog as well as the neighbor lady who was busy scanning the situation.

"You guys should go in," I told them.

"Why, we want to watch the sun rise," Heather said.

"Look, Heather." I waved my hands around. "The sun is up! And so are your neighbors. It's morning, a brand new day, the first day of the rest of your life and all that."

"Shit." Heather blinked at the sky. "How did I miss that?"

"I don't know, but you really should go inside. Your neighbor saw all of us out here and I don't think she was pleased."

Everyone got to their feet. Luann stared straight back into the yard. A stop-motion wonderment.

"I thought you said Mantis left with Tombs," she said to Rex.

"I thought he did." Rex threw up his hands. By then we were all watching Mantis cross the yard toward the house.

"What? You never seen anyone wake up behind a shed before?" Mantis shrugged.

I turned to get into the house as quickly as possible. I didn't make it before Luann could give me a look.

I took the longest, most incredible piss of my life. I could not believe how long it was or how totally fucking good it felt. I looked at the shower and smiled. Warm water. I was about to have it spilling all over me, warming me up and washing the lawn off me. I had the sense that a shower would solve everything.

Just as I striped out my clothes and stepped in, someone knocked on the door.

"Hey Angie." it was Mantis. "Let me come in and piss. I won't look, I swear."

"The door is locked. You got to wait a second." I stepped out of the shower and unlocked the door, once I was back behind the curtain I told him to come in. The curtain was a dark forest green and I was glad no outlines could be perceived.

"Thanks, baby," Mantis said and I heard his piss hit the toilet water.

Baby? Is that why Luann thought they were dating?

"How you feeling?" Mantis asked.

"Like something ran me over."

"I'll make some eggs. How does that sound?"

"Awful."

"Well, if we eat, we'll probably be able to fall back asleep."

"Is there enough food for everybody?"

"I don't think the acid heads are gonna need any food."

"Oh, so that's why they're still up."

The toilet flushed just as I got my hair lathered.

"Man, I really want to take a shower too."

"I'll be done in a minute."

I felt Mantis pause. I could feel him on the other side of the curtain just inches away from my naked body. A swipe of his hand against the curtain and I would be revealed. Me and my fat gut hanging out all over the place.

"What are you doing out there Mantis?" I asked squelching my horrible fear that the whole bathroom was full of people. People waiting to see the show.

"Couldn't I just get in there with you?"

"No. I thought you were going to make breakfast." My heart rate sped up to like a million beats a second.

"Okay, okay, send me out into the cruel world stinking like whiskey and lawn fertilizer."

"Oh, I bet you can handle it."

Mantis left the bathroom and shut the door tightly behind him.

I finished my shower quickly. I wanted to stay under the warm water forever but Mantis hadn't locked the door. And Alien, all drugged out and being an asshole in general anyway, wouldn't hesitate to do something really terrifically awful to me.

My clothes were damp and smelled really bad. I poked my head out the door, pulled the towel tight around my chest and made a dash for Heather's room. But when I turned the knob, it was locked.

"Oh!" Mantis turned the corner. "Now this is a good look for you." He came down the hall in slow steps.

"Shut up and give me a hanger." I pointed to the coat closet right behind him.

When Mantis handed me the hanger, he leaned into my ear and said, "My breath is too bad to kiss you anyway."

Kiss me? The whole morning was fucking weird. Not like morning at all. It was a party just all light and weird and sickly. But fun. Somehow, I was having fun.

I bent the hanger and stuck it into the knob on Heather's bedroom door. I jiggled it for a second, and it opened just as Mantis closed the bathroom door behind him. As soon as I got completely inside the room, Shelby and Colleen both looked up. They were in Heather's bed. Naked.

"Oh, sorry." I was blushing from ear to ear.

"Do you understand what a locked door means?" Shelby smirked at me.

"Well, I guess not. I thought it got locked by accident. Or something. Listen, it'll just take a second. I need a t-shirt and some shorts, then I'm out of here."

"Get all dirty rollin' around with that boy?" Colleen asked.

"I guess. I don't know what happened. I just woke up behind the shed."

"With that boy," Colleen reminded me again.

"Yes, with that boy."

I rummaged through Heather's drawer. It was taking longer than I wanted because I had to find something that would fit. I hoped Heather would still have the shorts from her old soccer jock days. Finally, near the bottom of the drawer, I felt the silky fabric and pulled out a pair of royal blue shorts. I found a plain white t-shirt that was big enough and hurried to put them on.

"All right, I'm leaving you alone now."

"Lock the door," Colleen sang and I did as she instructed.

Alien was in the hall waiting for the bathroom. "What were they doin' in there?"

"Sleeping," I said.

"Oh, c'mon. They were, like, lickin' each other's titties and stuff, weren't they? Just tell me."

I swung around to Alien. "Yes. They were lickin' each other's titties and pussies and sticking high heels in each other. Too bad you missed it."

"High heels?" Aliens eyebrows arched up. "That's amazing. That's so fucking cool. High heels? Lesbians are the shit, man." Alien talked to himself.

I rounded the corner into the kitchen, where I found Luann lighting a cigarette off the stove.

"Feeling better?" She asked.

"Not really."

I rummaged around in the refrigerator for butter and stuff. Mantis had only gotten far enough along with breakfast to put the eggs and bread on the counter. I lit the stove under a big silver skillet.

"You hungry?" I asked Luann.

"Hell, no. Rex wasn't kidding, he really did have some great acid in his freezer."

"Oh. Where's your mom?"

"She only hung around for about an hour."

"Oh."

Luann sidled up beside me as I tossed a pat of butter against the hot skillet.

"Did you fuck Mantis?" She asked, taking a long drag off her cigarette. She looked crazy. All big pupils and sweat. Nothing about her was glamorous.

"No!" I said, giving her a quick shake of my head. I turned to the refrigerator to look for bacon or sausage or ham.

"You can tell me the truth," Luann said.

I found a half-pack of bacon and swung around to meet her sweaty, twitching look.

"I would know if I fucked him," I said and lit the stove under another skillet.

Luann pulled her hair back with one hand and smoked with the other. She looked positively insane and I wished she would go away. Heather and Rex were still giggling and Alien was in the hall saying: "Dude, are you like whackin' the weasel or something? C'mon, I got to piss like a race horse."

Luann let her hair down and ran her cigarette under the faucet. "Well, don't think fucking him makes him like your boyfriend or something. That's not the way Mantis operates."

I threw a few strips of bacon into the skillet and watched them fry for a second.

"I don't want a boyfriend, Luann," I lied.

"Good." Luann said as she walked away.

From the living room Rex said, "A race horse? What the hell do you know about race horses, Alien? You grew up in the white fuckin' projects!"

"Yeah, right next to you and your horse-faced family!" Alien said.

"My horse-faced family!" Rex shouted and everyone laughed, including Luann, who had returned to the living room.

I took the bacon off and let it drain on a paper towel. Did Mantis just tell me to make him breakfast? He could make the eggs himself. I put two slices of bread in the toaster and went to the living room to see what everyone was giggling about.

"Are you frying bacon?" Rex asked.

"Me? No. Why, do you smell bacon?" I said.

Luann, sat up on her elbows. "You were just frying bacon, I saw you," she said. Her face was twisted up in a knot.

"Me? No. You must be hallucinating," I said.

"Fuck you. I just saw you. Aren't you even going to eat it? Did you fry it just to make us sick?" Luann was serious about this question.

"Damn, Luann," Rex said. "You need some more whiskey or something? She's just fucking with us because we're high."

"It's not very funny," Luann dropped her head back on the floor.

Everyone got ridiculously quiet. I turned to leave the room when Heather busted out laughing, "Bacon! Fucking Bacon!" Rex and Alien seemed to find this very funny and they laughed and laughed until finally Luann laughed too. I included acid on my list of Things Never To Do.

I leaned out into the hall. "I feel like shit," I told Alien.

"At least you're not waiting for God's fucking gift to get done bathing himself!" Alien smacked the bathroom door with his fist.

"Are you hungry?" I asked him.

"Me? Are you finally in love with me Angie? I've been waiting so long." Alien lowered himself to his knees and feigned a pleading expression.

"I just want to know if you want some eggs or something."

"Oh, right." Alien snapped back to his full standing posture. "Mr. Thing is in there washing his nuts for you right now. I almost forgot."

Just then the door swung open and Mantis appeared in a towel. "I don't have to wash my nuts, Alien. They're self-washing. I had it installed last year."

"Self-washing!" Heather shouted and she and Rex laughed, as Alien flung himself toward the toilet bowl.

"That's not funny either," Luann said. "Jesus, Mantis, aren't you even going to put some clothes on?"

"No, actually, Luann, I'm not. Does that bother you?"

"I don't give a fuck what you do," Luann said.

"Okay, that's it," Rex sat up on his elbows. "Luann drinks more whiskey."

Rex pulled the fifth we'd been drinking the night before out of his back pack. At least, I thought it was the fifth we'd been drinking.

"I'm not going to drink by myself," Luann said.

"Oh, the lady drives a hard bargain," Rex said and took a swallow from the bottle.

Mantis turned the corner into the kitchen. He had a pink towel wrapped around his waist. He was so skinny and so pretty. I couldn't believe I'd woken up with him.

"You can make the eggs," I said, finger combing my hair.

"I can do that," Mantis said just as the toast popped up. "You want I should butter that?"

"I can handle it," I said.

Mantis broke eggs into a bowl while I struggled with the paper around the butter.

"Angie," Mantis whispered. "Luann wants to kill me. We can't stay around her, okay?"

"Sure," I said.

Mantis cooked the eggs all scrambled. My stomach groaned. I pulled two plates out of the cabinet just as Luann came into the kitchen for another smoke.

My body took up a lot of space in any room. But Luann was different. She was as skinny as Mantis yet her silence exhausted everything around her. I wanted to be like her someday.

Luann got between Mantis and the stove. She moved the skillet of eggs to the side and lit her smoke. She didn't bother moving the skillet back over the flame.

"I thought you left last night," Luann said to Mantis.

"Nope," he said sharply, moving the skillet back.

"I can see that," Luann attempted a pretty smile but in her state it just looked weird.

"I'm making breakfast, you want some?" Mantis stepped back and threw his hands up over the top of his pink towel.

"No, but I would like to talk," Luann said, tilting her head back.

"What do you want to talk about?"

"Privately." Luann looked over at me.

"Not now, my eggs are about to burn." Mantis shouldered her out of the way and dug a spatula into the eggs.

Luann looked at him for a second then turned my way and mouthed the words FUCK YOU.

"Luann," Rex called from the living room. "C'mon girl, I'm not finishing this bottle by myself. Why don't you just party and deal with your shit later?"

"Shut up Rex, there's no shit to deal with," Luann spat and turned back toward the living room.

When Mantis and I passed by with our loaded plates she was taking another mouthful of whiskey while Heather giggled.

Heather's house had a guest room. To my knowledge no one had ever stayed in it, but that wasn't the point. The point was that there was one. And Heather's mom had gone through the trouble of decorating it. Jungle. The wall paper was all green vines and tiger heads. No bodies, just heads. The bedspread was a blend of tropical flowers and parrots. The nightstand and the chair by the window were made of wicker. And a full length mirror was mounted at the foot of the bed. It's plastic frame was made to look like bamboo, even though it just looked like plastic. On the bed was a huge stuffed monkey.

Mantis and me plopped on the floor at the foot of the bed, the stuffed monkey staring at us. Mantis scooped a big mound of eggs into his mouth and looked around.

"There should be a sound track to this room," he said.

I followed his gaze around but didn't have any comment. As far as I was concerned the room could have been empty.

"Why does Luann want to kill you?" I asked, taking a bite of bacon.

Mantis looked at me for a minute, chewing toast.

"I don't want to talk about Luann," he said.

"Well, all the same, she's giving me a hard time and I want to know why."

Mantis stared at the monkey, looked at me, looked away, chewed.

"Look Mantis," I threw my fork against the plate. "I'm not being an asshole here. Luann is mouthing FUCK YOU at me. You need to fill in the blanks."

A wealth of crazy acid laughter came from the living room. Alien yelled, "Someday, Rex, you're gonna be ugly too and you'll wish you'd been a better guy in your youth, that's how it goes. You wait and see."

"I won't live long enough to see that," Rex said. Then the living room quieted to its steady giggle.

"Okay," Mantis said. "All right. Luann. Her parents have these parties. And one night, I made out with Luann. At the time it didn't seem like a big deal. I mean, people make out at parties, right?"

"Right." I shrugged, as if I did stuff like that every night of the stupid week. Never mind that I'd never kissed a boy before Mantis. Never mind that I barely remembered making out with him. Never mind that I didn't even know what all was included under the heading of making out. Kissing? Over the pants, under the bra? In the pants? It was obvious that feigned nonchalance should take over my personality.

"So we made out and I slept on the couch in her parent's living room. Well, I pass out drunk. I get woke up by Luann on top of me. So, long story short, we fuck. That was like a month ago and she keeps acting like we are dating. It's dumb. It's her problem. I never tried to fuck her. She fucked me. I don't owe her anything."

I took another bite of the eggs Mantis had over cooked and pushed my plate away. Luann was a girl prize. As far as I knew, every boy in the world wanted to date her.

"So, why'd you make out with her if you didn't like her?"

"It's not that I didn't like her. We've known each other a long time. We were always friends. But she kind of freaks out on the guys she sleeps with. I mean, she's real bossy and sometimes she gets mad about stuff that doesn't make any sense. Like, when I woke on the couch, the day after the party, I left. I had to work and I was already late. If I lose this job, I could wind up back in detention. It's part of my probation. Anyway, Luann flips a nut on me for not kissing her good bye. She wasn't even on the couch with me. She's crazy."

"Did you tell her you were late for work?"

"Angie, it doesn't matter. It was just a thing that happened. That probably shouldn't have happened. Luann will get over it."

Mantis licked the grease off his fingers one by one. The monkey, reflected in the mirror, lurked over his shoulder.

"You gonna finish that?" Mantis pointed at my half-eaten plate.

I looked down at it and shook my head. It was the first time in my life I could remember not being hungry. Mantis grabbed the plate and scooped everything up with the piece of toast. He steered the shovel toward his mouth, but before he took a bite he glanced at me.

"Can we talk about something else now?" he asked.

"Sure," I said, focusing my attention on my nails.

"What are you writing these days?" Mantis squished the toast and stuff into his mouth.

"Writing? Nothing." I started to tell him I didn't write but changed my mind. "I've got a lot going on, right now."

"Family shit?"

"Yeah. My mom's getting remarried."

"Asshole?"

"That's not the half of it."

Mantis finished the rest of my breakfast then climbed into the big bed. He threw the monkey on the floor.

"You comin'?" he asked.

I looked at him in the mirror. His pink towel dropped to the floor. My stomach did a pirouette and my heart sped up.

"No fucking," I pointed at him in the mirror.

"No fucking. Cross my heart and hope to die," Mantis made the hand motions and I crawled in the bed beside him.

He kept his word and didn't try to fuck me. We curled up together and Mantis fell back to sleep. I listened to him snore for awhile. There was no way I'd fall back asleep. I slid out of the bed. Mantis woke as I gathered the dishes.

"You leaving?" he asked.

"Yeah, I should be home."

"Okay, I'll call you." Mantis reached for me. I leaned in and kissed him.

"You need my number, then, don't you?"

"You gave it to me last night. It took you three tries to get it written down, but you finally got it." Mantis laughed and snuggled back down into the bed.

CHAPTER 14

I listened to Mom and Rudy move through the apartment. Going through what was rapidly becoming their basic routine. Mom making breakfast and Rudy asking her where everything was: his razor, his belt, cream for his coffee. God, if only we did have a big house. We could get away from each other, sometimes. As it stood, I could hear Rudy fart in the bathroom.

I laid in bed listening to them for a few minutes. I put bits of my dream back together. I was kissing Mantis when he turned into Carrie. Carrie Shuren giggling and giving me smoky tongue kisses.

Kissing a girl in my dream didn't make me gay. That's not how dreams worked. No, it was a symbol of some kind. Aunt Jean had one of those dream dictionaries, I would look it up sometime.

I dragged myself out of bed. Going to school after everything that happened seemed like the stupidest thing in the world. But I did want to see Carrie. Maybe that's what the dream was about. I couldn't wait to tell her about everything. The party, Mantis. I wished she knew Mantis so she could see how cute he was. Then again, maybe girls like Carrie didn't really think dirty punk boys were cute.

"The toilet's busted," Rudy told me in the hall. "I ain't got time to fix it now. So, if you take a shit, you have to pull the plunger up so it will flush."

"Gross." I shouldered past him into the bathroom.

I brushed my teeth while Mom and Rudy talked about the toilet.

"Rudy, I'm off today, I'll just call a maintenance man. That's what we pay rent for."

"No. I don't want them in here. I got my weed and shit in here."

"So, put it away."

"I'll handle it when I get home, Rita."

"I can probably fix it myself."

"Oh, Jesus. Don't go fuckin' around in there, Rita. You'll probably break something else."

"Jean is coming over today. She can fix it."

"Why can't you just leave it?"

"Why can't I just fix it?"

"Okay. Fine. Be stubborn, Rita. I gotta go."

I heard Rudy leave out the door just as I reattached the toilet chain to it's arm. All fixed. Rudy could have fixed it as soon as he found it. Would have taken him a fraction of the time it took to argue with my mother. But that's not how Rudy did things, I guessed.

I dressed and popped a couple of Dexatrims out of their blister pack. I cupped them in my hand so I could sneak them with a glass of water before I left.

Mom was in the living room with her head on one hand. She was smoking in her little silk robe that now showed a couple cigarette burns of its own.

"Good morning," I said.

"If you say so."

"The toilet's fixed. Why did he make such a big deal out of it?"

"Because he's a man." She smiled then, and stood. "You want some breakfast?"

"No. I'm gonna get going." I waved her off and turned into the kitchen. I popped the Dexatrim and gulped down a glass of water.

"How are you gonna learn anything if you're hungry?"

"They don't teach us anything anyway, Mom."

"That's probably true. Well, make sure you come straight home from school. Jean is going to be here. We're gonna eat early since I don't work today."

"Okay," I said and left.

At school, I went to my favorite big bathroom and got my make up out. I was just smoothing concealer under my eyes when Mindy Overton walked in.

"Why the fuck are you always in here, Lezzylard?"

"Because I hate you." I was matter of fact.

Mindy smirked and leaned against the wall. I looked at her. God, she was perfect. Not sexy like Carrie, just perfect. Everything, her face, her clothes, her body. Everything, except her shitty, little, mean-assed personality.

"You waitin' for me to leave so you can puke? Just go ahead. It's not like everyone doesn't already know." I shrugged.

"What are you talking about?"

"Why are you here? Why do you get to school so early?" I asked.

"Why do you?"

"To put my face on, that's obvious. What are you doing just standing over there?"

"Shut up, fat bitch. Just get your make up on. Not like it's gonna help you."

"I'm not leaving until you do." I stared at her in the mirror while I put on lipstick.

"Fine, I'll use a different bathroom." Mindy turned and pushed her weight into the big bathroom door.

I grabbed my make up and my book bag and followed behind her.

"I'll go with you." I put a big stupid smile on my face.

"What is your fucking problem? Why don't you just leave me alone?" Mindy asked.

"Oh, you want me to leave you alone? Wow, what a great change in our relationship. All these years, I've just wanted you to leave me alone."

"You're going to be so sorry you did this." Mindy pointed in my face.

"What's the big deal Mindy? Why can't you be in a bathroom with someone else?"

Mindy and I were standing in the hall looking at each other. The bell would ring soon. Mindy looked over her shoulder at the first couple bus loads coming in and sighed.

When she looked back at me, her brown eyes were almost black. "So fucking sorry." And with that threat, she walked away.

I went straight to art class and finished my make up at the table before the second bell rang. Then I went into the hall to look for Shelby. I couldn't wait to tell her what I had done. I couldn't wait to hear about her weekend with Colleen. God, Shelby had SEX. She always said I'd be the first since I was straight. And I guess we could have both lost our virginity on the same night. I regretted not doing that. Would I always regret that? Shit, we've known each other forever, it would have been perfect. The second bell rang and there was no Shelby anywhere to be found.

I took my usual seat feeling frustrated and guilty. That's when Troy Mulligan got my attention and mouthed the words YOU'RE DEAD! He made his hand into a gun shape and pointed it at me.

Mindy and Troy. Troy and Mindy. I'd completely forgotten to think about the two of them being a brand-new couple. The latest thing, and it was after me, with no Shelby in sight.

I spent the rest of the morning looking over my shoulder. I was nervous enough to actually shake and every noise made me jump.

At lunch, I gulped down two Dexatrim and hurried out Stairwell B. I flopped down behind the annex. All I wanted was a cigarette. No, I wanted ten cigarettes. I wanted as many cigarettes as I could smoke. When I lit one, I was shaking. I took in a long drag and looked out over the empty tennis courts. I had to get away from the school. I really was in trouble. Mindy and Troy and all the rest of them were mean. They didn't keep their social standing just by being rich and beautiful. That's when I heard Carrie coming up behind me.

"Hey," she said.

A horrible hot blush spread across my face. My dream about her. My involuntary images of fucking her. Shit. I tilted my face off to the side, blew smoke away from Carrie and took another drag. I was in love with her and I didn't get it until just that moment, when her tiny little ass flopped down beside me.

"Hey," I said, looking at her always perfectly shaven legs with my head still turned a little. "Carrie, how the hell do you get your legs so smooth?" I asked, letting my blush fade.

"I shave every morning."

"You're kidding?"

"No. I hate hair. I mean, except for the hair on my head. I shave everything else every morning."

"Everything?" I asked feeling another blush rise into my cheeks.

"Yeah." Carrie giggled. "Don't be embarrassed. It's just a shaved pussy. You should try it. It's so clean. Especially during your period.

I don't know, women are supposed to be smooth, you know? Clean."

"I just hate to shave. That's all. I can't believe you do it everyday."

"Oh, you hate to shave but you love starving?" Carrie laughed and gave me a hard shove, falling against my body. And she stayed there. Like Mantis at the party. I wished I had a big bottle of whiskey. I wished I had a real personality. I wished I was thin, that Rudy was dead, that Mindy and Troy would disintegrate. And I wished Shelby was with me.

I took another long drag of my cigarette. Carrie lit a new one without moving from against my body.

"Brandon likes that, huh? I mean, you know?"

"Oh god! He LOVES it. It drives me crazy sometimes. Boys love shaved pussies and skinny girls.But don't think Brandon pays any real attention to me. Don't get it in your head that I have, like, an awesome boyfriend or something."

"Oh. Well, Brandon loves you though, right?"

"Sure, I guess. Brandon loves what he loves and it might be me, but it could be anyone, you know?"

"No," I said flatly. I didn't understand. I didn't understand one word she said.

"Be glad you don't understand."

"So, why do you go out with him?"

"He's cute, you know? And he's got style. Shit, my parents think he's so perfect. They would die if they knew he's always 'accidentally' trying to stick his dick up my ass when we're fucking. Like, just ram it in there."

"WHAT?"

"Yeah, he's fucking obsessed about it. He likes my pussy shaved and stuff but he barely gives a damn about fucking it." Carrie laughed, just a little, and stared off.

I didn't say anything. I smoked and concentrated on the warmth of Carrie's body next to mine.

"My parents would like it if I married the jerk," Carrie said, turning back to me. Her lips were inches from mine. Glossed lightly with a sheer red tint.

"Would you like it?" I asked.

"Oh please! I wouldn't marry him. I don't give much of a fuck about getting married anyway. I'm at least going to college first. And there is no way I'd wind up with Brandon. He already fucks around on me. Marrying him wouldn't change that."

"You don't even like the guy, do you?"

"He's all right. Same as any of those guys. It's just a couple more years. So, who cares?"

I care. Shit.

"Be glad you don't understand." Those words were becoming Carrie's slogan.

I lit another cigarette without jarring Carrie's body off mine. She turned her head and studied me. Her face inches from mine, again. Don't blush, don't blush, don't blush.

"You need bangs. Frame your face better." Carrie sat forward and pulled her purse between her legs. Her little gray mini-skirt slid up her thighs and into her lap. She produced a pair of folding scissors and a comb.

"You want to give me bangs right now?"

"Yep." Carrie smiled big and wide. She pulled her purse under her knees and leaned over me.

"These scissors are small, but they're sharp. I like your mascara. It has glitter in it." She took the cigarette out of my hand and stuck it between her teeth.

I stared at Carries knees as pieces of my long hair fell around them.

"There," she finally said. "That looks real good. You're going to like it."

The lunch bell rang and it was time for us to part.

"Hey, Angie?" Carrie turned as she walked away. "Mindy is real pissed off at you. She's going to get you back. And she really will one way or another. So be careful, okay?"

I was late for Spanish, again. But my heart was going too fast for me to care. Mindy had something in mind for me. What else could she do to me? Isn't Lezzylard as fucking humiliating as it gets? Even being called a hooker would be a step up. Fuck Karen Dryer. She could have stayed at school. She could have handled it.

I fumbled my combination lock three times before I finally got it open. I couldn't think straight once I did. I stared down at the books and papers in the bottom and could not focus on what I needed.

"Well, I hope you're happy." It was Luann's voice.

I whirled around to face her. Her full fucked up glamour was back. Wild black hair and bright red lipstick.

"I guess Mantis forgot to tell you about me. I could believe that. But now you know. You knew the other morning too."

"Knew what, Luann?"

"You knew we were dating."

"Mantis says you aren't dating. I asked him."

"Well, men are like that. They'll take a cheap fuck wherever they can get one."

I narrowed my eyes on her. "Apparently."

"Oh, fuck you, Angie."

"No Luann, fuck you, okay?"

I said this in absolute monotone. Luann Bartel was a huge disappointment. She was supposed to be so cool and so beautiful that she was untouchable. But there she was. Right in front of me acting like a fucking idiot.

"Fuck me, huh? You steal my boyfriend and it's fuck me?" Luann pointed her bony hand into my face, backing me into my open locker. I pushed out against her hands, stepping into the open space of the hallway.

"Why do you want a boyfriend who claims not to be your boyfriend?"

"Why do you want to screw others people's men?"

"Don't you yell at me, Luann. I didn't do shit to you."

"You know what you are, Angie? You're a manstealer!" Luann turned and walked away.

I stood in the tilting sunlight as the bell rang. I watched her perfect little butt switch away from me down the hall as it filled with people. Luann did not look back.

A manstealer? Me? It was, by far, the best thing anyone had ever said to me.

CHAPTER 15

I didn't bother staying at school after that. I fled out the back and ran past the tennis courts.

My mother's car wasn't in the parking lot. She and Aunt Jean were probably out shopping. Which meant Jean was shopping and my mom was sitting somewhere smoking and drinking Cokes, probably reading one of her mystery books.

The apartment was quiet. I walked around the place for a minute. Paced. Touched things here and there. My stomach felt pukey. I ran to the bathroom and heaved up two undigested Dexatrims. I watched them float. Two perfect little red pills bobbing in the clear water. When I turned to wash my face I saw my reflection in the mirror. The bangs. Carrie was right, they looked good.

The apartment was so totally alien to me. Nothing was as it should have been. Which was to say, everything was somehow contaminated by Rudy. It was either the shit he dragged along with him or it was stuff Mom used to have that no longer seemed innocent of his presence. Even I didn't feel innocent of his presence. Whatever that meant.

"Shelby," I said when she answered the phone at her house.

"Angie? Hey. What are you doing?"

"Nothing," I said.

"Are you at home? Didn't you go to school?"

"I went. I left. Let's go play some pinball."

"Oh. Um. Well, I . . ."

"Bring Colleen, then," I said.

"No. I mean, she's getting ready to leave. And I'm sick as hell." Shelby sounded so distant and vague I wanted to hang up the phone.

"I skipped out of school after lunch," I said, hoping Shelby would get irritated with me.

"Yeah? I'm so sick I can't even believe it. My temperature is a hundred and one. I feel like I'm gonna die," she said.

"You won't believe the things that happened to me today," I said.

"Can I call you back?" Shelby asked in a low monotone.

"Sure," I said and hung up.

So, that was how Shelby wanted to be. I guessed she and Colleen had fucked all weekend and now I was just some girl who called. I wanted to talk to Shelby. To tell her everything. But then again, fuck Shelby. If she had a girlfriend and that was that, then what did I need with her anyway? And what was all that nonsense about being sick? She should save that crap for her mom.

I pulled the refrigerator door open. I was starving. I analyzed everything for it's inevitable calorie content. Cheese is a hundred calories a slice. A can of Coke is two hundred. A slice of bread is seventy. An apple is eighty. Butter is the most evil force in all of humanity. I shut the door and looked at my feet for a couple of seconds. My big boats. Size eight. Weren't there women somewhere who wrapped their feet up tight so they wouldn't grow?

I needed to leave the apartment. Mom and Aunt Jean would catch me if I stayed around. Aunt Jean wouldn't care, she'd laugh. She hated schools. You'll leave school and you won't know how to write a resume or fill out a fucking tax form.

My mom, on the other hand, would be livid. She'd start talking about college. About buying my own house. She'd start talking, I guess, about not being her.

There was only one place for me to go. I swallowed two more Dexatrim, since the last didn't have a chance to get into my system, and went straight for the Field House.

"What up, party girl?" Pike looked up from his little notebook.

"What are you going to do when it gets cold?" I asked and flopped onto the sofa.

"You mean, what are we going to do when it gets cold? You spend a lot of time here yourself."

"Yeah, but I don't actually live here."

"Well, as the Buddhists say, I'll cross that bridge when I come to it."

"Buddhists say that?"

"Buddhists and people without a certain future." Pike shrugged and gave me that smile of his.

"What are you drawing?"

"Oh, wouldn't you like to know?"

"Fine, Pike, keep it to yourself. Today has been so weird."

"Like flying saucers weird, or just regular weird?"

"God, this girl, Mindy, I started a fight with her. I mean she started it, she's really mean. And I couldn't help it, I had to come back at her and now I'm fucked."

"Fucked how?"

"Just fucked. Her and her friends are pretty mean. Last year they spread all these rumors about this girl, Karen Dryer. They told everyone she was a hooker and it went on and on. It got so bad she had to leave school."

"Maybe we could live here," Pike said, looking around at the browning leaves of the trees that, for the moment, still hid us from the rest of the world.

"I don't know what I'm going to do."

"I got somethin' for you. I didn't want to do it alone, but . . ." Pike's back arched as dug through his pocket.

"Here," he said, holding up a little piece of white paper, folded over on itself.

"What's that?"

"Inez and I were walking around over across from the mall, you know where those sports bars and the Dunkin Donuts is? And we found this plastic baggie with eight of these little wraps in it."

"Yeah, so, what is it?"

"Crystal," he said with a big grin on his face.

"What? Like speed?"

Pike just nodded, holding the package out to me.

"I don't do shit like that, Pike."

"Me either. That's why this is the perfect opportunity. You know?"

"I don't even know how to do it," I said.

"I do. I've seen it."

"How do you know what it is?"

"Inez knew. She tasted it," Pike said.

"You can tell from tasting it?"

"Yeah, drugs all taste different."

"Oh," I said. I stared at the little packet Pike threw on the table.

"Well, what do you say? Shouldn't we at least try it?" Pike asked.

I sat up completely straight, picked up the little packet, turned it over in my fingers.

"Yeah, we should at least try it. Everyone should try it, right?"

"Well, as the Buddhists say, that's what life is all about."

"Do Buddhists say that?"

"Well, Buddhists and people with free speed."

"All right, you lead the way then."

Pike smiled. "I'm so glad you ran away from that hell hole." Then he closed his little notebook and emptied the white powder onto its cover. He took an old ID from his school in Tulsa and made lines out of the powder.

"They're too big!" I told him. "I've never done speed before, let's take it easy, okay?"

"Okay. I've never snorted anything," Pike said.

"I thought you knew what you were doing."

"This is what I know. Cutting out lines. I've seen people do that."

"So, how much are we supposed to take?"

"I'll do a line, and then tell you how it feels."

"Okay. But I'm still not sure I want to do any lines at all."

Pike tore a little piece of paper out of his notebook and rolled it into a straw. He looked like a professional. He put the straw in one nostril, closed up the other with his finger, leaned forward and snorted one line straight up his nose. I watched closely, all of this. Pike let out a stifled scream and fell back into his chair holding his nose.

"What? What happened?" I asked.

"It burns like fuck! Jesus Christ!" Pike shook his head from side to side.

"Are you sure it's crystal? Are you sure it isn't like Drano or something?"

"Oh, it's speed all right," he said with a sudden smile and handed the straw to me.

"I'm scared," I said.

"Don't be." Pike stood quickly and stretched. "Go on. Try it. Just try it."

I mimicked his little ritual, but I only did about half as much as he did. It really did burn. Like hell, actually.

I lit a cigarette while Pike put the rest of the powder back into its folded paper square.

"You're shaking." I pointed at his fingers.

"So are you." He pointed at my cigarette. I looked at the bright orange tip with smoke lifting off of it. It was shaking from side to side, more of a quiver, really. This seemed impossibly wonderful to me and I giggled.

"You like?" Pike asked, giggling himself.

We both started pacing around the inside of the small circle of trees. Trapped animals.

"God, if we got picked up for truancy like this?" Pike shuddered at the thought.

I smoked non-stop and the sun swelled like orange bubbles between the tree branches.

"Let me see that fucking notebook of yours. You're always scribbling in it."

Pike looked at me. "Jesus, you sound like you're accusing me of murder."

Pike was pale and his upper lip had a perfect line of sweat on it. Actually, his whole face was wet looking. And the sun bubbles too, wet.

"Do I look as crazy as you do?" I asked.

"You look wasted."

"Are my pupils big?"

"You could eat me up with them," Pike said. He pulled the notebook out of his pants and threw it on the couch cushion.

"You're not going to eat me up, are you Angie?"

"Not right this second." I reached for his notebook.

"Women are always eating things up. Hansel and Gretel and all of that. Life and death. You can eat death, if you want. You know that? Women could cure us of death if you all wanted to."

"Pike, you should think about something else. You're getting pretty far out there."

"See what I mean? Just eat it up like that."

I lifted the cover on Pike's little notebook. I flipped the pages sort of fast. All portraits. Head shots of people. I found one of myself.

"Oh god, these are great," I said, studying the way he had drawn me. No double chin. My eyes looked serious and almond shaped.

"I drew that one the day I met you. Right here."

"I like it. I really like it." I kept flipping the pages. Inez. Shelby. Heather. Alien.

"Alien's is super good. You got those bug eyes and everything."

"He was fun to draw. I'd do more of him but it might start to look like I was in love with him or something. Usually, I only draw women. I mean if anyone ever found that book, you know? It could be disaster."

"You should make bigger pictures."

"Can't carry it around," Pike said carefully taking the notebook out of my hand and putting it back in his pocket.

"Shelby draws too, but her stuff is more cartoony."

"Yeah? Well, it's something to do."

"You could sell those. You know, like start a business doing portraits."

"Start a business? Did you just say that?" Pike laughed. "Give me a cigarette."

"You don't smoke."

"Well, shit, I'm seventeen, I guess it's time to start," Pike said.

"You're seventeen?" I asked, handing him a cigarette.

"Yeah. So I'm small for my age, you gonna make a big deal out of it?"

"No. I just didn't . . ."

"Everyone thinks I'm like fourteen or something. Always wanting to beat me up"

"Is that why you don't want to go to school?"

"No. Who wants to go to school? I mean, you don't seem to enjoy it so much."

"Yeah, but I'm . . ." I stopped myself.

"Go on. You're what? Say it. I know what they call you."

"Fuck it. I don't want to say it. If you like it so much why don't you say it."

"I don't like it. I think it's mean. I'm glad you got into a mess sticking up for yourself. And Inez and Shelby, too. That's how it's got to be."

"So, what do I do now?"

"Fight them. Fight them and fight them until you win," Pike said.

"Easier said than done."

"Yeah. Especially if you think exactly what they think."

"What does that mean?" I asked.

"It means, if you think you're as worthless as they say you are, you'll never beat them."

"You're one to talk, hiding in a field all day."

"Maybe I already did my fighting, Angie. You think of that?"

"What, like back in Tulsa?"

"We're going to lose our minds in here," he said, looking beyond the trees to the whole world.

"I'm so fucking thirsty," I said, trying to swallow.

"We're going to lose our minds and die, Angie. Right here." Pike pointed to the dirt and smiled. His sudden sense of morbidity pleased him. This much I could see.

"Oh, you'd like that wouldn't you? Well, too bad. We got to go and find some water."

Pike giggled. I giggled. That speed business was a mess as far as I was concerned. I wasn't having a bad time. I was too high to have a bad time. But I wasn't having a good time, either.

"C'mon." I motioned to Pike and I ducked under the tree branches.

"Where are we going?" he asked, following behind me.

"You want to meet my mom?" I gave him a wide-eyed look over my shaking cigarette.

"What? Like this? You're crazy. She'd think I was a psycho killer."

"Well, we could go to Heather's. Wait, what time is it?"

"How should I know?"

"Okay, well let's go to the soda machine outside the K-mart. You got any change?"

Pike dug through his pockets as he walked. He handed me two quarters.

"I don't want to go right in front of that store," he said, almost panicked.

"All right, I'll do it. You wait here," I told him when we got to the big cement corner of the building that housed the Billy Bear Pizza and the K-mart. One huge perfectly rectangular block of gray cement. They didn't even bother to try and make it look like anything other than what it was.

I passed Billy Bear hoping no one would look me in the eye. I understood why Pike wanted to stay behind. I was shaky and sweaty, even in the cool October air. A layer of sweat had formed all over my body. The closer I got to the soda machine the more people there were. Coming and going from the K-mart. It's not a crime to buy a soda. But I felt like a criminal anyway.

I stuck my shaky fingers at the slot in the soda machine. I missed. The first quarter hit the ground at my feet. I picked it up, concentrated, sure everyone was looking at me. I got both quarters in and hit the Coke button. The machine rumbled and it seemed loud enough to fill up the world with its noise. I grabbed the can and hurried back toward Pike. Fuck speed. Fuck the hell out of it.

When I turned the corner. Luann was there, leaned against the wall, one leg crooked with her foot planted against the wall.

"Look who it is," she said.

"Where did you come from?" I asked.

"School, stupid. Where did YOU come from?"

"You cut out too?" Pike asked Luann.

"No, school's out, kids. I want some of whatever you two are on."

"Shit!" I said, after slurping down half the Coke.

"What? What is it?" Pike asked, looking around like a bona fide paranoid.

"Nothing, no, I just have to go home. Shit. We're having dinner with my Aunt."

I dug through my back pack and pulled out the little hand mirror Robyn gave me.

"Oh, poo." Luann made a pouty face. "You won't have time to steal Pike here from Inez."

"Inez isn't my girlfriend," Pike said.

"Jesus, guys are all the same." Luann rolled her eyes and lit a smoke.

"Fuck." I looked at my pupils in the mirror. They were huge. I pulled a tissue out, spit on it and wiped hard at the make up still on my face.

"Just go home girl," Luann said. "Just go home and face the music. It's only a matter of time before your mom finds out what a slut you are."

"Oh? When did your mom find out what a slut you are? Like ten years ago?"

"Whoa." Pike put his hands up between me and Luann. "What the fuck is going on here? Is this about Mantis?"

"I'm a manstealer, Pike."

"That's right Angie, yuck it up. It won't be so funny when you find out about him."

"If it's his fault, why are you blaming me?"

"Girls are such fucking back-stabbers! You knew I was seeing him and you fucked him anyway!"

"I didn't fuck him! AND he says you're not dating!" I pointed at her.

"Typical." Luann shook her head, turned away from us. She held her cigarette, with its little band of red lipstick around the filter, between her thumb and index.

Pike and I shared a look.

"So, you guys got anymore coke?" She looked back and when she did she had become a totally different person.

"Yeah," Pike straightened up. "I mean, it's crystal. You want to buy some?"

"Hell yeah, after a little taste, of course," Luann said. A long flirtatious smile spread her face.

"Sure. You got a place to do it?" Pike asked.

"Yeah, we'll go to my house. My parents might want some, if it's good."

"Lead the way," Pike said. He looked at me. "You'll be fine, just don't be nervous."

Pike and Luann took off as I listened to my heart beat like crazy. I took a deep breath and started my way home. At first I hurried. But why? So I could get home and be all fucked up in front of everyone?

I slowed myself way down. If I was going to be in trouble, I was already in it. I walked at a steady pace, scanning the backsides of everything. The back side of K-mart and Billy Bear. The big gray block with massive overflowing dumpsters serving as the view for Evergreen Apartments. The complex, my mother always told me, we were lucky not to live in. Did Mindy or Carrie or Troy even know it existed? A place where you wake up and look out your front window at the trash dumpsters of the store where you work?

Evergreen was always depressing. In the state I was in it looked like it was sweating. All the orange brick wet and pulsing. Perfectly rectangular buildings falling apart from the top down.

The figure eight-shaped pool was covered for winter, the rim sneaking slowly out of the ground. Even when it was open for season the water was always cloudy, almost greasy, somehow. If you turned your lawn chair one way you could see the K-mart dumpster. Facing another, the Kentucky Fried Chicken and the Dairy Queen dumpsters. The other two options for a view was the backside of a privacy fence that separated Evergreen from Carrie Shuren's neighborhood, or, possibly the most appealing, look at your own dilapidated apartment.

I stopped alongside the swimming pool and lit a cigarette. My teeth were clenched. I was nervous, but mostly I was mad. Mad as hell. Who were all these fucking people to tell me what I was or wasn't? The cover on the pool was waving and I understood completely why my mother broke her neck to live in Covington. You couldn't see Evergreen from any main road. The apartments didn't exist unless you lived in them. Evergreen was the place you went when the whole world turned its back on you.

I forced myself on, smoking hard. I walked through one of the sunken alleyways between the buildings. Cracking cement walls and browning miniature pine trees. What the hell makes a pine tree brown? They can survive anything. Anything besides Evergreen.

Between Evergreen and Covington was a short row of small brick houses. Older people who refused to sell their land, stubbornly staying put while apartments were built all around them. I cut through Mrs. Hamson's yard.

I dropped my smoldering cigarette butt outside our apartment building, took a deep breath and climbed the stairs. A mess of shopping bags covered the living room floor. Aunt Jean's packages. She loved to shop and she enjoyed the company of my mother while she did it. But mom didn't have shopping money. That's why she took her books along with her.

"Hey," I said, shutting the door behind me.

"Angie!" Aunt Jean came around the corner and gave me a big hug. I hugged her back, tight. My Aunt Jean was my favorite person in the whole world.

"Where have you been?" My mother stepped out of the kitchen, her hands dusted with flour.

"Oh, I just stopped and talked to some people for awhile. I must have lost track of time."

"Come see what I got today." Aunt Jean motioned me toward the packages on the floor.

"Oh, okay. Let me take a quick shower. I feel grimy from school."

"Sure, baby. I'll just help your mom with dinner. Take your time. We're making fried chicken and biscuits."

"Yum," I said, rushing for the bathroom. What a fuck-up. Aunt Jean is the cook. Her fried chicken is about the best thing in the world. That and her apple pie. Mom can't cook worth a shit, but Aunt Jean always acts like Mom is the one doing the cooking. It's one of those sweet things Aunt Jean does for her baby sister.

I took my clothes off and my stomach did a drop twist at the smell of food. How hell was I going to eat?

My pupils didn't look so big anymore. Maybe I was coming down. My heart was still beating like crazy though. The hot shower felt good. Maybe it could cure me.

I lathered up my hair and the tears came. The stupid tears. I felt so fucking guilty about Aunt Jean, about her dinner, about my mom, about Shelby. Like my childhood itself was running down the drain.

There was no way I could tell Shelby about Carrie or the speed. The tears kept coming and my mouth worked out silent sobs between drops of hot water. Mindy Overton. Luann Bartel. Speed. Aunt Jean. Everything was falling apart. I didn't want Pike to be friends with Luann. Why hadn't Mantis called me? All weekend I had expected the phone to ring. I sniffed up the remainder of my tears. I had become one of those silly women from TV.

I stepped out of the shower, wrapping my head in a towel and my body in one of the big beach towels that came with Rudy.

Carrie shaves everyday. She shaves everything. I had to admire it, but there was no way I could ever manage it. Smooth. Clean.

Everything was falling apart. My eyes were just about normal size again. Now, if I could just get my stomach in the mood for food, I'd be fine.

A lesson I learned that night: crystal meth makes everything taste like lard. The only decent dinner I'd see until Thanksgiving and I couldn't even stomach the smell of it. I remembered a story Alien told once about having to sit and eat pizza with his family while he was on acid. He said he just kept sneaking bites to the dog. Of course, we didn't have a dog.

"Here." Aunt Jean handed me a shopping bag.

"What's this?"

"Just something I got for you today."

Inside the bag was a fuzzy black scarf with little sequin sparkles sewn throughout.

"I thought you might actually wear a scarf this winter if it was black," Aunt Jean said.

"Everything does not have to be black!" My mother called from the kitchen.

"Well, she likes black. Me? I like turquoise."

Aunt Jean and I set the table.

"So, for Thanksgiving? You want anything special?"

"Apple pie," I said.

"Well, of course, anything else?"

Aunt Jean won a prize for her apple pie back when she was only twenty-three. It was still the best apple pie in the world and she still wouldn't give out the recipe.

I was setting the table when Rudy came in. His hands were black and so was the front of his shirt.

"I'm gonna hafta redo the exhaust on that thing sometime soon." He shook his head and kissed Mom.

"Go wash up," she said.

"Yeah, this chicken's about as dead as it's gonna get," Aunt Jean said.

When we all sat down to the table, I could feel the heat off all the food. Almost like it could burn me. The steam and the thin strands of smell that came from each one. Individual and combined.

"So, Angie," Aunt Jean smiled at me over the table. "You know, I'm looking at houses."

"No. Where at?"

"Well, I looked at one not to far from here. Nice brick place."

"That's really cool," I said, trying to take a bite of real mashed potatoes, my favorite.

"Jean, they are charging way too much for that dump," Rudy said.

"Well, that's an old neighborhood over there."

Rudy spoke through a mouth of food. "It needs a new roof and the plumbing is shot to shit. Them pipes ain't even gonna make it through the winter. And that's just what I saw today."

My eye's flitted around at Mom and Aunt Jean and Rudy. I had to take a bite of lard chicken to keep myself from laughing.

Aunt Jean gave Rudy a half smile. "Actually, them pipes are just fine. I been a plumber for over thirty years. Me and my husband ran a plumbing warehouse together for over twenty-five. He died last year and so, I sold the business. Gonna buy me a nice house with some fine plumbing."

"I'm just tellin' you what I saw in the basement," Rudy said, focusing on his food and trying to hide his blush.

"I see," Aunt Jean said. "Tell you what, when yous two go to buy your house I'll have a look at them pipes for you before you sign them papers. Save you a lot of headache."

Mom gave off a kind of funny little snort and Rudy shot her a look. I let out a peel of laughter I couldn't stop from happening. I was high again. When I looked at Rudy he was glaring and I laughed again, actually pointing right in his face as I did it.

"You're excused!" Rudy pointed his fork at me.

"Rudy!" My mom said through her smile. "Don't be silly. We're having a nice family dinner."

"Rita, I ain't gonna have this girl disrespectin' me at my own table!"

"Rudy, you are over-reacting," Mom said.

"Am I? You raised this girl up to disrespect her elders?"

"No," Aunt Jean broke in calmly. "Just fools."

"What did you say?" Rudy turned his attention to Aunt Jean whose thick hand was wrapped around a glass of Seagram's and Seven.

"I think you heard me," she said, picking a bit of chicken out of her teeth.

"Look Jean." Rudy waved his fork her direction. "This doesn't concern you. This is about my family and how things are gonna be around here. Where I come from, kids know their place, you hear?"

Aunt Jean took a long drink off her glass. Rudy shoveled another mouthful of biscuit and chicken into his mouth and Mom sat gape-mouthed, looking at me. I shrugged back at her not knowing if I should leave the table, laugh, or go on trying to eat that wonderful food that tasted like shit to me because I was an idiot.

"Well," Aunt Jean said slowly. "Where I come from, men know a good set pipes when they see 'em."

Rudy chewed and looked at Aunt Jean, who had ceased eating and smoked one of her little Swisher Sweets.

"Well, now I see where the girl gets her attitude. Raised up by the two of you," he swung his fork between Jean and Mom. "Man haters. You'll see, the girl'll wind up being one of them lesbians. Guess that'll make you two happy."

I was definitely high again. The table top seemed to be rumbling. It was everything I had to keep from telling Rudy that I wasn't a man hater, I was a manstealer and that even though I wasn't a lesbian, I was, in fact, in love with a girl.

"Man haters!" I squealed and Aunt Jean's smoky laughter followed mine.

"That's it!" Rudy threw his fork against his plate and stood. "You are excused! I done told you that! And as for you . . ." he pointed at Aunt Jean.

But before he could get anymore words out Aunt Jean laughed. "Am I excused too?"

"Rita, this is bullshit!" Rudy's attention landed on my mother. Her mouth fell open but nothing came out. What could she have said?

"All right, all right." Aunt Jean stood, nodding her head, just a lit-tle, at Rudy. "Me and Angie are gonna go for a little walk. You two finish your dinner. You have my apologies, Rudy." She stuck her hand out to him. After a bit of hesitation, Rudy took it. As they shook Aunt Jean said, "This is your house."

Rudy nodded and sat back down. Aunt Jean found a plastic tum-bler in the kitchen, mixed some more liquor and soda and left the house with me.

"Why did you apologize to him?"

Aunt Jean took a drink from her tumbler. "Had to calm him down before we left him with your mom."

I looked back at the apartment building. "You don't think he's gonna do anything?"

"No. I handed him his fuckin' nuts back. He'll be fine."

Aunt Jean and I walked toward a sad set of swings next to the manager's office. Most of them were busted but we found two next to one another and sat down.

Aunt Jean swung back a little. "That one—ain't nothin'. Just remember, the less they're worth, the meaner they are."

"Why is she doing this?" I asked as a couple of tears escaped my eyes.

"Who knows. She's got her reasons, I guess."

Tears flowed to my chin. Aunt Jean ignored them, giving her swing another little push back.

"You can always call me, Angie. Anytime. Anything you need."

My second high was crashing again and my guts felt as if they were hanging on the outside of my body. As if everything had been ripped out and left for trash.

Aunt Jean took sips from her tumbler. She let me cry it out for a few minutes.

"You know, I could teach you plumbing. Make a good living that way."

"I dunno," I said, sucking back the last of the tears.

"Your Uncle Maine always thought the world of you. Thought you might have a hard time of it, though."

"Why?"

"Said you were sensitive AND willful. Hard combination. He was like that too. You reminded him of himself."

"I miss him."

"Yeah, me too. I got lucky with Maine. You know, he's the one taught me to do plumbing? In case somethin' happened to him, I to be able to take care of myself. And he was right. Something did happen to him."

"You like plumbing?"

"Sure. I'm good at. Get to accomplish somethin' during the day. Feels good."

"Aunt Jean, did you know my daddy?"

Aunt Jean lit another of her Swisher Sweets, gave herself a push.

"Your father? I knew your father. Don't call him your daddy. Daddies stick around to raise their own. But, yeah, I knew your father."

"I haven't even ever seen a picture of him," I said.

"I don't suppose there are any pictures of your father. Your grandmother hated him. Like she had any room to talk. She had a wild man for a husband herself. Wrapped his drunk ass around a telephone pole, that one did. My daddy. Your mama's daddy."

"I didn't know that."

"Well, now you do."

"So, what about my father?"

"Oh, yeah. Your father. Well, let me see. He was a big man. Good lookin'. Real funny too. Your father had this real sarcastic sense of humor, but it was charming. He wasn't around very long. He heard you were on the way and sped off. Went to the bar. Actually, went to my Daddy's tavern and they got drunk together. Then your father came on back to the house an' asked your mom to marry him."

"He did?"

"Yeah, he did. Eyes all full of drunk feelings and shit. She didn't go for it, though. She told him to sleep on it and ask her again the next day."

"Did he?"

"No. He was gone the next mornin'. Just like that."

"What was his name?"

Aunt Jean gave her swing another push, regarded me easily, thoughtfully.

"Well, I guess you're old enough now, old enough to know. We called him Brownie, but his real name was Seth, Seth Thompson."

"Anybody ever see him again?"

"Well, when you was about twelve I saw him at the Kroger. Said he bought a house out in Arnold. That's the most I know."

CHAPTER 16

I managed to get myself up for school even though I had barely slept. That fucking speed kept coming back at me. Jolting me awake. When I wasn't having a nightmare, I was awake sweating and worrying. I was going to have to start actually writing out my list of Things Never To Do.

I found Carrie in the main corridor of the school.

"Hey, what are you doing here so early?" I asked her.

"Oh, I left some homework here last night. Nothing big. I just wanted to finish it up."

"I'm going to put my make up on. I got that glitter mascara you like. You wanna try some." I asked.

"Oh. I have to finish this thing. I'll see you at lunch."

In the big bathroom, I was alone. Somehow it felt creepy instead of comforting. Maybe it was the speed making my muscles so hard and tired. Nothing is going to happen. I pulled my big Zip-loc bag of make up out. Maybe Mindy would never come back to this bathroom. Maybe she would leave it alone.

The big bathroom door swished open.

"Oh, hi Lezzylard, I thought you might be here," Mindy moved into the bathroom wearing a yellow mini dress and a big smile.

I swung around to face her, dropping my mascara wand into the sink.

"What's with the good mood, Mindy? I thought you hated me," I tried to smirk and cover my shaking.

"Oh, I do hate you," Mindy said, letting the big door close behind her.

"You got something on your mind?"

"Besides, teaching you a lesson? No."

I heard a male voice outside the door. "Just move it!"

The door swung open again and there was Troy Mulligan.

"Oh, hey!" Troy said, pretending to be surprised to see both of us. "Is this one of those girl bonding moments, should I leave?"

I was in big shit. Why the fuck did I have to be so stubborn as to come back here? Willful? Whatever was about to happen, it was my own fault.

"No, Troy, you don't have to leave. You don't mind if he hangs around, do you, Lezzylard?"

I had the sense to start for the door, but Troy grabbed my arm.

"Don't go, fattie. The fun is just getting started."

"Let go of me, Mulligan! Don't you have anything better to do than hang out in girls' bathrooms?" I yelled as loudly as I could.

Mindy's hand quickly slapped over my mouth and Troy shoved me into the closest stall. I punched out at his stomach, but I never landed a hit. Troy stepped back, then grabbed my hair. I tripped backwards over the toilet and landed between it and the side of the stall. My head smacked against the pipes, pain ran down my through my spine. Troy leaned into my fall, holding my hair in a tight knot around his fist. Inez was right about the mohawk. I did, in fact, need one.

I let out a scream, this time it was Troy's hand that slapped against my mouth. "Shut up! I've let you and that dyke bitch get away with too much already."

I stopped struggling against him. I needed a plan. I could kick him in the balls when they got close enough. His hand was squeezing my face hard and he and I looked at one another closely, directly.

He leaned in closer to me and used his index finger and thumb to pinch my nose closed. I couldn't breathe. Troy laughed, getting closer to my face.

"You wanna give me a big kiss, Lezzylard? Huh? A nice big kiss for Troy?"

I bucked off the floor as hard as I could, landing my knee in his crotch. Troy's face lit up with pain, but he didn't let out any noise, his hand came off my face and I gulped in some air.

"Get her legs, Mindy! You dumbass!" Troy yelled, then gave his head a good shake from side to side. He felt some pain but he was keeping himself focused. He wasn't gonna get off me.

"You're gonna pay for that!" he said, thunking my head against the pipes again. I heard the hollow thump inside my head and little colored squiggles filled up my eyes.

Mindy was straddling my calves and I was completely paralyzed. If Troy threw his weight on my left arm, he'd break it over the toilet.

"Now you get to kiss it and make it better," Troy said, his free hand fumbled his zipper.

"Yeah!" Mindy squealed with delight.

They were crazed and I was in no position to stop them. My head throbbed, my legs were tight against the floor under Mindy and my arm was stuck between the toilet and the pipes, ready to splinter like firewood.

Troy's dick fell out of his pants. He came down on my chest with his knee. My arm strained against the toilet. Oh, god, please don't let my arm break!

"Open up, pig! Go on, kiss it, make it better!"

Troy rubbed the head of his dick against my pursed lips.

"C'mon, suck my dick, pig! I bet that dyke girlfriend of yours is gonna LOVE this! Don't worry, she'll get her chance soon enough."

Troy rammed his knee into my diaphragm, my mouth flew open and I sucked in a big gulp of air but it was like it didn't go into at all. There wasn't any air to make a scream with. He stuck his dick in my mouth. "That's it you fat bitch, suck my dick!"

It took a couple of seconds to get over the pain in my gut, then I did the only thing I could do. I bit down, hard.

Troy screamed. He let go of my hair and took a step back tumbling over Mindy and catching himself on one of the pale green sinks. Mindy lost her balance enough that I kicked at her and she was off my legs. I scrambled to my feet just in time to take a good right hook from Troy. His fist crashed into my eye and everything went silent. I fell into the wall without any thoughts at all. Pain expanded in a hot wave through every part of my body.

I turned to look at Troy who was coming at me again, Mindy still in a crumpled pile on the floor. My ears started to work again and I heard a voice shouting behind Troy.

"Stop! Stop it!" Mindy? "I mean it!" The voice was strained and terrified.

A skinny arm grabbed Troy around the throat before he could swing again. It was Carrie, her face streaked with tears.

"Stop!" she screamed. Troy grabbed her little arm and threw her off him to the floor.

Everything in the bathroom went dead quiet. My eye was throbbing like it had a heart of its own. Troy pulled his pants up and zipped them.

"Don't just sit there, stupid," Troy said to Mindy, who looked shocked. She stood slowly, turning her head to Carrie, who was on the floor crying.

"That was real stupid, Carrie," Mindy said in monotone with a quick brush of her hand against the back of her dress.

"This isn't over." Troy pointed at me.

Carrie got to her feet. Troy looked at her. His hand cupped over his prick and his stare steady, "Damn, you are one dumb bitch, Carrie."

Troy grabbed Mindy's arm and they left.

I touched my eye lightly with my index finger. It hurt real bad. Carrie ran some water in one of the sinks. I blinked the tears out of my eyes. I could see her face in the mirror, silent tears streaking either side of her face. "Angie? You okay?" She finally asked. I stepped cautiously out of the stall. I wasn't entirely sure my shaking legs would even be willing to carry me.

"Yeah." I nodded.

Carrie splashed water on her face, handed me a wetted paper towel. I looked at my reflection. It belonged to someone else. Carrie tossed all my compacts and tubes and brushes into the Zip-loc bag that overturned into the sink somewhere in the middle of everything.

"Let's go," Carrie said, shoving the Zip-loc in my back pack and handing it to me.

I followed Carrie silently. Out in the hall the first couple of bus loads of people were streaming in. Messing with combination locks and handing notes to each other. Another world. Two distinct layers of reality stacked in one space.

I followed Carrie out the back of Stairwell A, out to the side of the tennis courts.

"Why are you helping me?" I asked once we were outside in the relative safety of the fall weather.

"They can't treat people like that. It's just over the top," Carrie said, turning her face to me. Her chin was still wet from where she splashed water on herself.

We walked around the side of the tennis courts through the drifts of brown and orange leaves accumulated along the chain-link fence surrounding the courts. I kicked at them. When I was a kid, I'd visit Aunt Jean and Uncle Maine out in the country. They'd rake big piles of leaves for burning and me and their big dog, Buck, would jump in them. All so long ago it was just a dream. Buck died not long after Uncle Maine.

My eye stung. My stomach hurt. The back of my head started to swell. I'd been whacked against those pipes pretty hard. Nothing in the world was okay.

"Carrie, how did you find us?"

"I just . . ." Carrie stuttered.

I stepped in front of her and stopped.

"How did you find us?" I asked again.

"I just . . ." Carrie dropped her head and scratched at her palm.

"You just what?" I asked. A gust of wind blew our hair into our faces, a red leaf tangling itself in Carrie's pretty, naturally blonde hair.

"She told me," Carrie whispered.

"She told you? Mindy told you what they were planning? When?"

"Last night, yesterday." Carrie's voice was tiny. Her tears were flowing freely again.

"Well, which is it? Last night or yesterday? Did you know already when I saw you at lunch?"

"She said she was going to scare you. Back you down. I didn't know Troy was going to be involved. I didn't know they were going to . . . I DIDN'T KNOW!"

"Why were you so early for school?"

"Angie, I . . ."

"You were the look out!" I screamed, swinging my backpack at her head, steering it away just before it landed.

"Don't!" Carrie threw her arms up and dropped to her knees. "I'm sorry. I'm sorry. I didn't know, I swear I didn't."

"You should be sorry," I said, grabbing my backpack off the ground. Carrie flinched like I was gonna beat her over the head with it.

"I'm not going to hit you. I should beat the shit out of you, but I'm not," I said, through clenched teeth.

I looked at Carrie for a second. The wind sent another gust of leaves over her.

"Get up," I said

"I really am sorry, Angie. You don't understand," she said, still on her knees.

"Can you say anything besides that? Now get up before we get in trouble."

Carrie walked a couple of paces behind me all the way back to the apartment. A week before I would have been embarrassed to have Carrie see the inside of our apartment. Hell, the outside too, for that matter. I would have practically died of shame to have Carrie see my life, but I didn't care anymore.

Inside, I dropped my stuff on the floor and went straight for the bathroom to look at my eye. It was red and swollen. The skin tight, like the eye itself was straining to escape. I brushed my teeth and changed into different clothes. When I got back to the living room Carrie was still standing in the doorway clutching her bag and looking around.

"Don't be scared. I'll make some breakfast, we'll watch TV. It's gonna rain anyway."

"I'm not hungry," Carrie said, absently stripping her jacket off just as the sky cracked with thunder. Carrie jumped at the sound of it.

"Look, you have the rest of your life to photosynthesize or whatever, but I'm making breakfast and you can just shove that "not hungry bullshit."

I pulled everything out of the refrigerator. Cokes, eggs, butter, ham, cheese, pudding cups. Out of the freezer I grabbed a box of waffles, a package of frozen strawberries, a box of toaster hash browns and a chocolate pie. I put a skillet over the electric burner and let it heat while I searched the cabinets for syrup and salt and a couple packets of powdered hot chocolate.

"You should put ice on your eye," Carrie said from behind me.

"Do you think it's going to bruise?" I asked, watching Carrie wrap a bag of frozen peas in a kitchen towel.

"I think it's going to swell shut." Carrie gently pressed the bag against my eye. "Hold that there."

"What am I going to tell my mom?"

Carrie shrugged and moved past me to all the food I'd laid out on the counter.

"Wow, this looks so good. I haven't eaten anything but lettuce and grapefruit in a week."

"I heard about the grapefruit thing. Does it work?" I asked, letting the cool of the peas drift through the towel onto my eye.

"Doesn't hurt. Listen, I'll make breakfast. You sit. Watch some TV. I'll bring you a cup of hot chocolate."

I settled myself and the peas on the floor in front of Rudy's big screen. My whole body hurt. I was going to have bruises all over me. My mind ran with revenge scenarios, but they made my eye hurt worse so I willed them away. The rain began and it sounded so nice. I listened and stared at my reflection on the blank TV screen. Everything was a miserable wreck.

Carrie appeared with a cup of hot chocolate. "I'm gonna set it on the table. The cup is real hot. I love those little marshmallows," she said, watching them bob up and down.

"I'm gonna cut my hair off," I told her.

"Yeah? Well, don't do it today. You should think about stuff like that, you know, you don't want to cut it off because you're upset and then regret it."

I took the cup by its handle and looked at the marshmallows for myself. I hoped Troy's dick and balls hurt like hell. Maybe I'd left bite marks on that nasty thing. When I was a kid I used to save the marshmallows until the very end of the chocolate and slurp them up in one sweet, sticky glob. I hoped Troy's balls would turn black and fall off.

"I'll put the TV on for you, there must be something to watch. You guys have cable, right?"

"Oh boy, do we ever," I said.

The TV came to life. Carrie put the remote in my hand. "I like my strawberries real sweet, so I'm gonna heat them up with some sugar. That okay with you?"

"Sounds great," I said, changing the channels as rapidly as I could. I didn't want to watch anything. I just wanted to marvel at how many stations we could tune in.

Carrie opened the window and the wet smell of rain hit my nose. So many nice things in the world and my life couldn't truly touch any of them.

Carrie made two huge ham and cheese omelets with toaster waffles drenched with sweet strawberries and syrup. She cut up the hash browns and stuffed them inside the omelets. It was all so delicious. After she served me my plate, she took the bag of peas back to the freezer and brought me a bag of vegetable medley to replace it.

I had settled the television on *Donahue*.

"My mom thinks he's hot," Carrie said, taking a bite of waffle and waving her fork at the TV.

After all the starving we'd done together, the fantasy grocery lists and talks of multi-vitamins and photosynthesizing, eating with her was really fun. Carrie, my friend, my enemy, the only person who would ever know what happened in that bathroom besides Mindy and Troy.

I drew lines through a puddle of syrup with pieces of waffle and strawberry. Carrie shoveled forkfuls of eggs into her mouth, chewing and giggling as a tiny line of melting cheese dribbled down her chin.

We even went after that pie. We ate until all we could do was lay on our backs and digest. Sally Jesse Raphael had a guest who owned a photography studio. His business had been vandalized because his store front featured a picture of two men embracing.

"People are worthless," Carrie said, nuzzling her face into a sofa cushion.

"You don't have to tell me." I was sprawled out on the floor in front of the TV.

"Why don't you share the couch with me?" Carrie said sleepily.

"I feel like I could sleep forever," I said.

"Me too. Here, there's plenty of room for you." Carrie scrunched her feet up.

I took my vegetable medley and moved to the couch. I curled up on the end opposite Carrie. She threw Mom's pink afghan over our legs and wound one of her feet between my calves.

"Fuck everyone, Angie. Just fuck 'em," she said and we both fell asleep.

We very nearly did sleep forever. We slept far enough into the afternoon that Carrie worried she wouldn't get home on time.

"Shit, I don't have much time to help you clean up." Carrie rushed around collecting plates and Coke cans. "Don't you guys have a dishwasher?"

"No."

"Let me see your eye." She took my chin in her hand. "It looks pretty nasty."

"I'll be okay." I reassured her.

"Of course you will. Seriously, I have to be home to get my sister off the bus. I'll be an orphan if I don't."

Carrie left and I finished cleaning up. Not that Rudy wasn't going to notice there was hardly a mouthful of food left in the house. Carrie was right, my eye had swollen nearly shut. I studied the protrusion in the bathroom mirror. The white I could still see had filled up with blood and it was almost completely red. Maybe I should go to the hospital. No, people get punched in the eye all the time. I should call Robyn. She'd know what to do. She'd been punched in the eye at least as many times as she'd punched someone else in the eye.

The sight mesmerized me. The sight of my eye and the reeling of my still too-full stomach. It would be another day before I fully recovered from my feast with Carrie. I turned behind me and looked at the toilet bowl. Was Carrie going to throw up? Did all those girls do that? It was the standing rumor that all pretty girls threw up whatever they ate.

The water in the toilet was clear, almost appetizing. Mantis. Shit. What did I mean the water looked appetizing? Everything was a wreck. I knelt at the toilet bowl and watched my reflection. I stuck my index finger to the back of my throat. My stomach lurched, but nothing happened. I stuck my finger farther back, pushed harder. My stomach lurched again, my eyes watered. This time a mouthful came up. Once the taste of vomit was on my tongue, it all just came up. One, two, three big gushing stomachfuls of crap. Eggs, waffles, strawberries, chocolate pie.

My swollen eye took some strain. Both eyes stung with water. I straightened up to the sink, rinsed my mouth out, patted my tears dry. I felt pretty fuckin' good. I was empty. All I had to do next was figure out something good to tell Mom and Rudy and everyone else in the world about my eye.

I gave the apartment one last look over, wiped a greasy spot off the coffee table. After that I had nowhere to be. So I took Mom's pink afghan and went to one of the laundry rooms where me and Heather and Shelby used to play strip club. I curled up on the big table meant for folding clothes and fell off to sleep again.

CHAPTER 17

"What the hell happened to your face?" Rudy's voice boomed as soon as I walked through the door.

"I had an accident," I said as my mother rounded the corner from the kitchen.

"Oh my God!" Her hands flew to her face. "What happened?"

"I was on my way to school, through the parking lot and somebody opened their car door right in front of me and I just ran right into it. We didn't see each other."

"Oh, that's terrible! Let me put some ice on it." Mom grabbed the bag of peas and wrapped them in the same green kitchen towel Carrie had used.

"So, what's the other one look like?" Rudy smiled under his little mustache. Mom stuck her head through the breakfast bar. "Don't start that Rudy," she said.

"Do you really believe she got hit by a car door, Rita?" Rudy took a long drag of his Marlboro.

"You didn't get in a fight, did you?" Mom asked me with her crumpled, concerned face.

"No, Mom, I didn't. I told you, I got hit by a car door. I mean I walked into one. I don't fight."

Rudy spoke slowly as he peeled himself off the wall. "Well, you might want to start fightin' with whoever done that to your face." Rudy turned into the kitchen. His advice was, somehow, nearly fatherly.

"Rudy, she told you she wasn't fighting. She had an accident, okay?"

"Okay. Case closed." I heard Rudy pop a beer open. "But, you mind telling me what happened to all the food in the house?"

"Yeah. I know I'm not supposed to have anyone in the house. But Carrie walked me home after I got hit with the door. She saw it. And we made breakfast and she put ice on my face. It was kind of an emergency."

"You had a whole pie for breakfast?"

"Yeah. I guess we did. Don't be mad. I was upset."

Rudy raised his can of Busch my direction, his index finger extended beyond its top. He let his mouth fall open like he was about to speak.

"Leave it alone," my mother growled.

"Case closed. If you gonna baby her for the rest of her life, it ain't my business." Rudy brushed past us, flopped onto the couch, and turned the TV on.

Neither of them asked if I was hungry. Mom heated up two Hungry Man TV dinners in the microwave. Rudy's first. Then her own. They both sat on the couch and I sat on the floor. Mom offered me a space next to her but I declined. We watched *Die Hard* on HBO. It was the first time the three of us had done anything like that together.

Whenever I looked at Mom, she gave me sad smiles. She was happy to have Rudy and me to herself in this way. My eye, though, made me look like a monster. This I knew. And just the thought of telling her the truth about where it came from made me sick.

When the phone rang I nearly jumped out of my skin. Rudy looked at the phone and stood.

"Hello? Yeah, she's here. Who's calling please?" Rudy asked looking over at me. "Your name is what?"

"Angie. Some boy for you, calls himself Manless." Rudy shoved the phone into my hand.

"Hello?"

"Hey, Angie." His voice was low, but it was definitely Mantis.

"Hi," I said, looking up to see Rudy watching me from the recliner. I turned the corner so my body was hidden next to the part of the wall between the dining area and the breakfast bar.

"Whattya doin'?" Mantis asked.

"Watching a movie with my mom and her boyfriend," I told him, completely amazed by how normal it sounded.

Mantis wanted to meet me the next day after school. I told him about the car door. My mom and Rudy could hear me. In fact, I had the feeling the TV had been turned down just to accommodate their listening. But I was more than happy to have them overhear the car door story. The story had gained details I hadn't quite delivered to my mom and Rudy. The car was light blue. The guy who opened the door was bald, probably someone's dad. It was a four door sedan of some sort. The bald man had helped me afterward, giving me his handkerchief and some aspirin, which I gulped down with some Dr. Pepper offered by a passing student. Yes. The whole story was something I could see in my mind.

"So, you want to meet me tomorrow? When you get out of school? I'm off work, so whenever is fine with me," Mantis said. I wanted to tell him I wasn't going to school the next day or ever again. But Bruce Willis's voice still seemed quiet. I agreed to meet Mantis at Billy Bear Pizza after school. I told Mantis I looked really awful with my eye and everything. He said he didn't care, he just wanted to see me. I hung up the phone.

"That your boyfriend?" Rudy asked, turning the sound on the TV back up as I began to speak.

"No, he's a new friend is all."

"You sure? A shiner like that? Some guy callin'? Sounds like a boyfriend to me."

"Mantis did not do this," I said.

"Oh, right, sorry. You got hit by a car door. I almost forgot," Rudy said, smiling at my mother. This time I actually saw his thumb work up the volume on the remote control.

"What are you tryin' to say?" I asked Rudy without enough energy for anger.

"I ain't TRYIN' to say nothin', girl. Boy calls himself Manless must need to make up for it somewheres. Like your face, fer starters, I guess. Anyway, we're gonna have to meet this kid."

"Mom!" I yelled at her. She tried to seem extremely interested in that stupid movie. "You can't just let him do this to me."

"Rudy," Mom said calmly. "If Angie says he's not her boyfriend, then he's not."

Rudy cocked his head to me, "Either way, we need to know who your friends are. Who yer associating yourself with. Especially with this black eye business."

I could have stabbed Rudy. The pleasure he took in telling me what to do. The way he reveled in stealing my mother from me. I had nowhere to go and Rudy loved every second of it.

"Mom! You can't let him do this!" I shouted, my eye pulsing again with its own little heartbeat.

"Hang on, everybody. Just hang on." Mom stood, took the remote from Rudy, and muted that stupid goddamned movie. "Angie, Rudy might be right. You have made some new friends this year and we should know who they are."

"Okay," I said, wanting to preserve my date for the following day. At least one decent thing could happen to me. "Can we do this meet-the-fam business later this week?"

"No." Rudy stuck his finger out at me.

"Wait, Rudy. Just wait. Yes, we can all meet later this week. I want to meet this Inez and this Pike I've heard you talk about. Maybe we can all go out for pizza or tacos or something. Right Rudy? You wouldn't mind taking Angie's friends out for a treat would you? It's as important to you as it is to me, right?"

"It isn't like she don't feed them half the time anyway."

My mother turned to him with a swish of her hip. I made a note of the move in case I ever got thin and had to manage a man of my own. "I'm saying we can all meet halfway on this. Angie will bring her friends out for dinner with us later this week, and you'll pay because kids don't have money."

I looked hopefully at my mother. She gave me a kind of secret smile and swished her hip the other way.

"Okay. But, if we decide your friends are not appropriate for you, then that's that. No more talk. No whining."

"Appropriate? Where'd you learn that word?"

"If I told you, I'd have to tell everyone and then I wouldn't sound so smart all the time." Rudy smiled and lit a cigarette.

I called Shelby.

"How are you feeling?" I asked.

"Terrible."

"Are you gonna be at school tomorrow?"

"Not unless there's a miracle."

"Good. I mean, I'll come by and see you."

"You sure you don't want me to call the school?" Mom asked me with her perfect morning lipstick in place.

"No. I'm going to school. I'm fine. I promise," I put two fingers against my blue, mostly yellow eye. It was Mom who winced.

"Take a couple of aspirin," she advised. "You really got a good whack."

"Yeah, the timing was amazing. What's with the white being all red? Is that blood?"

"Yeah. I guess it is. I really wish you would stay home," she said, putting two aspirin and a glass of water in my hand.

I swallowed them back. "No, really. I want to go, I have a . . ."

"Rita, where are my clean socks?" Rudy yelled from the other room.

"They're in the laundry basket," Mom called over her shoulder. By the time she turned back to look at me, I was at the door.

"Well, I'll see you tonight then sweetheart. But take these." She fished through a bowl of junk on the breakfast bar and produced a pair of sunglasses.

"Thanks," I said.

"Are these clean? I thought you did wash yesterday," Rudy yelled again. Mom gave off a sigh and turned down the hall toward him.

Since I was alone for a second, I took two Dexatrim with a gulp of orange juice straight from the container. Something else Rudy had forbid me to do.

"Good morning, Mrs. Beckham. This is Rita Neuweather," I said into the phone outside the K-mart.

"Oh, good morning Rita. Is Angie sick again? I was just getting ready to call you. We noticed she wasn't in class yesterday."

"Yes. I apologize for not calling. It kind of slipped my mind. Her allergies are just getting worse and worse. I lined up a program, a test group really, in Chicago. She'll be out for about two weeks."

"Two weeks? We'll need a doctor's note for that."

"Oh, yes, of course. I'll have Angie bring it when we get back."

"Oh, no. Ms. Neuweather, we are going to need it before she leaves," Mrs. Beckham sounded, suddenly, impatient.

"There's no time. We're at the airport right now."

159

"Well, we can't excuse the absence without it, so make sure she has it the day she returns to school."

"I definitely will," I told Mrs. Beckham and hung up the phone. My stomach was a wreck. There was no way that was going to work. But I certainly couldn't go back to school. Whatever happened, I couldn't go back to school.

CHAPTER 18

I found Pike exactly where I expected to find him. Stoned, surrounded by the skinny Field House trees with a few leaves still clinging to their branches. I could see him in there from a hundred feet away.

"C'mon," I said. "We have to get over to Shelby's. Everything is fucked up."

Pike stood, closed his little notebook, and stuck it in his pocket.

"What's with the sunglasses?" He asked as we made our way through the field of knee-high grass.

"You don't want to know."

"Do you have a bruise under there?" Pike asked.

"Oh, mind your own business, already. I'll tell you soon enough. When we get to Shelby's."

Robyn opened the door. She was wearing a stained pink sweat suit and her eye was pretty messed up. Her hair was flat and greasy looking. "You quit school or something, Angie?"

"I wish."

"You got a bruise under there?" Robyn pointed to my face.

"It's a long story."

"Always is when someone knocks you around." Robyn flopped onto the couch and brought a big bowl of ice cream up to her face.

"Nobody knocked me around, Robyn. I got smacked with a car door."

"Whatever you say." Robyn shrugged. She was beyond depressed.

It didn't make me feel any better to have a matching shiner with Robyn.

Shelby was curled under her covers.

"Hey, wake up." I nudged her leg.

"Hi. What are you doing here?" Shelby asked. Her nose was red and stuffy looking.

"How do you feel?" I asked.

"I've been better. Why are you wearing sunglasses?"

"I got smacked with a car door. My eye is all messed up."

"You have bangs. They look good. Let me see your eye." Shelby sat up. She looked awful. How could I think she was lying about being sick? That's something I would do, not Shelby.

I took the glasses off.

"Oh Jesus!" Pike said, shielding his eyes with his arm.

"God, that's nasty. What happened?" Shelby asked.

"I was in the parking lot at school . . ."

"Do you have those glasses back on?" Pike asked from behind his arm.

"Yes. You can look now."

"Fuck, I think I'm scarred for life."

I told Shelby and Pike the car door story. I used the bald man and the Dr. Pepper and all those details. I had to make sure to keep them the same.

Then I made up some other lies about Mindy and Troy. Well, they weren't all lies. I confessed to having followed Mindy and threatening to follow her from bathroom to bathroom. I told the truth about Troy telling me I was dead. But I lied about the rest.

"Why did you do that? Telling her she was born to be fat should have been enough," Shelby said.

I told Shelby that Troy had threatened her while he and I were in art class. I didn't say anything about him being in the bathroom or his stupid dick or Mindy's twisted excitement.

"Wait, how did I get into this?"

"I dunno. But, just let it cool off for awhile. Stay home this week."

"Stay home this week? No. I gotta keep my grades up. You know that. I can't stay home just because these people think they're tough."

"This is pretty serious. They're real mad about this."

"So what? They already call me a dyke. What are they gonna do, call me a hooker? Shit. That would up my status."

"Shelby, please. Stay home."

"Angie, how did you do this? How did you get me into this?"

"I didn't!"

"God, everything was bad enough for me without this. You should have used your head with those people. You know how they are and now, thanks to you, I gotta get a knife or some mace or something just to go to school. I really didn't need this shit."

"And I didn't really need to wind up being called a lesbian because of you! Ever think of that, Shelby?" I didn't know where my anger came from, but it came.

"What?" Shelby's eyes narrowed.

"MY life would be a HELL of a lot easier if you weren't a lesbo! I stand up to these assholes and you blame me? Blame yourself!"

"Get out."

"What?"

"Get out of my house, Angie."

"You guys." Pike's voice was low and focused. "Don't do this."

"You can leave too, Pike." Shelby's look was so icy calm Pike took a step back.

My eyes filled up with tears, stinging my fat eye under the sunglasses. Finally Pike nudged me a little and we left.

We walked quietly past Robyn in front of a re-run of *One Day at a Time*. The laugh track was going as I shut the door behind us.

"What am I gonna do?" I sniffed my tears up. It hurt too much to cry.

"You two will work it out. It's just a fight," Pike said.

"I can't believe I said that."

Pike patted my back and let me steady my breathing.

"Tell me about something else, Pike. Talk about something else."

"Well, okay. So let's see. Something else." Pike rubbed his chin. "Oh, well, Luann's parents are not exactly what you think they are."

"They're not real hippies?"

"Well, they're into that flower power business and everything. They like to smoke pot. But they have some really strange political ideas. Like, the whole house is covered with tie-dyed sheets and American flags. There's a huge Love it or Leave it! poster over the couch. Over the COUCH. You know, where most people hang a piece of art or a family portrait or something."

"What happened over there?"

"It was weird sittin' there watching them do lines of speed under that poster while they're sitting on their tie-dyed couch. I asked if I could use their bathroom and Warren—that's Luann's step dad—was like, It's a free country, son."

"Did they buy that speed off you?"

"Yeah. Well, I traded it for some pretty good weed."

"Inez will be happy," I said.

"Yeah, she is. She came over there the other day."

"Oh," I mumbled. I didn't like Inez and Pike being friends with Luann. They were my friends. Luann had plenty of her own friends.

"I was glad to get rid of that shit. I don't like it. Hell, I still haven't slept. I did some more over at Luann's that night, but I haven't done any in, like, more than twenty-four hours."

"Jesus, Pike. You've been awake for two days?"

"This is my third." Pike held up three fingers.

"Well, I know I can go my whole life without doing it again."

"Inez seems to like it though. She got all wasted over there and Warren went off on some long tangent about American rights being taken away and how everyone should get as many unregistered guns as possible and bury them in their back yards. He even has a whole procedure for oiling them and wrapping them for burial."

"What? Those people are crazy."

"Yeah, well, Inez pipes in and tells them about that Randy dude, the one that licked puke out of her mouth? Well, she tells Warren that Randy has guns and brags about them being unregistered."

"That's like totally illegal, right?"

"Oh man, it's, like, so illegal. But this whole thing gets even weirder. Warren gets all interested in what Inez is telling him and Luann calls a couple of these jock boys over to the house. Like, all Izod shirts and loafers and shit. I was pretty high and all of this was, like, so surreal. I think those dudes go to Mehlville, too."

"What were their names?"

"The one guy was Troy. I didn't get his buddies' names. I just wanted to leave but I was kind of scared of all this and Inez seemed like she was real interested or just real high or something and I didn't want to leave her there all alone."

"What did Troy look like?"

"Big fucker. Cropped brown hair. Why, you know him?"

"Yeah, I think I do."

"Well, he's in on this thing with Warren to steal this Randy asshole's guns or some dumb shit like that."

"What? Is Inez gonna be in on this?"

"Well, she agreed to show Troy where this guy lives. But it gets worse, Rex is definitely in on it. They got him set up to pop the lock on the guys house, AND, get this, he's going to borrow his brother's van to carry the shit."

"Rex?"

"Yeah, he was there too. You know how he is all hung up on Luann and everything. I'm never going there again. You should talk to Inez. She's gonna get herself into a world of trouble with those hippie whatevers."

"Yeah, I'll talk to her."

Pike and I walked along Sunworth road not saying much of anything. Our bodies seemed to be naturally gravitating back to the field house. That place was like a magnet. Only problem, it was rapidly losing its cover.

"Pike, the Field House is closed for the season. You know that right?"

"Yeah, I guess I do. So what should it be? Hanging out behind dumpsters?"

"No, let's go to a laundry room. They are nice and warm in the winter and definitely covered from the street. There's a laundry room every third building at Covington. Open from seven to ten every day. It's gonna be your best bet for winter."

We spent the rest of the afternoon hanging out in one of the Covington laundry rooms. Pike smoked weed until he looked cross-eyed.

"God, I think I may even be able to get some sleep."

Pike curled up on the big table people used to fold clothes and let his eyes shut. His eyes darted back and forth underneath their lids. I watched him for a little while. Every once in awhile he would jerk kind of violently, but he didn't wake. Whatever he was dreaming wasn't so pleasant.

I propped myself up on a washer and read from my book. The one about serial killers. Charlie Manson and The Family. Poor Inez. Where do people come up with the tortures they put us through?

The book said Charlie Manson was what he was because he had a bad childhood. He was passed around between family members and they say his mother might have been a hooker. Seemed having a hooker for a mother automatically made a person a killer. Well, the sons anyway.

In Manson's case, he thought he was the second coming and apparently so did some other people. And they all got together and cut a few rich people up. He gets more mail than any other prisoner in the country.

I looked at Pike's sleeping body, his eyes still bouncing mercilessly around his head. If it was true that pain and abandonment turned people into killers, then everyone I knew would eventually become a monster. Furry and unkind like that thing in the magazine.

I read and thought and watched Pike sleep until it seemed about time for me to meet Mantis.

"Pike. Pike wake up. I gotta go."

Pike blinked his eyes at me and gave me a sleepy smile.

"What's the hurry? We have the rest of our lives."

"That's what they say."

Pike woke himself up, shaking his head from side to side and yawning somewhat compulsively.

I shoved my book back in my bag. Pike slid himself off the table and yawned again.

"Hey, I'm meeting Mantis at Billy Bear. You want to come?"

"Do I want to come along on your date?"

"No, do you want to walk over and play a little skee ball ball? That's what I meant."

"Okay. I'm trying to help Inez win that panda she wants."

"What is her deal with that thing?"

"Its sad eyes." Pike shrugged.

I didn't have the proper motivation for skee ball ball. Pike was rolling along just fine. One fifty after another. Between Inez and Pike, that panda bear was just a few tickets away.

"You're not even trying," Pike said, rolling another fifty.

"I have a lot on my mind. Did Luann say anything else about me being a manstealer or whatever?"

"No. She was busy organizing a militia. Like I told you, it's pretty weird over there."

"Why is Rex getting himself hooked up with that shit?"

Pike shrugged, putting more tokens into the machine. "Money. His life is pretty fucked. Five brothers, no mom, drunk dad. They basically live in a shack. I'm serious. He's on his own, you know?"

I nodded and rolled again, although I didn't know. I didn't know anything about Rex. His life was a mystery. I'd tried, a couple of times, to ask him about himself, but he always found a way to get around the subject.

"Besides," Pike said. "Luann is Rex's obsession. And she loves all this crazy business. Shit, it's what she grew up with."

Pike stood back, counting his tickets. He folded one over the next as he counted them, the same way Inez did. I felt a hand touch the small of my back.

"Those glasses make you look very mysterious," Mantis said.

"Hey," I said, softly turning my face away as a giant blush rose over its surface. But Mantis caught my cheek with his hand and planted a little kiss on it.

"I'm gonna go find Inez. Don't tell her I'm collecting tickets for her, okay?"

"Okay," I agreed, letting Mantis's hand find my ass.

Pike shook hands with Mantis and left. We didn't stick around long after that. We went to the apartment where Mantis lived with his brother.

The place was a mess. Actually, it was beyond a mess. Dark and smelly and looking like it had been ransacked.

"Bachelor pad," Mantis said, stretching his arm out in front of him. I looked for something not completely filthy to sit on. Mantis fished a couple of beers out of a refrigerator the size of a small television.

"Where do you sleep?" I asked. The whole apartment consisted of two rooms.

"Right here." Mantis patted the couch. Despite the fact that the whole couch was covered with a thick layer of man grease I sat down next to him. He handed me a cold can of Busch.

"So," he said. "Let me see your eye."

"It's really nasty looking." I popped my beer open, not wanting to show him at all.

"C'mon. It can't be that bad." Mantis gingerly removed the sunglasses from my face.

"Oh shit!" he said. "That's amazingly awful!"

"I told you!" I snapped the glasses out of his hand and put them back on.

"God, I guess a car door will do that." He laughed.

"You're laughing at me!"

"Yeah, no, I mean, c'mon, it's funny!"

"No, it's really not."

"Oh, it's funny." Mantis put his hands on my waist. "It's at least a little funny." His fingers worked at tickling me. I squirmed trying not to spill my beer, "Mantis, quit!" I screamed the way a person does when they are being tickled and they don't like it. I was involuntarily laughing and getting madder and madder as each second of tickling passed.

"See it's funny! I told you!" Mantis straddled me. He quit tickling and started kissing me with hard, breathy stabs of his tongue.

I was so relieved he'd stopped tickling me, it took a second to register we were kissing. And a second after that, even, to consider whether or not I liked it.

I pushed him back a little. "Where's your brother?"

"I dunno. Either at work or at his girlfriend's house." Mantis took my sunglasses off again. He took the beer out of my hand and settled both of them on the mound of crap covering the side table. "Besides, it's not like he'd mind." Mantis smiled and pulled my face back toward his.

I couldn't decide if I wanted to be there or not. I kissed Mantis back, but it was more like a tongue duel than I thought a kiss should be. Where was he trying to put that thing? In my lung? Did he kiss me the night of the party like this? It wasn't the way I had fantasized it over and over in my head since that night.

He kept pushing my head back against the arm rest. It hurt. My head was still tender from the pipes. I didn't want Mantis to feel it and ask me about it, so every time he tried to run his hand through my hair, I stopped him.

Mantis stuck his hand under my t-shirt and pulled the cup of my bra down. My left tit fell out. His palm cupped it and his tongue circled the inside of my mouth. Then he grabbed the nipple real quick with his thumb and index finger and he pinched it. Hard.

"Ow!" I pushed him back.

"Did that hurt?" he asked, his hand still resting on my tit.

"Yeah, it hurt. You're not popping a zit here."

"Most girls like it," he said, doing it again.

"Ow! Stop!" I pushed his hand out from under my shirt. "I doubt most girls like that. It hurts."

"Well, it's normal for girls to like that sort of thing. So sorry, okay?" Mantis got off me looking like a cross between a hurt puppy and one of those serial killers I'd been reading about.

He stood, grabbed his beer, took a hard swallow, ran a hand through his mess of dark hair. He looked back at me. At me with my big grotesque eye and my abnormal sexual responses.

"Maybe you're just sensitive because you're about to start your period."

I pulled the cup of my bra back over my tit and the little throbbing spot that was my nipple.

"Maybe," I said, reaching for my beer and my glasses. Of course, I wasn't about to start my period. It was like three weeks away. But the idea seemed to please Mantis, so I went with it.

"Girls' breasts get sensitive right before they start their period." Mantis explained as if I couldn't possibly have known this for myself. "Maybe I should have asked you. But, really, you should have told me. I don't want to hurt you so you have to tell me when you are about to go on the rag. Okay?"

I took a drink of beer, eyeing Mantis from behind my sunglasses. I should tell him? Like in the future? Like he wants to be my boyfriend? My stomach did a couple of flops and I finished the beer.

"Okay?" Mantis asked again, leaning forward meaningfully.

"Okay," I agreed, and Mantis took the empty can out of my hand and replaced it with a full one.

"Good," Mantis said, popping the top on his fresh beer. He might as well have said: Good dog, good girl! But I ignored it in favor of thinking about a cute boy like Mantis being my boyfriend. Aunt Jean had once said, Men have egos the size of Texas and you got to stroke that whole fucking state if you want them to act right at all.

"Don't mess with Texas," I mumbled to myself.

"What?"

"Nothing."

Mantis sat back down beside me but left a whole cushion between us. Punishment for not wanting to have my nipples pulled off? I picked a *Playboy* off the floor. I flipped its glossy pages.

"That magazine sucks," Mantis said, leaning into me to look at it.

"Then why do you have it?" I wanted to know.

"My brother gets them. I can't afford the good ones. The Easy Wash only pays $3.35 an hour. And you'd be surprised how much this shit-hole apartment costs."

"You work at the car wash?" I asked, still flipping the pages of the *Playboy*.

"Yeah. I wash cars. Wait, go back. That girl has a super-hot ass."

"This one?"

"Yeah," Mantis dug his fingers into my skin.

I dropped the magazine back to the crowded floor.

Mantis ran his hand up under my shirt again. He was rubbing at my tits over the bra.

"But as soon as I get my driver's license I'm gonna start delivering pizza."

Mantis pushed closer to me. "I'll be easy," he whispered. "Just let me play with them for a minute. You can look at that magazine, if you want."

Mantis pushed my t-shirt all the way up and popped both tits out of their cups. He kissed my nipples. Gently sucking on one and then the other. Mantis put his cold beer can against my left nipple while he slowly licked my right. I liked it. I liked it a lot. I relaxed, pulled off the sunglasses again.

"They look so big coming out of your bra like this, don't they?" Mantis breathed these words into my chest.

We kissed some more and Mantis was easier, slower. I liked the kissing this time. And the touching. But I didn't like my stomach showing. When Mantis ran his hand over it, I nearly jumped out of my skin.

"What?" Mantis asked, pulling his hand back.

"I'm ticklish. You know that," I said. I pulled my t-shirt down.

"No, no, no," Mantis whispered, trying to push my t-shirt up, again.

"I should go. I have to be home for dinner. I'll be in trouble if I'm not," I said.

I was putting my tits back into their holders when Mantis said, "What? You're gonna leave me here with a case of the blue-balls, like this?"

"The what?"

"Blue-balls. Guy's balls turn blue and ache if they get filled up with come and it has no place to go."

"That's not true," I said, standing and getting all my stuff together.

"Yes, it is true and it's dangerous." Mantis was really trying.

"Nice try Mantis. I might be a virgin, but I'm not stupid."

"You're a virgin?" Mantis's eyes nearly popped out of his head.

"Yeah." I shrugged.

"You should have told me that."

"I just did."

"I wouldn't have gotten all worked up if I'd known."

"Well, I wouldn't have come over here if I thought you expected to get fucked."

"You got me all excited. You're a virgin, you don't know. But you have to think about what you're doing to a guy, you know? What you're doing to him when you make out and stuff. So now you know."

"What exactly is it that I know?"

"You'll wind up being called a cock tease and stuff. Shit, I'd call you that myself if I didn't know you were a virgin."

"I have to go," I said, confused as hell.

Mantis grabbed my arm and leaned into my ear. "Sure you don't want to touch it. Just a little?"

"No. I don't want to touch it Mantis. I have to go. Besides, wouldn't that just give you a bigger case of the blue-balls, or whatever?"

"Have you ever touched one?"

"No."

"Well," Mantis was whispering and unzipping his jeans at the same time. "You could see what it's like, maybe put your mouth on it for a minute. Just for a minute."

"You want me to suck your dick?"

"You'd still be a virgin, Angie. I won't even come in your mouth."

Mantis was pulling his dick out of his pants when I broke his grasp and stood.

"Mantis, put it away. I'm not going to suck your dick or touch it or fuck you or anything. AND I'm NOT about to start my period, either. You just don't know how to touch tits!" I said all of this in one big angry rush and left.

I added dick sucking to the list of Things Never to Do.

CHAPTER 19

Pike and I hung out for the next couple days. Shelby still wouldn't talk to me. I almost smoked pot a couple of times, but I was doing pretty good with food. I hardly even wanted it anymore. I weighed 163. I'd lost nine pounds. Only nine, but it was something. And I was off food for the first time in my life.

I tried Shelby on the phone again. Robyn said she'd gone back to school that morning. My insides dropped out in a cold glop.

"You wanna go to Heather's?" I asked Pike. I was too nervous to just sit around. I had to get to Shelby when she got out of school. I had to make her talk to me. I had to do something.

"She made the appointment!" Heather was crying when she opened the door.

"What? What appointment?" I asked.

"For the tit! I'm getting a tit for Christmas!" Heather wailed and flopped onto her mother's couch.

"Should I leave?" Pike asked.

"No," Heather said. "It's no secret I only have one tit!"

"You don't want the fake tit?" I asked, sitting beside her and resting my hand on her back.

"I don't know. I don't want to have surgery. I don't want to go back to school after Christmas being, like, all, you know, altered."

"Did you tell your mom?"

"Yeah, I told her. I told my dad too, he's paying for half. I think he's really the one who is pushing for it anyway. Like he should care so much about my tits! Like anyone should!"

"Can't you get them to wait?" Pike asked.

"No, it's for the best. That's what they say. My dad even said I would thank him later. He said, once I was married I would understand his decision. His decision! You hear those words?"

"Married?" Pike wrinkled his face.

"Yeah. I guess I don't get to decide about being married either. And, apparently, men don't marry one-titted girls." Heather sobbed into her hands.

I kept petting her back. Tears welled in my own eyes. Men didn't marry fat girls either. These things were self evident.

Heather finally sniffed up the last of her tears and turned her swollen face to me, "I want to . . . Jesus Shit! What happened to your eye?"

"Oh, I got whacked with a car door, it's a long story."

"It looks awful."

"Actually, it's getting better."

Heather went to the bathroom and washed her face while Pike rolled up a joint.

"This'll make her feel better." Pike nodded at the joint.

"Fuck, you guys are almost religious about that shit." I shook my head.

"Well, it takes the edge off, which is what my grandmother used to say about church, so you might be onto something there." Pike nodded.

I left Pike and Heather to their worship and headed for Shelby's. Robyn was there by herself. Shelby hadn't made it home from school yet.

"Hey, car door." Robyn rolled her eyes. She seemed to have pulled herself together. Her hair was fixed the way she, and only she, liked it and she was wearing her tight blue jeans and jewelry.

"Your eye looks a lot better," I told her.

"Yeah, a clobbering heals quicker than you think it will. Haven't you noticed?"

"I didn't get clobbered, Robyn. It was an accident. Shit happens, haven't you heard?"

"Oh, I've heard all right. I've heard plenty. But you weren't hit by any car door. You ought to tell me who did that. That's what you ought to do instead of lookin' me right in the eye an lyin' about it."

"Robyn, can we just drop this, please?"

"Nope. This is the only conversation we're gonna have until you tell me the truth. I don't care if it takes years." Robyn opened the fridge for a beer.

"What the hell difference does it make to you, anyway?"

"Look, if a girl made that mess on your face, I'll teach you how to fight an' win and you can drag her ass through the mud. If some guy did that to you, I'll make him pay like he never imagined. So, who hit you?"

"Nobody."

"I can do this longer than you can, Angie. Trust me." Robyn leaned down to my face, her right eye mirroring my own.

"Did you make Vince pay?" I asked, trying, I guess, to back her down.

"Who hit you?" Robyn asked mechanically. She stared into my eyes for a second then turned and pulled a box of toaster strudel out of the freezer.

"Where's Shelby, anyway?"

"Who hit you, Angie?" Robyn turned on the toaster oven. It's orange glow spilled onto the counter and my eyes filled with tears. Before they could run down my face, I headed for Shelby's room.

"It's up to you, Angie," Robyn called after me.

Shelby wasn't home so I laid in her bed soaking up her smell. It was only about an hour away from dinner when Shelby finally got home. She was followed by Colleen.

"What do you want?" Shelby asked when she found me curled into a ball on her bed.

"I want to talk to you," I said.

"Oh," Colleen gasped at my eye. "That looks worse than Robyn's."

"It's fresher," I explained.

"Angie, we're not speaking, remember?" Shelby said.

"Just let me talk to you for a minute, Shelby."

"All right, then talk," Shelby was more pissed than I'd ever seen her. I looked over at Colleen.

"She stays," Shelby said.

"I didn't know it was ever going to have anything to do with you. It was about Mindy Overton and Inez and me."

"And I deserve to get lumped in with it because I'm a lesbo. Isn't that what you said? That all this was my own fault?"

"Shelby! Stop! I didn't mean anything." My tears rolled.

Colleen sat on the edge of the bed staring at her feet. I collapsed into the unmade covers and cried. I could take anything—Rudy, Troy Mulligan, anything—aside from Shelby being mad at me.

"Shelby." Colleen's voice was calm. "You're being cruel."

I heard the door open and Robyn's voice: "You find out who hit her yet?"

"Hit her?" Shelby asked.

"Yeah, you don't believe that dumb-assed 'a car door hit me shit,' do you?"

"Angie, did somebody hit you?" Shelby asked.

Her tone was so calmed from what it had been, I almost screamed the whole story out. But instead I buried my face deeper in her pillow and said: "NO!"

"You are too old to be fuckin' my sister," Robyn said and it sounded as if her mouth was full.

"And you are too seventies to be standing here right now," Colleen said. I couldn't help it, I started to laugh. And I knew I had to dig my face out of the pillow in case Robyn went nuts. When I looked up at her she was chewing at a piece of toaster strudel and staring blank-faced at Colleen. It was the official Robyn Moment. The one where it could not be determined if she would laugh or try to strangle someone. I don't think Robyn ever knew what would become of the Robyn Moment until it happened.

I glanced at Shelby, who gave me the traditional raised eyebrow. For the first time ever, I was thankful for Robyn's skittish temper.

Robyn finished chewing, swallowed, and laughed. "Great, I actually like my sister's dyke girlfriend. Or are you the boyfriend?" Robyn asked.

"Don't be typical," Colleen said with a simple directness that made Robyn smile. Again. It was unprecedented.

Robyn looked at Shelby. "Guess it's time to come out of the closet, as they say. When you gonna tell Mom?"

"You wouldn't." Shelby's forehead creased as she stared at Robyn.

Robyn shoved the rest of her pastry into her mouth, chewed it for a second, and held her palms up. "No, I wouldn't. But you will."

With that Robyn left the room.

Colleen stared at the closed door. "She's something else, huh?"

Shelby shifted her attention back to me. "Troy threw a note at me today in art class. It said "You're Next" and there was a little smoking gun drawn by the words. What did that mean?"

"I dunno." I shrugged.

"So he didn't have anything to do with your eye?"

"No, I already told you."

"So what did he mean? What did he mean I was next?"

"I don't know, Shelby. Just be careful. I'm sorry you wound up in all of this, I really am."

I left Shelby's, but not before Robyn could ask: "Who hit you Angie?" At least Shelby had cooled from pure rage to simple hatred. I could work with that.

I walked home the Monroe Street route. I rounded the hedge that curved around Carrie Shuren's house. Carrie and her problems. Her friends were shit. Big deal? I was a shit friend. So was Carrie. My friend, my enemy, Mindy's lookout. None of us could be trusted.

I opened the apartment door to the crack of one of Rudy's beer cans opening. That tinny little noise that followed Rudy and Robyn through life like a sound track.

"Your eye looks a lot better," my mother said, putting a plate of bite-sized pieces of iceberg lettuce and tomato wedges on the table.

"Did you talk to your boyfriend about meeting us?" Rudy asked from his constant position of hovering directly over me.

"He's not my boyfriend and no, I haven't talked to him about it."

"And you don't plan to, do you?"

"Yes. Yes, I plan to, Rudy. I just haven't yet, okay?"

"Are you all right?" Mom looked at me. I noticed the delicate crows feet around her eye.

"Yeah. I guess. I just came from Heather's. Her mom made the appointment for her tit."

"Breast, Angie. Say breast. Well that's wonderful. It's so nice that her mother has managed a way to afford it."

"Heather doesn't want it," I said. I flopped down in a chair and tried to ignore Rudy sucking off his stupid Busch beer.

"Well, surgery is very frightening. Remember when I had that surgery on my ACL?" She tapped her knee with a vegetable knife. "About ten years ago. I was terrified. If I could have still gone to work, I wouldn't have done it at all," she said, then laid out a plate of fried pork chops.

"What's going on? She's gettin' tit surgery?" Rudy asked.

"Only one of her breasts ever developed." Mom explained from the kitchen. "It's a shame really." She was shaking her head from side to side as she settled a bowl of instant mashed potatoes on the table.

"Yer shittin' me," Rudy said with a great wallop of a laugh. "She's only got one tittie?"

"Rudy, say breast, please."

"She's real upset about the surgery. She doesn't want to go through with it," I told my mother, who surveyed the table for what was missing.

"Well, she's sixteen. And it's all very scary, but it's for the best. She'll thank her mom someday."

"Yeah, she can't go through life all lopsided," Rudy said with another laugh.

"Rudy, stop!" Mom said, but she failed to conceal her smile. "Okay, let's eat."

I put some lettuce and tomato on my plate. Mom slid the jar of Miracle Whip toward me. Just plain Miracle Whip. It was her favorite way to dress her version of a salad. I declined. Instead I pulled some meat off one of the chops and made a sandwich.

I wasn't really hungry. My life had become upsetting enough to actually disrupt my appetite. I ate about half the sandwich and just sat in the chair listening to my mother and Rudy chew. Rudy's little mustache twitched slightly as he leaned over his plate, conquering its contents.

"Anything else happening, Angie?" Mom asked, trying to bring something besides silence to the table.

"No." I twisted a bread crust between my fingers.

"When I was a kid, this eye lid." Rudy pointed his fork toward his left eye. "It dragged. Means it was droopy. Anyway, they gave me a surgery for it. I didn't want to do it neither."

"I didn't know that," Mom said.

"Yeah, said it was for my own good. But I don't know. It was terrible, the surgery and everything. Hell, maybe I'd look all handsome with some droopy eye lid. Guess we'll never know."

"How old were you?" I asked.

"Ten or so. Isn't no fun havin' people make you do that shit. Hell, that's just the way you are, right? I mean, Rita, you'd still love me wouldn't ya?"

"If you had one big breast?"

"Funny. Very funny, Rita."

CHAPTER 20

The Easy Wash opened at eight. Which didn't leave me much time to kill between leaving the house as if I were going to school and finding Mantis. At least, I hoped to find him. I stopped by the Hardee's. The smells were there, those delicious greasy smells, but I ignored them.

I ordered a diet Coke and a cup of ice water from the woman behind the counter. In her little paper hat and brown smock, she looked like anyone. My stomach jumped around, lusted after the smell of biscuits and hash browns. No way. I didn't care what my stomach thought it wanted.

I took my Coke and my ice water to a table in the corner between two windows. I dumped a package of Slim-fast into the ice water and stirred it around with a straw. All the powder just sort of clumped up on the ice. I swallowed back some diet Coke, waiting for the Slim-Fast to dissolve into the melting ice.

I put on my make up. It didn't make sense to try to cover any of the bruise around my eye. It was still too nasty for that. Make up would have just made it more gross. The Slim-Fast never melted. It just stuck to the remaining ice in sticky pink blobs. I stared into the cup, wishing for Carrie. She, among all people, would understand.

I walked over to the Easy Wash. It was weird the way there were all these stores and restaurants and things but not a single sidewalk. I still feared I'd be picked up for truancy. Just the act of walking around out there seemed like a crime. There certainly wasn't anyone else on the street.

Cars were lined up in a U shape waiting for the first wash to begin. None of the cars actually looked dirty. The Easy Wash had taped some smiling jack-o-lanterns in a hallway lined with windows where customers could watch their cars going through the soapy water and brushes. I used to love Halloween. I looked around at everyone in their work shirts. None of them were Mantis.

"You need somethin'?" one of them finally asked.

"I'm lookin' for Mantis," I told him. The guy smiled and scanned me from head to toe. I blushed and twisted my head to watch a car passing under the sprays of water.

"Mantis? Hey," he called over his shoulder to another guy who was standing behind a cash register counting money. "This lady is lookin' for Mantis."

"Oh, yeah?" the guy stopped his counting and gave me that same body scan. "You Angie?"

"Yeah," I said, confused as to how or why that guy would know my name.

"Hey, Stinky." The counter guy called out to another guy who was drying the windshield of the day's first car. "This here is Angie. She's lookin' for Mantis." He stuck his thumb at me meaningfully.

Stinky poked his head around a column to smile at me. "Well, he don't come in today. You should try him at home. What happened to your eye?"

"Fight."

"How's the other one look?"

"Like the butt end of an Easter ham," I said over my shoulder as I left.

At the edge of the parking lot I turned and they were looking at me, joined by a couple other guys in gray shirts. They all smiled and waved and I smiled and waved back.

"What are you doing here?" Mantis asked from a haze of sleep.

"I didn't go to school. I thought we could hang out."

"Come in." Mantis scratched at his bare arm pit and yawned. "Got to make some coffee. You like coffee?"

"No," I said, staring down at the couch. Mantis didn't even bother putting a sheet on it when it became his bed. The TV was going too. A commercial for a Time Life series of books on the Civil War.

"You sleep with the TV on?" I asked.

"Yeah." Mantis stood in the doorway stretching himself. "Can't hear the neighbors that way."

"Oh." I shrugged and an uncomfortable silence fell between us as the TV preached and the coffee maker gurgled.

Mantis was smiling and rubbing his stomach. "I thought you hated me."

"Hate is a strong word."

"You were pretty mad the other day."

"Yeah. But that was the other day."

"I see." Mantis pulled himself out of the doorway and headed through his brother's bedroom for the bathroom.

I got nervous. I wasn't exactly sure what the hell I was doing there. I really did think Mantis was pretty much an asshole. Still, I wanted him to be my boyfriend. I wanted somebody, something. Sex. It just seemed like the time had come. Everyone else had something of their own.

"Your eye looks a lot better," Mantis said as he came back into the room. "You can sit down. I just have to wake up a little is all."

Mantis poured himself a cup of coffee and I sat on the couch/bed and stared at a rerun of The Dukes of Hazzard. I never could stand that stupid show. The girls in elementary school used to have crushes on the guys in it, but I never had any interest.

I never had crushes on anyone back then, except maybe a kind of crush on Jennifer Randall in the second grade. But I guess that didn't really count because I wasn't a lesbian. I mean, it wasn't like I had ever imagined I was kissing her or anything like that.

Coffee roused Mantis pretty quickly. He pulled a long-sleeved black t-shirt off the floor and put it on. He probably never washed anything.

"Where's your brother? He can't be delivering pizzas at this hour."

"Oh, he's over kissing his girlfriend's ass, as usual. She's always freaking out about something. I don't know what her problem is. I'm just glad she doesn't like to hang out over here."

I looked around the dark, smelly room, with its beer can and over-filled ashtray décor. Why would anyone want to hang out here? God, if we were going to have sex on that stupid couch would there even be a sheet or something to throw over it? It was so filthy I didn't even like sitting on it in my clothes.

Mantis and I watched TV and smoked all morning. I managed to get a little more information out of him. He was on probation for stealing a car.

"Why'd you steal a car?"

"There used to be this place in Belleville. This garage that did body work and shit. Anyway, if you snagged a car and got it to them they'd give you five hundred bucks. So I stole this Cadillac from over on Butler Hill. Nice car. It was open, too. Tombs used to have this piece of shit El Camino with a busted steering column and he'd have to start the thing with a screwdriver, so I kinda knew how to do it. Had to fuck with it for awhile, but when it started, shit, nothin' in my life ever felt so good."

"Then what happened?"

"Well, I didn't get so far. It was New Year's Eve. I thought that would be a good time to get the car since no one would be home. But, turns out, that's the time to rob houses, not steal cars. Goin' over the bridge into Illinois, cops set up a road block to catch drunk drivers. No place to go once you got there. I tried to jump out and just make a run for it over to the old Koch Hospital. You know that place?"

"Yeah, I heard about it. Supposed to be haunted by hundreds of insane veterans or something."

"Yeah. Whatever. Maybe like a handful of junkies and a couple of crack heads. If there were ever any ghosts in there they were probably scared off by the sight of the living dead. Anyway, I tried to break for that place. I hopped the fence onto the service road and everything, but a cop pulled right up on my ass. I tried to deny I'd been in the Caddy, but it was pretty hopeless. So, they took me into custody. That's what they call it when you're too young to be arrested."

"And you got probation?"

"Shit. I got six months at St. Paul's Juvenile Corrections, after I completed three months at Riverside."

"The rehab?"

"Yeah."

"Why did they send you to rehab?"

"They just do that shit automatically now. With juveniles anyway. Something crazy with that whole Nancy Reagan Just Say No or whatever. Didn't meet one person in there with an actual drug problem. Couple of drunks, a slew of pot heads. Other than that everyone was like me, waitin' for a spot at St. Paul's to open up."

"So, you were locked up for nine months?"

"No, I only did three at St. Paul's. I got out early for gettin' my GED. Wouldn't had to go at all if my bitch-ass mom would have gotten me a lawyer."

"What, she couldn't afford one?"

"Shit. My mom's loaded since her father died and left her all kinds of money. She lives out in Chesterfield now, for fuck's sake."

"I've never been to Chesterfield."

"No one from South County has ever been to Chesterfield. I think you get arrested if you get caught out there. She wouldn't get me a lawyer because she said getting what I deserved would set me straight. Proves what she knows about the fucking justice system, don't it? Anyway, after I got out of St. Paul's I came here to live with Theo and do my two years of probation. I got another eight months left. Then I'm free."

"What are you gonna do then?"

"Quit that fucking job." Mantis finally stopped fiddling with his lighter and looked at me. He gave me a kind of sideways smile. "I'm sorry about the other day."

"Well, maybe we should forget it." I shrugged.

"You're pretty cute when you're pissed though. Your eyebrows go up and down real fast."

"They do?" I reached over and rubbed the knuckles on his right hand.

"Yeah." Mantis turned his body toward me.

"You're not gonna tease me all over again, are you?"

I poked my lips out, looked him in the eye and shook my head from side to side.

Mantis leaned in and kissed me. He worked his hands under my sweat shirt.

"No pinching," I whispered.

"I'm not gonna hurt you."

We kept kissing and it was good Soft and not too fast. Mantis got me out of my sweat shirt and bra. He pushed me into the couch and lowered himself between my legs. I pulled his t-shirt off him and stroked his chest. I loved the way his ribs slid along under his skin and the little circle of chest hair that had begun below his throat.

Mantis held himself up with his hands on either side of my head. "I got an idea." He reached over me for the television remote. The cord dangled over my face as he studied the numbers for a minute. Then all this flesh burst onto the screen.

"Theo gets the Playboy channel too." Mantis looked at me hopefully and dropped the remote to the floor.

I turned my head and watched a blonde woman with huge tits take her bikini top off. She licked her lips and got on all fours, arching her back the way the girls in the magazines did. It made her perfect ass slip out of her denim cut offs. It was that Daisy Duke thing. Mantis rubbed against my crotch and licked my tits. Every once in awhile he looked over at the television for a second.

Mantis shoved his hand down the front of my stretch pants. "We got to get you out of these."

"Wait," I whispered.

"Oh, no, Angie. Don't back out on me this time, please?"

"I'm not. I just want you to put a sheet or a blanket or something over this couch."

"Is it scratching your skin?"

"Yeah," I lied. It was too greasy to scratch anything.

"Okay, hold on. I should get a rubber from Theo's room, anyway."

Mantis stood and I watched his smooth back walk away. When I turned my head to the television, a brunette was washing her tits in a bubble bath.

"Here," Mantis handed a sheet to me. I got up and threw it over the couch. It was a kind of wheat color and it had a big lighthouse on it.The sheet didn't seem particularly clean either, but it was an improvement. As I bent to pull the sheet all the way to the end of the couch, Mantis caught my hips and landed me on all fours. I arched my back the way I was supposed to and he ran his hands over my tits and down to my stretch pants, which he pulled off in one motion. I heard his zipper.

I felt the flesh of his dick against my ass. When I turned to look at him, his head was swiveled toward the television watching a redhead eat a banana.

"I wanna see it," I said, rolling back over on my back.

Mantis wiggled out of his jeans and knelt between my legs.

I reached down and felt it. I liked it so I just held onto it. Mantis came back close to my face.

"Relax, it'll be fine."

Of course, it was anything besides fine. When he started it felt like someone was trying to drive a truck up my cunt. I screamed.

"Okay, okay," Mantis stopped and looked at me. "You are so tight. Just hang on, okay. It'll be fine."

Mantis kept at his pushing and breathing and reassuring me. The pain went through my body like hot liquid. Tears spilled out of my eyes.

"Okay, okay." Mantis stopped again and looked at me. "You okay? It hurts, huh?"

"Yes," I croaked.

"It hurts my dick too," he kind of laughed.

"Don't stop," I said. "I can't be a virgin forever."

I tried to find something enjoyable about what was happening.

"I'm sorry, Angie," he said. "We may have to work on this, over time." His brow was sweating and he was smiling.

When he pulled the condom off, there was a little raw spot on his dick. We giggled about that for awhile.

"You're my first virgin," he said.

"I'm my first virgin too."

I was high from the whole experience. High and sore.

"Look," Mantis said.

I looked down to see a big red bloodstain marring the picture of the lighthouse on the sheet.

"I'm sorry," I said.

"I think it's cool."

Mantis took the sheet off to the laundry basket while I dressed and found something more suitable on the television.

"Let's order a pizza. I get 'em free from the Cecil Whittaker's cuz of my brother."

So we spent the rest of the day watching TV and eating pizza and giggling. I couldn't feel anything but love as I drifted off to sleep.

When I finally opened my eyes, it was completely dark except for a streak of white light coming through the front door under the feet of several people who were talking rambunctiously. Then a bare bulb in the ceiling lit up.

"Oh, hey, Mantis. Oh, sorry dude." The man's eyebrows went up when he saw me curled up on the floor next to Mantis.

I wiped the sleep out of my eyes and looked around at the three men who had just come through the door. They were all smiling and when Mantis stood the shorter of them gave him a slug in the arm. I understood what was happening and was thankful to be dressed.

I stood. "Anybody know what time it is?"

"Six-thirty," the tallest of them told me.

They passed beers around to each other. Not that they weren't already drunk.

"You the virgin?" One of them asked, handing me a beer.

I didn't know what to say. I looked over at Mantis who was grinning from ear to ear. I understood the guys at the Easy Wash, then.

"Hell yes!" The short one said and gave Mantis a high five and the others guys held up their cans.

"C'mon baby." One of them nudged me. "Open your beer, this one's for you."

I cracked open the beer and shared in the toast. Compliance seemed the best line of defense.

"Check this out," Mantis said, running off for Theo's room. He returned holding the bloodied sheet in front of him.

"Oh shit! You okay, kiddo?" The tall one asked, laughing into his fist.

I nodded. Fought off tears. Drank from the beer can and sat quietly stunned as they talked about playing pool for money. My legs were shaking with both pain and nervousness. Mantis sat down and draped his arm over my shoulder. I waited for a second, letting my legs stop their shaking and the guys get deeper into subjects that did not involve the loss of my virginity.

"I have to go," I told Mantis.

"I'll walk you out."

"Bye, nice meetin' you," The guys all told me one by one and I just wiggled my fingers their direction.

Once outside I looked at Mantis, who was still smiling.

"Angie, I don't want you to do that with anyone else."

"Why did you show them that sheet?"

"Because it's cool."

"It was private," I said.

"Angie, it's all right. I'm tryin' to ask you something."

"What?"

"Be my girlfriend. You know, going out together? Just you and me. Nobody else involved."

"Why?"

"Why what?" Mantis asked.

"Why do you want to be my boyfriend?"

"Because I like you. What, you think I'm just after your money?" Mantis asked this with such a deadpan I busted out laughing.

"Okay. You and me. But no more telling everyone else our business like that. Cool or not. Promise?"

"Promise," Mantis said and gave me a long kiss.

I walked home in pain and confusion and excitement. It looked like I finally had something of my own.

I did feel different. I had heard that was a lie. Heather said she didn't feel any different after she fucked Mike Patterson. Why would I feel different? I've been fucking myself for years.But I did feel different. Maybe it was the pain. I was so sore I was surprised I could walk home. Even my calves were sore. I must have been flexing them or something. I had a cute boyfriend.

I wondered if Mom and Rudy would be able to tell. To tell that something had changed. Of course they wouldn't. The two of them were absolutely oblivious to anything that remotely resembled reality.

I was glad to find an empty apartment and a note when I got home.

Angie,

We went to Tim and Kathy's. Home late.

There are burritos and waffles in the freezer.

    Love,

  MOM

PS. There's a bag of peanut butter cups to give out for Halloween. Have some if you want! xxxoo

The diet in itself probably constituted child abuse.

They say sex burns calories so I heated up a burrito. The fullness I felt from the pizza had worn off. I felt ravenous. Just as I got the burrito out of the microwave, the phone rang. It was Shelby.

"We have to talk."

"Okay," I said. Shelby sounded dire.

"Troy Mulligan is going around saying you sucked his dick while Carrie Shuren watched."

"What?"

"Yeah, it's all over school. Mindy backs it up. She says you're a total cockmonster, I quote. And that what gets you off is having other people watch."

"What about Carrie?"

"What about her?"

"What is she saying?"

"She says she doesn't know anything about it. That, like, why would she want to watch anyone suck Troy Mulligan's dick? But, of course, Mindy and Troy say she's just too embarrassed to admit it. Brandon broke up with her. Made a big deal out of it too."

"Shit."

"Oh, and check this out, Troy tells me that you said all I needed was a good dick to suck on."

"When did he say that? In art class?"

"No, him and Mindy followed me into the bathroom. Can you believe?"

"And that's all they said?"

"Well, Troy was acting all macho when he came in, but he got kinda nervous when Barbara Duchamp came out of one of the stalls."

"Did she hear him?"

"Yeah."

"What did she say?"

"Nothing. What's Barbara Duchamp gonna get herself involved with anybody's shit for? She's on her way to Harvard or whatever the fuck."

"Shelby, be real careful about those two following you into the bathroom, all right?"

"Why? Mulligan gonna make me suck his dick?"

"You don't know Shelby. You should be careful."

I hung up with Shelby and leaned my head into the wall. All I really wanted to do was tell her I had a boyfriend, that I wasn't a virgin anymore, that everything had changed. All I really wanted was to sit with

Shelby, listen to her records and eat junk food. Talk about Mantis and Colleen. All I really wanted was Shelby.

I couldn't keep myself out of high school forever, much less Shelby. It simply wasn't possible. I jumped a little when the phone rang, again.

"Hello?"

"You're a little cockmonster, aren't you?" Then the line went dead. It couldn't be long until everything blew completely the fuck up.

CHAPTER 21

Rudy's stuff was stacked all over. There were even two boxes stashed behind the bathroom door which kept it from opening all the way. I assumed most of the boxes were in their bedroom. I wasn't sure since it had been ritually sealed from me. Their bedroom door was always close whether they were in it or not. I did the same thing with my own bedroom. I wanted Rudy out of my space and he wanted me out of his. Rudy moving was my preferred solution, but I didn't mention it.

Mom was making a lunch for me when I found her in the kitchen.

"You know," she said. "With Rudy around, you could buy your lunch if you wanted. I have extra money now."

"Okay," I agreed, looking at the peanut butter sandwich I would only discard or possibly give to Pike.

Mom dug into her purse. "Here's two dollars. Is that enough?"

"Do you have another one?"

"Sure." She produced another bill.

"Thanks," I said, giving her made-up face a kiss.

Mom moved the peanut butter sandwich from the brown bag to Rudy's lunch box. This is what she's doing for me. This is what she thinks is best for me.

I left the house with the three dollars and nowhere to go. I searched the laundry rooms until I found Pike.

"You," Pike pointed at me. "Have to stop Inez from doing what she's doing."

"Wait. What are you talking about?"

"Tomorrow is Halloween. Inez is actually talking about making a cut if she can unload a few of the guns. AND every time she talks about it, the number of guns she swears are in the house gets bigger and everybody gets all excited about it and it's real fucked up."

"I thought you weren't going over there anymore."

"I had to find Inez. You have to talk to her, she won't listen to me."

"What the hell am I supposed to do?"

"I thought you were going to talk to her, anyway," Pike said.

"I haven't seen her." I threw my hands in the air.

"Yeah? Why would you just see her? You should have found her and talked to her."

"Are you mad at me?"

"Irritated. I'm irritated with you."

"I didn't know you wanted me to find her and talk to her."

"Isn't she your friend? I mean, aren't we?"

"Yes. Of course!"

"Well then get off your bullshit and help." Pike looked away.

"Okay. What should we do?"

"Inez is still at Luann's. They stayed up all night. You should go get her."

"Get her? I can't go to Luann's. You know that."

"Luann is at school. Besides no one ever said you couldn't go there. In fact, you HAVE to go there. Luann or no. Inez will listen to you."

She will listen to ME? "Okay. Let's go."

"Fourteen-twelve Lemay Ferry. You can't miss it. There are four old houses between the Venture and the Taco Bell. Hold outs. You know the sort."

"You not coming?"

"No. I've had enough of those drugged-out libertarian-nationalist-militia-hippie types."

"I don't even understand those words all strung together like that."

"I've taken a crash course."

I watched Pike smoke his joint for a second.

"I'm not, like, in with all those people. They don't know me. If they are as paranoid and high as you say, why would they even let me in?"

"You have a point. All right. We both go."

We left the laundry room just as the sky began to gray. The air was full of fine mist and it seemed like the perfect time to perform a rescue.

"It's going to rain," Pike said, looking up at the clouds.

"Oh, how can you tell? Your arthritis actin' up?"

"Shut up." Pike nudged my arm.

We didn't talk the rest of the way to Luann's. By the time we got there we were slick from head to toe with mist. Pike took a deep breath and knocked.

A gray-haired man opened the door with creepy caution. If I had been a cop I would have arrested him instantly.

"Oh, hey, Pike, my man. Come in."

"This is Angie." Pike motioned toward me.

The guy took my hand and kissed it, an act I had never before seen in person, much less have happen to me. "You sure got a lot of pretty girlfriend's for being such a skinny fuck." The guy slapped Pike on the back with a good thwack.

"Yeah, well, I'm a smooth talker," Pike said.

Pike and I followed the guy up a short set of stairs and into the living room. The shades were open, letting gray daylight fill up the floor while The Beatles sang "Happiness is a Warm Gun." Inez was sitting on the hearth of an extremely decayed fireplace holding a long spoon over its flame.

"Inez!" Pike said when he saw her. "What the hell are you doing?"

Inez swung her face in our direction and the reality of it hit me. She was a complete wreck. Her eyes were red and saggy but her pupils were inflamed and jetting around in their sockets at ninety miles an hour. Her skin was kind of translucent except under her eyes where it had folded over itself in black half-moons. There were freshly burned star patterns visible on her hands.

"Pike!" she said happily, without removing the spoon from its place over the fire. "Don't worry, it's not what you think."

A thin stream of laughter came from the couch, where Luann's mom was stretched out in a tie-dyed shirt that blended in perfectly with the tie-dyed couch cover.If she'd kept quiet, she could have remained camouflaged all day.

"We're just gonna smoke it with some weed, okay with you daddy?" Luann's mom smiled and her off-colored teeth showed. Above her was the poster insisting Love It Or Leave It!

"Yeah." The gray-haired man came back to the room with a few cold beers. "That okay with you?" He fell into the couch next to Luann's mom and put his skinny bare legs up on a coffee table cluttered with books and beer cans and ashtrays. It looked kind of like Mantis's place, only less safe.

Inez pulled the spoon out of the fire and examined its contents. "All done."

"Here." The man handed her a long cylinder I had recently learned was called a bong.

Pike looked over his shoulder at me. Fear. I was nauseous. The big black dog I'd heard Pike tell a story about came into the room and stuck its horrible wet nose straight into my asshole.

"Whoa!" I jumped.

"Jerry!" Luann's mom called. "Don't be fresh!"

"Dog gives the best rim jobs in town!" The guy laughed.

Rim Jobs?

"Inez," Pike said calmly. "Come hang out with us."

"Okay. Let's hang out here." Inez shrugged as she began carefully scraping the crusted bowl of the spoon into the bowl of the bong.

Pike opened his mouth like he was going to say something, but nothing came out and he shut it.

"Yeah," the guy said. "Not like it's a nice day out or anything. I brought yous two beers anyway." He pointed to the unopened cans on the table.

"No thanks," I said, staring at the silver can tops.

"Well," the guy said. "I think I'll help myself. It's a free country after all." He popped the top and lifted it toward me in a kind of toast. People, apparently, will toast anything. Bloodied sheets, drug addictions.

"Here." Inez offered the bong to Pike.

"No thanks."

Luann's mom let out that thin stream of smoky laughter again. "What? Are you kids, like, Mormons or something?" She and the guy laughed.

"Inez," I said. "I need to talk to you. Something has happened."

Pike looked over his shoulder at me with a steady gaze. A hopeful look. Prying Inez away from this mess was a delicate procedure. This much I had come to understand.

Inez stood and handed the bong to the gray haired man, "Don't smoke it all. I'll be right back."

Inez followed me down the short set of stairs, behind me I heard the guy say, "At least smoke a joint with us."

I stepped out onto the concrete porch that was slowly crumbling away from its foundation. Inez looked even more ghastly in the mist than she had in the smoky interior of the house.

"What happened to your eye?" She asked.

"It's a long story. Listen can you come with us?"

"Where are you going?"

"Let's just go hang out, you, me and Pike. This place is creepy."

"No. Let's stay here. It's fun. Rex is coming over in a little while. We got a bunch of speed and pot and beer."

"I don't do speed or pot. Let's go walk around."

"It's going to rain." Inez looked at the sky. "Wait," she said. Her eyes narrowed and her lips curled back. "Pike has been talking to you. Look, Angie, I don't need any fucking intervention, okay? I don't need anybody telling me what to do. Not you, not my dad, not Pike, not anyone, you understand?"

Inez had become Robyn.

"Yeah, I understand. I'm not telling you what to do. I just want to hang out."

"Save it, Angie. You can stand around in the rain all day actin' like everybody needs you if you want. It's a free country," Inez said, turning a sharp and abrupt shoulder to me. She grasped the old aluminum handle on the screen door and yanked it so hard it came right off in her hand.

"Troy Mulligan hit me!" I yelled into her shoulder blades.

"What?" She turned back as sharply and as quickly as she had turned away.

"My eye. That's what happened. He hit me. And that's not all," I said this with a rising lump in my throat. A flood of tears were on their way.

"He HIT you? He PUNCHED you in the eye?"

"Yes."

"I'll fucking kill him! Where does he live?"

"Inez." My tears were sure and thick down my already wet face. "I don't need you to kill him. I need you to hang out with me. To leave here and come with me and Pike. I haven't told anyone else what happened, okay?"

"Shelby?"

I could only shake my head and let the tears drip off my chin.

"Oh, God," Inez said. Reality surged across her fat pupils.

I stood in the mist that quickly turned to a light rain. Inez gave me a long look with those darting eyes. "I'm gonna get Pike and my bag, okay? I'll be right back." She looked at screen door handle. "Fuck it," she muttered and threw it in the dirt. Water puddled around it.

So that was it. She'd leave for me but not for herself. So that's how it was. That's how everything was. I'd come clean for Inez but not for myself.

After a few minutes Pike and Inez emerged from the house.

"Let's get the fuck out of here," Pike said, giving me a pleased nod.

Once we were out on the main road, Inez grabbed my hand. She held it tight in her own, her face still a disaster. I smiled at her a little while Pike pretended to be more interested in the Venture parking lot.

"So, tell me everything," Inez said.

"I will," I stammered and squeezed her hand. Inez squealed. I'd crushed one of her mounding blisters.

"I'm sorry!"

"It's okay," Inez said. She was searching Pike's profile.

"When did you do those?" I asked.

"I dunno." Inez shrugged.

"They look painful," I said, pulling Inez's hand up to study it. I wanted all conversation directed away from my eye. Away from the truth I had blurted to Inez.

"Yeah," she said, looking away from Pike, who would not look at her. "They heal up quick though. I like stars." Inez smiled.

"Are we going back to some laundry room?" Pike looked at me.

"What laundry room?" Inez asked Pike, who looked away before their eyes could meet.

"No laundry rooms!" I said. "We'll go back to my house. Pike! Damnit! Stop! Okay? We'll go back to my house and we'll talk and watch TV and stuff. And we're all gonna act like friends."

Pike was still staring away as we crossed in front in the liquor store and the karate shop everyone was always breaking into.

"Pike!" I insisted.

"Okay, right," he said, looking back at us. "TV and talk and all that."

"Is that sarcasm?" Inez asked with huge tear drops situated against her bottom eye lids.

"No," Pike took up Inez's other hand. "Everything I say just sounds like that."

Inez smiled and I winced and the rain started to come down on us harder.

"Hurry," I said, sprinting toward the apartment.

Inside, Inez bustled. She looked everything over. The pictures on the wall, the brown dining room table, the big TV.

"Wow, that thing is fucking huge," she said.

"Yeah, you want to put something on? The remote is on top."

I raised my eyebrows at Pike and motioned toward Inez, trying to indicate that he should speak to her. But he just shook his head and shrugged.

Inez turned from the TV. "What the hell happened, Angie? With Mulligan?"

"It's a long story." I turned into the kitchen and grabbed three Cokes out of the refrigerator.

"So, tell it," Inez said. "Tell us what happened to your eye."

"Yeah." Pike chimed in behind her. "I've been dying to hear the real story."

"So you didn't believe my car door version?" I asked Pike, handing him his Coke.

"No one believed that story, Angie."

"Oh."

I settled myself on the couch next to Pike and began at the beginning. I told them about fucking with Mindy. I told them about the note Troy threw at me. I told them about Troy and Mindy following me into the bathroom. I told them about hitting my head on the pipes. I told them about Troy's stupid dick and Mindy sitting on the floor while Troy called her a dumbass. I told them about Carrie. I told them everything I could remember. The event had already become cloudy in my mind.

Pike listened carefully to all of this while Inez paced back and forth picking up random objects and setting them back down.

"Why didn't you tell anyone?" Pike asked. I just shrugged.

"Why didn't you go to Principal Linden?" Inez asked.

"Why would I?" What the hell would Linden do about it? What the hell could anyone do about it? It was a thing that happened and no amount of telling could undo it.

"Well, something has to be done about it," Pike said. "You can't go back to school and they're threatening Shelby, too. You should have told on her, Angie. She could be in a lot of trouble."

That's when I broke all the way apart. I sobbed like there wouldn't be another day after the one I was in. Inez stopped pacing and held onto me. I cried into her denim jacket.

"Shelby's been back at school for three days! I don't know what to do. If something happens to her, it's gonna be all my fault!"

"We have to get Shelby out of school," Inez finally said.

"How?" Pike asked.

Inez thought for a moment. "Robyn."

And that was it. There would be no more cover for me.

CHAPTER 22

"Anything else I should know?" Robyn asked.

"No. That's everything," I said.

"You kept this to yourself knowing that something bad could happen to my sister!"

"Let's just focus on the task at hand," Pike said.

Robyn turned to Pike, her fists going automatically into her hips. "You could have done something about it yourself, Dickass! Fuckin' pussy."

"I just found out!"

Pike and Robyn stared at each other intently as Inez let out a huge, pained scream. We all turned and looked at her. She crumpled onto the floor and slid under the table.

"What the fuck!" Robyn threw her arms up over her crazy hair.

"She's all high."

"What?" Robyn stomped toward the table and stuck her head underneath it. "Look at me," she demanded of Inez.

"No!" Inez hid her face under her arms and scooted herself further under the table.

"What the fuck is up with your hands? They're all raw and burned! Did you do that to yourself?"

"She likes stars," I offered.

"She WHAT?" Robyn stood and looked at me like I was fucking crazy.

"Don't freak her out, Robyn, okay?" I appealed.

"All right, all right." Robyn stood up straight. "I'm going to change my clothes and think of something to tell that fucked up school. Then I'm going to go get my sister. You two find out what she's high on. Got it?" Robyn asked. Without waiting for any affirmation from us, she disappeared down the basement stairs.

"Inez." I knelt down and calmed myself. "You can't stay under the table all day."

"No more yelling," she said.

"No more yelling." I nodded.

I managed to get Inez propped up on one of the chairs. Pike sat down next to her but he wouldn't look at her.

"I'm sorry, okay?" Inez said into her sleeve.

"Let's just get through the day, Inez," Pike said.

I tried to melt into the wall. Relief had come over me. A relief that made me very, very tired. I was glad, somehow, that Robyn was in charge of everything. Shelby would never speak to me again but that was beside the point at the moment.

Robyn returned to the kitchen in her tight blue jeans and a pink sweater that fit so snug over her tits they looked like big pieces of round bubble gum.

"There's some hydrogen peroxide in the bathroom, clean up her hands." Robyn pointed at Pike. "Those burns are already getting infected."

Robyn thumbed through some things in her purse while I watched from my place along the wall.

Robyn glanced over her shoulder. "What's that one all messed up on?"

"Crystal meth," I said.

Robyn sighed. She took her little address book out and looked up a number.

"What should we do?" I asked.

"About which thing, Angie?" Robyn was so completely annoyed.

"About her?" I motioned to Inez.

Robyn stuck the phone against her shoulder and her chin and returned her hands to her big purse. She pulled out a prescription bottle and tossed it my way. I actually caught it. I turned the bottle over in my hand. Valium.

Robyn talked to Mrs. Beckham for a minute. Something about a sick aunt and how Robyn would be there in a few minutes to pick Shelby up. Robyn sounded annoyed with Mrs. Beckham too.

Robyn hung up the phone and threw her purse over her arm.

"Give her a couple of those. I'll be right back and none of you are going anywhere. You just stay put."

By then Pike was gently cleaning the burns on Inez's hands.

"Ouch," she said miserably.

"This can't hurt more than burning yourself," Pike said.

We waited around the table in silence. When Robyn finally pulled up to the house with Shelby, my stomach dropped out and my hands shook. Inez was calmed from her crying and watching Pike, who was arranging pieces of stray cat food into shapes.

Shelby gave me a long sad look as her coat dropped to the floor.

"Angie," she said softly. "Why didn't you just tell me?"

I shrugged and looked away from her. Shelby took two careful strides toward me and pulled me into her arms.

"I'm sorry. I'm so sorry," I whispered into her neck.

"It's okay. I mean, I'm not hurt or anything. Why didn't you go to Principal Linden? Why didn't you . . ."

"I didn't want anyone to know. I just didn't want anyone else knowing about what happened."

"Okay," Shelby said, and rocked me back and forth.

Robyn threw her keys on the counter. "That was fucking stupid, Angie. Now we have to figure out what to do."

"Go to the school. Get them expelled," Pike said.

"Not enough," Robyn said.

"They have lots of friends at school. It wouldn't end if they were kicked out," Shelby said.

"The fucking school let this happen in the first place. You guys got to hunt them down somewhere else," Robyn said.

"Robyn, what are you saying?" Shelby asked.

I held my breath.

"I don't know just yet. All I know is, nobody is gonna stick his dick in my mouth. So we find them. We make them pay."

Pay. That's what Mindy said about me. This was all pay back.

"Guns," Inez said.

"No guns!" Robyn said.

"I mean them. They're getting guns."

"How do you know that?" Robyn asked.

"They hang out over at Luann's sometimes. Mulligan and his friends. I just saw them last night. They are, like, all top-shelf and shit, but they like to get high too."

"I'm confused." Robyn rolled her eyes and took a seat at the table.

"Party jocks," Pike said.

"Okay, so what's with the guns?"

Pike and I exchanged a look. I held my breath waiting to see what Inez would say.

"They are going to steal some guns and sell them. But they might keep some for themselves too, if there's enough. That's what they were talking about last night."

"This is out of control." Robyn bent her head forward.

"What do they want guns for?" Shelby asked.

"I dunno. Just to have them, I guess," Inez said.

"You feel okay?" I asked Inez.

"Yeah," Inez nodded.

"Well, don't get too comfortable. That shit comes back on you. Gives you another ride. I don't know why," Robyn said.

Robyn looked weary. She lit a cigarette and smoked silently while we all watched. Watched and waited for her to fix everything.

"When are they planning to do this?"

"Halloween party," Inez said picking at one of her blisters.

"What Halloween party?" Robyn asked, crushing her cigarette out in the little amber colored ashtray on the table.

"At Luann's. They do it every year. At least that's what they were telling me. Big blow-out. They spend months making shit for it. Costumes and weird shit for the yard. You know, like a haunted house thing."

"Yeah, so? I ain't lookin' for a good party." Robyn shrugged.

"Well . . ." Inez looked up at Robyn.

Pike looked at me. Shelby looked between me and Pike with her head tilted a little. She knew we knew something she didn't.

"Well, what?" Robyn demanded.

"They are the ones buying the guns," Inez said.

"Who are? Who are the ones buying the guns?" Robyn demanded.

"Luann's parents," Inez said and started to cry again.

"What are you crying about?" Robyn asked, her frustration level rising again.

"They're her friends," Pike said, putting his hand up between Robyn and Inez.

"Some friends," Robyn said. "Get you this fucked up on speed and all messed up with stolen guns and shit. That's great. Sounds like some real good people to know."

"Like you should talk," Shelby said with a smirk.

"Shelby, ram it up your ass already, okay?"

"I'm just pointing out the obvious, Robyn," Shelby said.

Pike put his arm around Inez.

"Do you know where they are planning on stealing these guns from?" Robyn asked Inez.

I held my breath.

Pike froze.

"Randy," Inez said quietly.

"Randy? Randy who?"

"Your friend."

And that was it. The official Robyn Moment. Three seconds, no breathing.

She blew.

The amber colored ashtray went flying across the room. Robyn kicked over the chair as she stood.

"That's great! That's just fucking amazing! Those little worthless pieces of shit are planning on stealing from Randy?" Robyn's went across the room to the cabinets. The cat screeched and darted when she came in its direction. Robyn opened and slammed the same cabinet a few times, then took a bottle of Jim Beam out and poured herself a nice glass of it. She broke ice cubes and slammed the trays against the wall behind the sink. The rest of us froze exactly where we had been except for Inez. She slid back under the table.

"How the fuck do these kids know Randy has guns?" Robyn asked, taking a long drink.

"Luann's mom was at Heather's party that night remember? Her mom even said something about Randy having illegal weapons." Pike covered for Inez who was apparently incapable of not telling the truth.

Robyn calmed again. "That's who we're talking about here? Those bossy fucking hippies?"

Pike and I both nodded.

"Oh, well shit," Robyn laughed then. "I thought we were talking about the mob or some bike gang."

Robyn relaxed against the sink and sipped at her whiskey, delivered, once again, from rage island.

"So what's their plan?" Robyn asked the space Inez had previously occupied. "Where'd she go?"

"She's under the table again," I said. "She doesn't like yelling."

"Oh, okay, she likes stars, she doesn't like yelling. Anything else I should know about her preferences?"

"Just stop yelling, Robyn," Shelby suggested.

"Well, they're not gonna get too far with those guns. They're all legal. Randy doesn't believe in illegal weapons."

"They think just the opposite," Inez said from under the table.

"Halloween is tomorrow," Robyn said. "Okay, I'll call Randy when he gets off work. You guys stick around. You're gonna have to tell him the story. I'm gonna go get some shit done and have a couple of beers somewhere."

We all watched Robyn's car pull out of the driveway.

"What about Rex?" Pike finally asked.

"What about him?" Shelby asked, sticking her arm in a box of vanilla wafers.

"He's going along with this. He's gonna borrow his brother's van and drill the lock and everything."

"What? Since when is Rex friends with Troy and Curtis?" Shelby asked.

"Rex wants to make some money. That's all." Pike shrugged.

I watched everyone's mouths very closely as they spoke. Persia came back into the room and none of it was real. How could I be so nervous and so calm at the same time?

"They're going to get him in trouble," Inez said.

"Yeah, he's definitely gonna get in trouble with them. Hell, Randy is gonna beat the shit of him. That's trouble," Pike said.

"He has to back out," Shelby said. "You have to call him and tell him to back out."

"With the cops, I mean." Inez shot us a hard look.

"Cops?" Pike asked.

"Yeah. If they get caught or whatever they're going to say it was all Rex. You know, that he drove and drilled the lock and stole the guns. I heard them talking about it."

"When were you going to mention this, Inez?" Pike was pissed again.

"I just did!"

Pike jumped at the phone and dialed it. No Rex. Haven't seen him.

"I wonder if Heather knows he's in this," Shelby said.

"I'll try him at Heather's." Pike grabbed the phone again.

"We can't let Robyn find out Rex had any part of this," Shelby said.

Heather and Rex showed up about an hour later. Heather carried a big green duffel bag and Rex had a bright red one.

"Are you guys going somewhere?" Shelby asked.

"I'm fucking sick of my mom and her boyfriend and my dad. Why don't they just get fucking tit surgery on themselves?" Heather said.

"Where are you going?" I asked. Heather and Rex couldn't leave right then!

"I'm gonna stay with Rex and Evan for awhile. Forever, maybe." Heather dropped the bag she was carrying.

"So Troy and Curtis are already plannin' to give me up?" Rex asked Pike.

"Inez heard them, not me," Pike said.

Inez looked miserable. "If you guys get caught. They're gonna to say it was all you."

"Fuckers," Rex mumbled.

"I told you to stay out of this." Heather pointed at Rex.

"The thing is, Robyn knows now. She's gonna call Randy," Shelby said.

"Who's Randy?"

"The guy's house you're going to rob!" Shelby said.

"How should I know his name? I'm rippin' him off, not askin' him on a date."

"He's friends with your brother!" Shelby told him.

"Who? Randy Tucker? Oh, shit." Rex swung his head from side to side.

"You have to get out of it," I told Rex.

"So what should it be? A sick grandma? A job interview? How am I supposed to back out?"

"I dunno," I said.

"Tell them the van is broke down," Pike said.

"Hell, it might even be. Evan's van is broke down at least as much as it's runnin'." Rex said.

Rex got a hold of Curtis and told him the van was broke down. Curtis told him not to worry, they'd pick him up in the Mustang.

"Now, what should I do?" Rex asked.

"Just don't show at the pick up spot." Heather shrugged.

"No. They know where I live. If Evan finds out about this he'll be so pissed! Rippin' off one of his friends? Shit, I don't even want to think about it."

"We'll figure something out," Shelby said.

"I'm gonna make sure there isn't no ammo in the house. That way nothing's loaded." Randy propped against the sink.

Vince and Mark and Randy were all standing around the kitchen, drinking beer and being pissed.

"You better make damn sure there isn't a single bullet anywhere," Mark said to Randy.

"Don't worry. I know exactly where all my shit is."

"Grab some more beers out of the fridge, Angie," Robyn told me.

I passed cold Busch beers around and took one for myself. Rex took two, shoving one in his pocket. He was nervous.

"You gonna let them rip you off?" I asked.

"I'm gonna let them think they're ripping me off." Randy nodded and popped his fresh beer. "Don't want them breaking any of my windows though."

"Just leave a couple open," Vince said.

"With the screens out and everything? Don't you think that will look suspicious?" Randy asked.

Vince dipped his head and didn't say anything.

Robyn cleared her throat, "Just remember, I need to talk to the Troy kid. You let me have him."

"Sure, we grab 'em, you stab 'em!"

"Nobody gets stabbed!" Mark said.

"I just want to talk to him is all," Robyn said.

"And I just wanna see her talk to him," Randy smiled at Mark.

"You're a cold motherfucker, Randy." Mark winced.

I opened a can of beer for myself. If I could just get my stomach to relax I would be fine. I looked at Rex and shrugged. Somebody needed to think of something, quick.

"You know," Rex finally stood from his listening position in the hall. "Those two asked me about drilling a lock for this deal. I told them no, but I could . . ."

"Wait, you knew about this?" Randy asked.

"I didn't know it was your house or anything. I never asked them that because I didn't want to do it anyway." Rex shook his head.

"We can't let them drill my lock! You know how much that costs? Shit. We're gonna have to grab them before they go in," Randy said.

"No. You can't do that. They got to have your stuff on them, be in the house, you know? That's the law," Mark said.

"The cops aren't gonna be there anyway," Randy said.

"Look, you gotta do it the right way. You gotta be in the right. Cops or no cops, you gotta follow the law and be in the right, you see what I'm saying?" Mark leaned toward Randy.

"Yeah, I see what you're sayin'."

"You're just cheap, man. Don't want to spend that dollar." Mark laughed.

Rex stepped all the way into the kitchen, "What I'm saying is, I could call them and tell them I'm in. That I wanna go along. You could leave the door open. I'm the one who's supposed to take care of the lock anyway."

"That's a good idea. Be good to have someone inside, anyway. Keep an eye on things. That way we don't got to worry about them having guns or something already. A baseball bat, anything. You know? Cuts out a lot of fucking worry on our end," Randy said.

"Call 'em up," Mark said to Rex.

"I'll have to go find them at this other place. I'll call back here in an hour." Rex grabbed his jacket and left. Smooth as could be, Rex became a double agent. And it was the sexiest thing I'd ever seen.

CHAPTER 23

In the morning, Rudy swung my bedroom door open. "Manless is on the phone for you."

I was standing in just a t-shirt and panties. "Knock next time," I said as the door shut behind him.

I pulled on my shorts with the elastic waistband. They were loose. Really loose.

"Mom!" I called once I was in the hall. "Tell him to knock before he just comes in my room! He can at least act fucking civilized, can't he?"

"Angie, don't say fucking. I mean it," Mom said from the living room couch. She was curled up under her pink afghan, smoking. Her face was done and she was wearing her little robe.

"Okay, but tell him he has to knock!"

"Rudy, you DO need to knock before you go in Angie's room." She spoke to the figure standing behind me.

"My parents never had to knock on any doors in their own house," Rudy said.

"She could be dressing or something, Rudy." Mom said.

"Yeah, it's the or something that bothers me."

"This is hopeless." I threw my arms up in defeat and went for the phone. "Hello?"

"Hey. Everything all right?" Mantis asked.

"No. My mom's boyfriend doesn't know how to knock, he just walks in on me whenever he likes!"

"God, that's gross. How about you get out of the house and meet me?"

"Sure. Where?"

Rudy's voice came booming again, "Oh, hell no! You ain't goin' anywhere with old Manless until we meet him. Tell him to come over here."

"What?" I asked without shifting the phone from my mouth.

My mother stood then, letting the afghan fall to the floor at her feet. "That's not a bad idea. He could come by here. I'd like to meet him too."

"Hey, Mantis? I can't go anywhere with you until you come over and meet my mother and her boyfriend."

"Fiancée," Rudy yelled.

"Fiancée," I said into the phone.

"Oh. That sounds like fun," Mantis said.

"Doesn't it though?"

"Well, I could do that. I mean, it has to happen sooner or later."

I told Mantis where I lived and he said he'd be over in about an hour.

"You happy?" I asked Rudy.

"It ain't like meetin' this friend of yours is all I got to do today," Rudy shrugged and took a sip off his coffee.

"I know, Rudy. It's work, work, work for you. You a workin' man. I get it. You don't have to remind everyone every fifteen minutes," I said and walked straight past him to my room. I closed the door behind me but I still heard Rudy ask, "She on her rag or somethin'?"

I turned on my stereo, found some clean clothes. Black stretch pants and black cardigan sweater. Loose. All loose on me. I was losing more weight. I wanted to pull out the scale and weigh in. I hadn't done it in awhile. But who knew when Rudy would bolt in. My bedroom door was hollow, like every other door in the apartment. I couldn't even put a chain lock on it. It would tear right off.

I was brushing my hair, when Mom tapped on the door.

"Come in," I called.

She had changed from her robe into a pair of stretch denim pants that clung to every curve she had, and an equally tight long sleeve black t-shirt with an airbrush design of a wolf on it. She loved that shirt. I thought it was tacky.

"Rudy will knock from now on," she said, shutting the door behind her.

"What the hell is the matter with him?"

"I dunno. No manners, I guess. He'll learn. We all have to learn to live with one another. It's an adjustment," she said, taking a seat on the corner of my unmade bed.

"Mom, let me use some of your concealer. I just want to cover up what's left of this bruise around my eye."

"You can hardly see it anymore."

"Look, though, it's still kind of yellow and even a little green," I said, leaning in so she could examine the lingering injury on my face.

"Yeah, it is. So, this boy, this Mantis, he really is your boyfriend, isn't he?"

"As of the other day, yeah."

"Well, I'm not surprised. You've really lost a lot of weight recently. I knew it would come off, eventually. Now everyone can see that pretty face of yours."

"Which I don't want ruined by this thing on my eye," I told her.

"Well, you are sixteen. I guess, it's okay. Wait here," Mom said and left the room. When she returned she was carrying several little tubes and a compact. She shut the door again. We sat on my bed and Mom put make up on my face. God, I thought, none of this would have happened if she'd just let me wear make up to begin with.

She dotted concealer under both eyes and worked it gently into the bruise, then she handed me the compact and I put powder over everything. She also brought black mascara and a plum colored lip gloss. It was sheer and shiny.

"You don't need eyeliner. You're lucky. If I don't wear eyeliner you can't tell where my eyes are."

I had never noticed this problem, but it had been awhile since I'd seen her without make up. Maybe she was starting to morph now that she was engaged.

"Didn't Rudy even get you a ring?"

"We are going to do wedding bands, skip that whole two ring business. We can't really afford it. Besides, it's kind of silly, isn't it?"

"I dunno." The whole thing was pretty silly as far as I was concerned.

"Did you talk to Heather again? She adjusting to the idea of getting her breast fixed?"

"Why does everyone say "fixed?" It's not like anything is broken. It's purely cosmetic, as they say."

"Yeah, I guess fixed is the wrong word. I don't know how to put it, really."

"Maybe Heather likes having only one tit, I mean, breast."

Mom seemed unconvinced. A huge knock came at the door and we both jumped. Then it came again, and again, like the door was going to break open.

"I'm knocking! See? This is me knocking!" Rudy banged the door some more.

"Come in," Mom said and rolled her eyes.

"How was that?" Rudy asked. "Better?"

"What is it, Rudy?"

"Am I interrupting?"

"Kind of," Mom said.

"Well, some lady is on the phone for you, Angie," Rudy said. He walked away from the open door.

It was Heather's mom.

"Angie, do you know where Heather is?"

"No."

"Angie, yes you do. You need to tell me."

"I really don't know," I said.

"Let me talk to Rita." Evelyn was angry.

I handed the phone to my mom and looked over at Rudy who was looking at me.

"That make up looks nice," he said. "Kind of a lot of trouble, though. I mean for someone who ain't your boyfriend."

"You're a broken record, you know that Rudy?"

"Ain't the first time I heard that one." He laughed and returned to his newspaper.

I hung around in the dining room listening to Mom's side of the conversation.

"Well, Evelyn, I'm sure we can find her. Angie can do some calling around."

I shook my head at her.

Mom hung up the phone and looked at me. "Angie, DO you know where she is?"

"No," I told her.

"Well, you know where she might be, right?"

I shrugged.

"Well, you should tell her to call her mother. Okay? I know you can find her, Angie."

"She could be anywhere." I said.

"Just give her the message, okay?"

"Okay."

Mantis showed up in an almost clean black sweat shirt. He left behind his leather jacket and combat boots. Instead he was wearing a pair of Adidas tennis shoes and a tan coat. Shit, he even combed his hair. But he still looked like a degenerate.

"This is for you." He handed a box of Russell Stover caramel candies to my mother. They were her favorite, though Mantis could not have known. Still, she was charmed.

"Hey," Rudy said and stuck his hand out. "You certainly have a way with the ladies, but I ain't so easy."

"I wouldn't expect so." Mantis shook his hand firmly.

Rudy smiled.

"Hi." Mantis wiggled his fingers at me.

"Hi," I said.

"So, what's with the name? Where you get a name like that?" Rudy asked.

"Oh, when I was a kid, I had a couple of exoskeletons of preying mantises. I used to read about them a lot too. Did a report for school and all that. My brothers started calling me Mantis and it just stuck, I guess."

"Just stuck, huh? What name did your daddy give you?"

"Edward. Used to call me Eddie."

My mother smiled and offered him a Coke. I made myself a glass of ice water. No more regular Cokes for me. I liked the feeling that I needed to pull my stretch pants up.

We all sat at the table. It was stupid but not, somehow, especially uncomfortable.

"You go to school?" my mother asked.

"No, ma'am, not anymore. I work full-time."

"Oh, yeah?" This pleased Rudy, both the ma'am and the work.

"Yeah, I wash cars right now. But I'm going to start delivering pizzas soon. Me and my brother want to open a pizza franchise in a couple of years."

"Really? Which one?" Rudy asked.

"Cecil Whitaker's," Mantis said with a nod.

"Well, I hear that business is pretty good. The pizza business, I mean," Rudy said and offered his pack of cigarettes up to Mantis.

"No, I don't smoke," Mantis lied.

"Suit yourself," Rudy said and lit one for himself.

The conversation died off. Both Mom and Rudy seemed fairly satisfied with Mantis and his demeanor. Which might have changed had I offered up the blue-balls and the bloody sheet and all that. Everything is a matter of presentation.

"So, we're going to go play some pinball, if that's okay with you?" I said getting to my feet.

"Sure, go have fun," Rudy said and went to the kitchen for his first beer of the day.

Once Mantis and I were on the first floor landing of the apartment building, I started snickering.

"You look like a dork!" I said.

"Do I?" Mantis made a funny face with his tongue sticking out.

"Yeah, nice work with the hair." I reached up and grabbed his head, scratching my fingers through his hair. Mantis gathered me up around my waist and kissed me.

"I missed you," he said into my neck. I wanted to believe in the Mantis that was kissing me at the moment. I wanted to believe in the Mantis who brought my mother chocolates and called her ma'am. I wanted to believe, so I did. Kind of. I believed it for the moment.

"C'mon, let's go," I said.

"You don't really want to play pinball, do you?" he asked.

"Why? What do you want to do?"

Mantis smiled a sinister little grin and kissed me again.

"That can't be ALL we do, Mantis," I said trying to give that little hip swish my mother did with such perfection. It felt awkward, but it seemed to have the desired effect.

"All right, what about pool?"

"I don't know how to play pool."

"I can teach you. My brother has been teaching me. That way, at least I can watch you bend over that table."

"I didn't hear that!" my mother appeared at the base of the stairs in her red coat with the black fuzzy trim she had saved up for a couple of winters ago.

Mantis blushed and shoved me back like I was a disease. Mom laughed and pointed and ruffled his hair as she walked by.

"You two should go now. This is no place for necking!"

She pushed open the door to the outside and held it for us.

"Have fun!" she chided and pinched my arm as I walked by.

"Yes, ma'am." Mantis smiled.

"Rita. The name is Rita," she said, and made a bee-line for her Chevette.

"I'm gonna get my own pool cue," Mantis said. He chose two from a rack on the back wall. "This is how you check 'em," he said, rolling one after the other across the table.

"Mantis, listen, there's some crazy shit going on. I need to tell you about it."

"This thing about Rex and the guns and all that?"

"Yeah."

"I heard. This is how you rack up the balls," he said, showing me a plastic triangle.

"What did you hear?"

"Well, I saw Rex last night. He said the whole thing fell through. The guy found out about the plan or something?"

"Is that all you heard?"

"When you put the balls in here, put a stripe between two solids and a solid between two stripes, like this."

"Is that all you heard, Mantis?"

"Yeah, mostly, that's all I heard."

"What's mostly?"

"Well, I heard there is some kind of revenge thing going on. Something against those jock fucks . . ."

"You know them?"

"Shit, everybody knows them. Those assholes are always trying to buy some drugs or fuck somebody's girlfriend or some shit. That one son of a bitch raped this girl last year. Tombs went ape shit, but the guy said if anyone tried to call the police or anything he'd turn everybody in for dealin' drugs. Not like he wasn't buyin' 'em or anything. Shit, his main dealer was the girl he raped. Took her stash too, fuckin' asswipe."

"Who? What guy?"

"Curtis, somebody. Curtis Allen or somethin'."

"Alroy? Curtis Alroy?"

"That's it. Yeah, you probably know him. He goes to Mehlville."

I sucked in a breath. I had to tell Mantis the whole story. He was going to find out anyway.

Mantis held up a white ball, "This is a cue ball, you never sink this. It always stays on the table."

"Mantis, there's more. You have to listen to the whole thing."

"I'm listening," he said, placing the cue ball on a white dot on the table.

"No, I mean, you have to really listen to me." I stepped up to the table and blocked the ball with my hand.

Mantis looked up. "All right."

We sat at a messy table and I told him. One quick steady stream of words.

"That's what happened to your eye?"

"Yes, that's the truth."

"We'll get some people together, we'll take care of him."

"I don't want to play pool," I told him.

"I'm gonna have that son of a bitch killed!" Mantis pointed his finger at me.

"Don't be so angry."

"Oh, what am I supposed to do, nothing? Just sit here and act like everything is fine? Some motherfucker shoves his cock in your mouth and I'm just supposed to be calm? Happy about it even? Is that it Angie?"

"Keep your voice down and don't yell at me!"

"It's not you I'm mad at, okay?"

"Well, it sounds that way."

Mantis punched the table top and empty glasses went clanking into the napkin holder. People turned to look at us.

"Mantis! Stop!"

"I'll kill him. I'll kill him for you."

"For me? You punching things doesn't do shit for me except make me sorry I told you at all!"

"It just hurts that someone did that to you."

"Then say that. Pay attention to me, not him, damnit."

CHAPTER 24

Mantis said he'd walk part of the way to Carrie's with me. I needed to talk to her alone for a minute. She owed me.

Mantis was fuming, hands shoved deep in his coat pockets. I guessed he didn't know what to say. If Shelby had been with me she would have made up something about the origin of Lawn Deer, or the proper name for having applesauce licked out of your pussy.

"I can just go from here.I need to think, anyway." Not that I couldn't have been doing plenty of thinking in our silence.

"It's okay. I don't want to leave you alone."

It was sweet. Sort of. But I was alone. Completely exposed with no one to talk to.

"Did you know Lawn Deer are the only animals indigenous to the suburban landscape?" I asked.

"What?" Mantis looked irritated.

"Never mind. I think Pike is over at Rex's. I know Heather is. I'll just meet you there later, okay?"

"Okay," Mantis gave me a long hug and a kiss.

I knocked on Carrie's door. My pulse thumped in my wrists. The door opened and a man looked at me.

"What can I do for you?"

"Is Carrie home?"

"Yes."

"Can I talk to her?"

"Have we met?" the man asked.

"No, sir. I know Carrie from school."

"Well, I'm Mr. Shuren, and you are?"

"Angie. Angie Neuweather. It's nice to meet you."

"Well, just a moment, then," he said and closed the door tightly.

It took a long time, but Carrie finally emerged onto the front porch.

"Hi, Angie." She seemed genuinely pleased to see me.

"Hi," I said and we awkwardly looked at one another.

I followed Carrie over to the side yard where Shelby and I had watched Brandon paw at her and beg for sex.

"Look at you," Carrie said. "You are getting so thin! God, I've just been gaining."

"I can't tell."

"Don't lie. I look like a pig. But you look great."

"Thanks. Listen, I heard about what they're saying. At school."

"Oh, about me being a pervert and everything?"

"Yeah. That."

"I'll probably have to change schools." Carrie was serious.

"I'm sure no one believes any of that stuff."

"They don't pick me up for school anymore. I have to take the bus."

"Oh."

She was silent for a moment.

"And Brandon. He broke up with me. Which is fine, I totally don't care about that. But he's acting like he's all morally outraged and disgusted and stuff."

"What about Mindy?"

"Oh, she backs up Troy's story. Says she's gonna make you pay when she sees you."

"I have to get her back," I said.

"Yeah. You have to get me back, too. Don't you?" Carrie's eyes fixed on mine.

"Maybe," I said.

"I shouldn't have let that happen to you."

"No. You shouldn't have."

"I don't feel good about it, Angie."

"I don't feel too good about it either, Carrie."

"I didn't ask you to forgive me."

"There's a party at Luann Bartel's place tonight. Can you get Mindy there?"

"Mindy wouldn't be caught dead there and besides, we're not friends anymore, remember?"

"What if you told her Troy was fucking Luann?"

"Troy is fucking Luann?"

"I dunno. But what would happen if you told Mindy that?"

"She'd bust an artery."

"You could act like you're trying to get in good with her again."

"That would work. She thinks everyone wants her."

"Can you bring her to the party?"

"Well, I already have my mom's car tonight. If she agrees, maybe I could pick her up. I don't know though, she might ask Sarah to go. What are you going to do?"

"Make her suffer."

"I wish I had a cigarette." Carrie dug her bare toe into the grass and studied it for a second. "I'll try. What time?"

"Ten or so. You know where the place is?"

"Sure. Brandon used to buy weed there all the time. I always thought he was fucking that girl. Not that it matters."

Robyn was leaning over the kitchen table studying the faces in a Mehlville yearbook.

"This guy?" Robyn asked as soon as I sat down.

"Yeah, that's Troy."

"Oh, this is gonna be fun." Robyn smiled. Revenge suited Robyn the way round suits a wheel.

"This is Mindy," I turned a couple of pages and pushed the book back toward Robyn.

"Looka' that bitch. I can tell just looking at her," Robyn said. She picked up an ink pen and drew a beard and mustache on Mindy's dumbass face.

I headed off to Shelby's room. I found her and Colleen curled up together on top of Shelby's neatly made bed.

"What's up?" I asked.

"Man, you have a serious knocking problem." Colleen gave me a half-smile.

I jumped back out the door, closed it and knocked.

"Who is it?" Colleen sang and I could hear Shelby giggling. God, she was happy.

"It's me!" I said, swinging the door open and giving them the stupidest grin I could.

"Asshole," Shelby laughed.

"Carrie is going to get Mindy over there tonight," I reported.

"Are you sure you can trust Carrie Shuren?" Shelby asked, sitting up.

"Yeah. Well, no. But she wants to see something bad happen to Mindy."

Colleen rubbed Shelby's back gently. I liked Colleen. I liked her more and more all the time, but I still wanted her to go away. I needed to know if Shelby bled. And if she did, how much? I wanted to know if Colleen made her come and if she did was it better than making yourself come? Did Colleen show everyone a bloody sheet? And what about the toast? I didn't imagine Shelby's lost virginity had been toasted by a group of drunken party dudes. Man, she just didn't know what she was missing.

"Has Heather called here?" I asked Shelby.

"No. But her mom certainly has, like, five times. Robyn told her to go shit up a pole the last time she called. So maybe she'll drop it."

"She still at Rex's place?" I asked.

"Guess so."

"Mantis should be there too."

"Oh, I see," Shelby tilted her head. "He your boyfriend now?"

"Actually, yes, he is."

"What?" Shelby sat bolt upright. "You didn't tell me!"

"There hasn't been time. We'll talk about it later," I said, giving a quick look over to Colleen.

"Oh. Well, I'll just see you tonight then," Shelby said and gave me a pouty little face. Where the fuck did she learn that?

It was cold outside. Cold enough for a coat, but the sun was shinning. Everything was orange and blue and crisp. I knew where Rex lived but I had never been inside. Actually, I'd never been to his house, period. I just knew where it was, Rex being a staple of my sex life and all. My imaginary sex life. The way I figured it, I would live my whole life, long and to the fullest and all that and still want to fuck Rex.

By the time I got to his house, I'd had, like, six fantasies about fucking him. Well, one about kissing him, one about him kissing my tits and one about him fucking Carrie. God, I hoped like hell she wouldn't let me down. I hoped with every part of me Carrie wouldn't let me down.

CHAPTER 25

Rex's house was a couple hundred feet off the busy Lemay Ferry, just like Luann's house. Far enough back to nearly eclipse the world beyond its perimeter. I crunched down his driveway, under the shade of the trees.

Heather sat at the kitchen table, where a pile of neatly rolled joints were stacked next to a pile of weed on a plate. Pike was right, Rex's place was basically a shack. The kitchen floor was a piece of stained plywood. The table was covered with crumbs and dishes and papers. There was a mound of melting butter stuck to the counter.

"You are not going to believe it." Heather swung her beer can my direction. Her eyes were almost bright red and the lids were sagging halfway down.

"Believe what?"

"I talked to my mom today. And she said if I get the surgery, she and my dad will get me a car!"

"They're bribing you?"

"Yeah. Good bribe, though. We could do anything we wanted. Anytime we wanted too."

"So you agreed to this?"

"We could go somewhere this summer. Like Chicago or New Orleans. Wouldn't that be cool? New Orleans?"

That idea sounded so good. Going somewhere else.

Rex really did have a lot of brothers. They were all coming and going. Taking showers, using the phone, popping beers. Heather and Rex were talked how many bags of weed it would take to fill up a whole room. I think they were talking specifically about the kitchen.

Evan, Rex's oldest brother and the one who looked the most like him, came through the door with a case of Milwaukee's Best. Evan was really hot. My eyes lit on him and I couldn't move them.

"You find the hand drill?" Evan asked Rex.

"Yeah. It's jammed, though. It doesn't work."

"So what? You don't need it to work."

"That's true." Rex shrugged.

"Heather, stop giving him pot. He doesn't need to be completely wasted while this whole thing goes down," Evan said.

"We're gonna sell these." Heather touched the pile of joints.

"Did you get a bag for me too?" Evan asked.

"It's on your bed." Heather nodded slowly.

Evan smiled at her and she dipped her head a little. God, did Heather fuck Evan sometimes too? If her mom knew how many hot guys Heather got her hands on, maybe she'd drop the tit thing all together.

Mantis nudged me toward the door and we stepped outside. He produced two beers from his coat pocket.

"You nervous?" He asked.

"Yeah."

We sat on a stack of wet, stinking wood pallets.

"What the fuck do you think this shit is for?" Mantis asked, rapping his knuckles against one.

"Nothing, apparently."

We could see Luann's yard. There were string lights looped through the trees and Warren appeared under the motion light dragging a life size dummy through the gravel.

"Their Halloween parties are fun. They go all out. You see all them tombstones and shit they got set up?"

"Oh, yeah. What's that?" I asked, pointing to a shadowed object under one of the huge pine trees that lined their driveway.

"Casket. They got everything. And always plenty of beer and weed and shit."

Luann's life wasn't so glamorous. Shitty house, fucked up parents, people her age running in and out buying drugs all the time. What the hell am I doing here watching Heather stumble around a plywood kitchen while I plan to beat up Mindy Overton?

I took a gulp of beer. Everything in me was slipping and blurring. It was still Rudy's world I would go home to. My mother there, still trying, but gone all the same. No matter what happened tonight, my bedroom door would still swing open or be pummeled by Rudy's fists. And then there was Mantis. Next to me. Cute and smart and mine. But he couldn't be trusted. And where the hell was Shelby, anyway? Wasn't she supposed to be here?

"You should spend the night with me tonight," Mantis spoke into my neck, his breath warming the prickly flesh under my ear. Even if I couldn't trust him, I needed to feel like that. I needed to feel my body wake up.

"What? On that little couch of yours?"

"It folds out," he said.

"Oh yeah?" I tried my best teasing voice. "We'll see."

"Okay, what's going on over here?" It was Colleen. That meant Shelby had arrived. I pushed Mantis off to the side. Shelby had a big grin on her face.

"Show time," Rex said, emerging from the house. Heather was behind him with her hands on his shoulders.

"Don't worry," she said.

"I'm fine," Rex told her. But he didn't look fine. He looked scared.

"Remember," I piped in. "The front door is open."

"Yeah. Yeah. I got it. See all of you soon." Rex headed the direction of Lemay Ferry. He was meeting Troy and Curtis in the liquor store parking lot. We all watched him trudge down the driveway.

"God, I hope this works out," Heather said, crossing her arms into her thick black coat.

"Don't worry," I said, somewhat unconvinced myself.

CHAPTER 26

A car pulled down Rex's driveway and shut off. It was Robyn. I could tell by the silhouette her hair made when she got out of the car. She crunched along the driveway in high-heeled black boots. The heels were low—two inches tops—and they were almost as wide as her foot. They were sexy, but they could do business, too.

"Mark here yet?" Robyn asked. The light hit her beer can and it looked like a shiny, silver knife.

"No, not yet," I said.

"Bastard. It's time." Just as Robyn spoke, headlights turned a spotlight on us.

"Let's go!" A man's voice called through the white glare.

Evan came racing out the door, poking his arms through the sleeves of his jacket as he went.

"Good luck." Heather leaned in and kissed my cheek, moving me forward with her palms against my back.

"I should go with you," Mantis said.

"Sit down stud boy. That's my job," Shelby said.

We went for Evan's van.

"Wait, you two don't need to come along," Evan said.

"They're coming with us!" Robyn yelled.

"Yeah. Let them see the show, Evan," Vince called.

Evan shrugged and we all jumped in the van. It was on, as they say.

Evan followed behind Robyn and Mark, making a caravan that whirled down the exit ramp and onto Highway 55.

"Where are we going?" Shelby asked.

"Arnold. You know the water tower that looks like a big flashlight?"

"Yeah."

"Randy don't live far from it."

It took forever to get there. I had to piss like mad and my stomach was clenched so tight acid came up and burned my throat. I'd never been nervous like that before.

After we got off the highway, the caravan twisted through a series of narrow roads with no white lines.

"God, it's so dark out here," I said.

"No street lamps," Evan said, bobbing his head to Eddie Money coming out of that staticky radio.

We took one last big curve and the caravan pulled over onto a grassy shoulder and stopped.

"That's Randy's place down there." Evan pointed.

"At the end of the cul-de-sac?" Shelby asked.

"Um, yeah. Don't call it culdysac out here, though."

"What do you call it?" I asked.

"Dead end." Evan shrugged.

"I gotta piss." I looked at Evan.

"Piss then. Isn't nobody gonna notice you."

I climbed out of the van and squatted in a mound of weeds beside it. The hot piss made steam and it smelled, somehow, very good to me.

When I got back into the van, Randy was at the driver's side window.

"You know what to do?" Randy asked Evan.

"Course," Evan said.

"All right, well, me and Mark are gonna be around back. Vince has got the wheel on Mark's truck. So, I'll see ya in a few." Randy spoke only to Evan. Shelby and I could have been in Alaska for all he cared.

We sat in the dark. Evan listened to the radio on low and none of us spoke. Then headlights came around the curve behind us. Evan eyed the car as it passed.

"Got a red Mustang," he said.

My lungs froze and my stomach turned out more acid into the back of my throat. Shelby put her hand over mine and we watched the Mustang pull into the driveway and stop. The occupants took a few minutes getting out of the car.

"Amateurs." Evan shook his head. "Don't even know how to move on something when they get to it."

Randy had left on the porch light. We could see everything perfectly as Curtis, Troy and Rex stepped out of the car.

Troy and Curtis leaned against the driver's side door of the Mustang as Rex approached the house. He carried his jammed hand drill as if it would be necessary. Troy and Curtis did their best to look casual. God, they looked like those people leaving the liquor store while Inez performed. Forced nonchalance so suspicious a blind man would question their motives.

Rex swung the door open and threw his hands up like they'd just won the lottery. I mean, who would have expected the door to just be open like that? Rex stepped back, and Troy and Curtis tried to affect a stroll as they rushed inside.

Rex watched through the open door for a moment, pulled it closed, and turned toward the line of dark cars a house down. He gave an exaggerated and sustained thumbs up sign.

"Okay," Evan muttered.

All three cars started, but kept their lights dark. Rex moved to the back of the Mustang and opened the trunk. Troy and Curtis came out of the house. Troy had long rifle-type guns in both hands. The light from the porch bulb hit them with a sick yellow-black glow. Curtis had a long black case in his hands. They hoisted the goods into the trunk, then talked with Rex.

Once Troy and Curtis were back inside the house, Rex turned to the cars and gave the same sustained thumbs up.

"What does that mean?" Shelby asked Evan.

"It means everything is on track, but don't move in," Evan told her with obvious relish.

Troy and Curtis came back out of the house, hands full of stuff. Another long rifle-type gun and a series of small cases. All of the stuff was dumped into the trunk of the Mustang. Troy and Curtis turned toward the doors of the car and Rex stuck his arm straight up and brought it back down. The way they did on *Happy Days* to signal a drag race.

The whole caravan moved forward in a smooth line. Evan pulled his van up on the grass in front of the door. Vince pulled Mark's truck up to the other side of the Mustang, and Robyn wedged her Cutlass long ways across the end. They were boxed.

Troy came face to face with the nose of Evan's van, he let out a yelp and ran off to the left side of the house, but Evan was already out of the van and grabbed him by the shirt.

"C'mere you little bastard," Evan snarled.

"Get the fuck off me!" Troy clawed the air.

Troy was a big kid and even though Evan was bigger, he had to struggle to keep a hold on Troy.

"We got you now, you little son of a bitch!" Randy came around from the back of the house and together they got Troy under control.

Randy was wearing Rex's ski mask with the Dead Kennedys patch on it.

Shelby and I followed behind the struggling Troy to where Curtis had locked himself inside the Mustang, its trunk still open and piled with Randy's things.

Rex mocked Curtis. "Where you gonna go, man? Huh?"

Vince and Mark and Robyn were gathered around the car, all smiles.

"Especially without these." Rex taunted Curtis with a dangling key ring.

"Get out of the car!" Vince yelled.

Curtis was pissing himself.

"Fuckin' let go of me!" Troy lunged his shoulder back at Evan, shaking Evan's grip a little. Evan responded by smacking his forehead against the hood of the Mustang.

"Keep still," Evan growled.

Rex jumped on the hood of the Mustang, holding up a key chain. He bounced the front end of the car then took a huge jump, wrinkling the shinning metal beneath his boots.

"Oh c'mon, man, stop," Curtis's muffled voice came from inside the car.

Rex went face first against the windshield, "Get out here and make me, you fuckin' dick. Get out and make me get off your car." Rex got back on his feet and jumped again and again into the metal.

Vince swiped the keys out of Rex's hand and unlocked the driver door.

"Here we come, ready or not," Vince sang.

In an instant, Curtis was out of the Mustang, held by Vince and Mark. Rex sat down on the hood and laughed at them. "Man, I'm so glad I'm not you right now."

Troy and Curtis were slammed against Evan's van. Held by four grown men.

"Now look, we're all just gonna have a little talk, okay?" Randy spoke through the ski mask.

Robyn went around to the trunk and opened one of the small cases. Out of it came a small silver hand gun. My guts locked and I thought maybe I had to piss again. I'd never seen a gun anywhere except in the movies and seeing Robyn with one in her grasp was more frightening than I'd expected.

"See that?" Randy asked Troy. "See that gun?"

"Oh, here, let's give you a good look," Robyn said, pointing the silver gun directly into Troy's face. Troy's body tried to recoil into the side of the van but there was nowhere to go.

"You getting a good look at that, son?" Randy asked.

"Yes. Oh god," Troy muttered, breathing heavily. His face was so pale and twisted he hardly looked like himself.

"That's my property," Randy put his mouth right up to Troy's ear, poking his lips through the ski-mask.

"C'mon guys," Curtis begged.

Shelby gripped my arm.

"Jesus," Curtis sputtered.

"Boy, you two are getting awfully religious out here," Vince said. "Ain't they? All God and Jesus?" Everyone laughed. As scared as I was I laughed too.

"They're not loaded, they're not loaded," Troy murmured to himself.

"Yeah? How the fuck would you know? Huh? Did you check?" Robyn asked.

Troy was visibly sweating and I was getting antsy. Right down to the tips of my toes, which were curling and tickling.

"DID YOU CHECK?" Robyn asked again, waving the gun in his face.

"No," Troy said. His body going limp. They were breaking him. Turning him to mush right in front of me.

"Well, then, you don't really know shit, do you?"

Troy fell further into Randy and Evan's grip.

"Look," Robyn said coolly. "I'm not gonna ask you everything twice, okay? So, let's you try and answer me the first goddamned time I ask you something."

Troy nodded and the first of his tears began.

Robyn grabbed him by his hair and yanked his head back. "A nod is not an answer!"

"Okay, okay." Troy barely had any breath in his lungs.

"So, again, you don't know shit, do you?"

"No."

"Say it."

"What?"

"Say that you don't know shit."

"I don't know shit." It occurred to me that Troy might pass out. I laughed. God. Fuck. I hated him. I hated him so much. I didn't care if Robyn did shoot him. Both of them.

Robyn kept her eyes steady on Troy but moved the barrel of the gun toward Curtis. "Get that one on his knees," Robyn said.

"You heard the lady, on your knees," Vince said as he and Mark shoved Curtis to the ground.

"So," Robyn turned the gun back on Troy. "I heard you liked to get your dick sucked."

"What? No."

"No?" Randy asked, laughing at Troy. "C'mon, boy, at least pretend like you a man."

Robyn smiled that amazing hateful smile of hers. "Let's try it again. You like to get your dick sucked?"

"Yes." Big tears rolled down Troy's face.

"Yes, what?"

"Yes . . . I like . . . to get my dick sucked. Oh God. Please."

"I heard you like an audience too, that's why your buddy here is gonna watch you get your dick sucked. Just the way you like."

"Please. This is crazy. I'm sorry!" Troy struggled the words out around his tears.

"Let him go," Robyn told Evan and Randy.

They dropped their grasp on him, but Troy did nothing except cower.

"Drop your pants," Robyn told him.

Troy didn't move.

Robyn slammed his body into the van, "What's a matter party boy? I thought you liked to get your dick sucked! Drop your goddamned pants before I blow your fucking head off!"

Troy's hands went for his belt buckle. He was shaking so hard he couldn't get a hold on it.

"Let's go, c'mon," Robyn said.

Randy and Evan were still on either side of him. Laughing.

Troy finally got his buckle open and his fly undone. He pushed his pants down to his knees. He was taking in sharp breaths and tears ran down his neck.

"All the way, c'mon. I'm gonna suck your fuckin' dick, just like you want!"

Troy bent and pushed his pants all the way down to his ankles.

Robyn shoved him back up against the van, his bare legs shaking and turning inward.

Robyn took the barrel of the gun and lifted his jacket and shirt a few inches above his penis.

"So there it is. Make sure that one gets a good look," Robyn said to Vince who pulled Curtis's hair and forced his face toward Troy's exposure.

"Say you want your dicked sucked," Robyn said, her eyes level with Troy's, the tip of the gun barrel grazing Troy's penis.

"I . . . want my . . . dick . . . sucked." Troy blew each word out of his mouth with tremendous effort.

We all stood there like that for a minute listening to Troy cry with his penis hanging limply in the cold air and Curtis being forced to observe it.

Finally, Robyn dropped his shirt and jacket. She backed up a step and through seething teeth she said, "I ain't gonna suck that worthless thing." And she spit right in his face before she walked away. Troy slid down the side of the van into a crumpled ball and held himself between his legs.

Seeing him like made me angry. I felt a hatred so deep all I could do was act on it. I ran at him and kicked him in the head as hard as I could. The toe of my boot caught him right behind his ear with a dense thump. Troy's body shot to the side, landing on his bent arm. It should have been louder—the kick should have been louder.

"You come near me again, I'll bite it off and ram it up your ass!" I guess I balled my fists, reflex or something, but Shelby grabbed me from behind.

"Enough. That's enough now," she breathed into my ear. Suddenly I realized I was crying too. Crying as hard as Troy, only my sobs were furious rather than frightened.

"I'm going to KILL HIM!" I screamed, struggling against Shelby's grip. Troy brought his arms up over his head. That act, that act of fear and self-defense, infuriated me. I was the monster and the more fear I sensed, the more fear I wanted to produce.

That's when the cherry lights came whirling around the curve.

CHAPTER 27

"It's the cops, Angie!" Shelby said into my neck. I stopped struggling against her. Rex fled to the back of the house. Two cops jumped out of one of the patrol cars and ran after him.

Shelby dropped my arms, I threw a look at Robyn.

"Who called the pigs?" Robyn asked Randy.

"I don't know," he said.

Troy struggled to get his pants up and wipe the tears off his face. I caught his eyes. Pathetic. We'd done him in. I held his gaze for a second. I now owned a part of Troy Mulligan.

Two cops strode slowly between the cars, cherry lights still circling. One of them was a real big guy. Not just tall but heavyset. As he closed in on us, he pulled his flashlight out and gave each of our faces a good jolt of bright white light. By the time he was done we were all squinting and hanging our heads away from it.

"I can't wait to find out what's goin' on here," he said.

"Who's house is this?" the smaller cop asked.

"Mine," Randy stepped forward.

"Okay, everyone else, over here," the big cop motioned to Evan's van with his flashlight.

"Officer, these people pulled guns on . . ." Curtis was trying to talk to the cop.

"You'll get your chance, son. Just be quiet. I want to see every-one's ID."

"If this is your house, why'd I see you take that ski mask off when we pulled up?" the smaller cop asked Randy.

"It's Halloween." Randy shrugged.

"Ain't that the truth? So, tell me what happened here." The cop took a pad out of his pocket and leaned back on his heels.

"Well, I come home with my friends here, and those two are over there, filling up the trunk of this car with my guns. So we blocked them in, and grabbed them."

The big cop was looking at Curtis's ID. "That true?"

"No, it was him!" Curtis pointed to Rex, who was being dragged back around the house by the other two cops. His mouth was bleeding.

"Oh, my god!" I said. "What did you do to him?"

"Shut it!" One of the cops holding Rex said.

"He was with us," Randy said.

"Then why you runnin', son?" the cop pushed Rex over the hood of Curtis's car and cuffed him.

"I didn't do anything!" Rex spat blood as he spoke and the other cop kneed him in the gut.

Rex dropped onto the driveway at my feet and moaned.

"Got a nice attitude on him," one of the cops said.

I stared down at Rex, his mouth bleeding, his knees curled into his stomach. His kicked-in stomach. I just stared. There was nothing else to do.

"I told you to get your ID out," the big cop said, shining that light in my face.

"I don't have one."

"Why not?"

"I don't drive."

"How old are you?"

"Sixteen."

"What's your name?"

"Angie Neuweather."

"Neuweather? I used to know some Neuweathers."

"My family is from just south of here," I said, still staring down at Rex.

The cop put his flashlight down and looked at me until he caught my eyes. He studied my face for a second.

"Ever been in trouble before?"

"No."

"That's good," he said, and moved on to Robyn.

We all stood around while everyone's name was ran and Randy's paperwork on the guns was checked. They made Rex lay on the ground for at least an hour while they noted everything.

"He didn't do anything!" I protested.

"Keep quiet." The cop shined his light in my face. I dropped my head.

Finally it was decided that Troy and Curtis and Rex would all be taken into custody and the guns would be taken as evidence.

"You a karate man?" the big cop asked Randy.

"No, why?"

"Trunk's full of all this stuff." He held up what appeared to be a Chinese star. "All those outfits too. Where'd you boys get all this?" He asked Troy and Curtis. Neither said anything.

"Gonna wait for your lawyer, huh? Well, I'll just make a note about you not cooperating. That okay with you boys?"

Troy and Curtis were lowered into the backseat of a patrol car.

"Watch your head," a cop said.

The big cop looked over at Rex as the other two cops lifted him to his feet. His boots were untied.

"I didn't do anything and I don't have a record," Rex said.

"We gotta take you in," the big cop said, completely matter of fact. Radios were sending garbled messages. Beeps went off between them. The cops nodded and gestured to one another. I was dying to pace. Just start on a pacing jag and go until morning.

The cop bashed Rex's head against the car as he shoved him in the backseat.

"Resisting arrest," he said and slammed the door shut.

"Needs a legal guardian to pick him up," the big cop told Evan.

Evan nodded his head. "Thank you, sir."

Before the big cop got in his car, he walked over to me. "You think of anything else, about tonight, you can give us a call." He put a business card in my hand.

Then the two cop cars pulled off without their cherries. And one cop jumped behind the wheel of Curtis's red Mustang and headed after them.

"Fuckin' pigs." Evan said to their brake lights.

"He shouldn't a run," Randy said.

"Shit, I almost ran," Evan laughed.

"Why'd he give you a card?" Shelby asked me.

"I dunno," I said, looking down at the card. The name on it was Seth Thompson.

CHAPTER 28

On the way back, Robyn smoked and drove the highway. Shelby stretched out in the back and I was bolt upright in the passenger seat.

"Angie, relax will you? You're giving me the creeps," Robyn said.

I leaned back, took a deep breath. "Is Rex gonna be okay?"

"Yeah, as soon as they let him go, he'll be fine. They're just makin' a point."

"A point?"

"Yeah, that's what I said. Here take a cigarette, Angie. You're a wreck." Robyn dropped her pack of Marlboro Lights into my lap.

I lit up a smoke and watched the houses along the highway.

"And there's another half to this plan?" Shelby asked from the backseat. "I'm exhausted."

"You don't have to do anything except keep your eyes open. Angie does the rest."

"What are you going to do?" Shelby asked.

"Fight Mindy." I blew out a long stream of smoke.

"What?" Shelby sat up. "Where?"

"Luann's party."

"You really think Mindy's going to show up?"

"Carrie told her that Luann is fucking Troy. She'll show up."

"Wait. Slow down. You can't trust Carrie Shuren. No matter what you think! AND what did Luann do that was so bad you'd sic Mindy on her? Look what Mindy did to get YOU back. You shouldn't have done that, Angie."

"It's not gonna go that far, Shelby," Robyn said.

As I took another drag of cigarette, my insides loosened and slipped around.

"I didn't think about Luann getting hurt," I said to the window.

"Everybody, just relax. Angie, you'll get to Mindy before she gets to Luann."

"Were late though," I said. I was, all the sudden, absolutely alarmed. "What time is it?"

"It's 9:50. Were fine. We left plenty of time to take care of Troy."

"What if they got there early?" I asked.

"Oh shit," Shelby said and fell back into the seat.

"Will you two stop already. Nobody is gonna be anywhere early. Okay?"

Robyn leaned in and turned up the radio.

The three of us pulled into the driveway at Luann's. Warren was a vampire, cape and everything. He stood over a big barbeque grill with a beer bottle in one hand and a pair of long-handled tongs. He was putting a hot dog in a bun for a man with big tits under his t-shirt and a blonde wig tangled in his long dark beard. People were in little groups talking and eating. One guy had a big screw going through his head. All grown ups. All Crystal and Warren's friends. My knees were actually knocking.

An electric cord snaked out of the open window to a crock pot Crystal was stirring. Around her were stacks of paper plates and cups and plastic forks. She was dressed like a sexy witch. Tits popping out of a tight black dress that showed off her big, curvy figure. She had a warty, pointy chin stuck on her face.

"This shit drives me crazy. Costumes and shit," Robyn said as she turned the car off just a few feet from the barbeque pit.

"You parked in the yard, Robyn," Shelby said.

"So write me a ticket." Robyn got out of the car.

"Witches brew!" Crystal called to a crowd of people I realized went on and on into the darkness.

"Where's Luann?" I asked Crystal. I half expected to find Mindy and Luann wrestling each other on the ground.

"Luann? Around back somewhere. Have some cider, it will warm you up." Crystal smiled and winked. I took the hot cup.

"We were a real mess when you came by the other day. That happens sometimes," she said.

"Yeah." I walked away.

I went slowly through the dark, methodically, placing one foot in front of the other. The hot cider slopped on my hand. I wasn't in a hurry to find Mindy. This was a dumb idea. This was a really dumb idea. But it was going to happen anyway.

I walked all the way around the house until I was about to come from behind Crystal and back to the front again.

"Why can't you just drop it?" I heard Mantis's voice come from the darkness. I stood completely still, listening.

"Why should I drop it?" It was Luann.

"What do you want me to do?"

"Tell the truth. Isn't a problem for most people."

My mouth involuntarily unhinged and I said, "Yeah, Mantis what's the truth?"

"Angie? Where'd you come from?"

"Let's just get around to this truth thing."

"Yeah, tell her, Mantis," Luann said with a great big laugh.

"Luann and I had sex more than once. There, you happy Luann?" Mantis leaned into Luann just as headlights from the neighbors drive way spilled over them. Luann was in sexy devil costume. The light glinted on her horns and shut off, returning all three of us to darkness.

"So you two were dating?" I asked.

"Yes," Mantis said.

"Tell her the last time you had sex with me," Luann said.

"The morning after Heather's party. After you left," Mantis said.

"So, are you dating Luann now?"

"No." Mantis said.

"Is that true Luann?"

"We aren't dating anymore," Luann said.

"Well, I'm not going out with Mantis anymore, either. You can take him back if you want."

"Angie! That's not fair. We weren't going out yet."

"Shut up, Mantis." I went straight for the lit driveway with barbeque smoke rising all around it.

When I turned the corner, Warren was putting hot dogs in buns for Shelby and Colleen.

"You find Luann?" Shelby asked, stuffing a hotdog end into her mouth.

"Yeah, I found her. Mindy hasn't been here."

"You look pissed," Shelby said and stuffed the whole rest of the hotdog and it's mustardy bun into her mouth.

"You are never gonna be able to swallow that," I said.

"Uh-huh," Shelby struggled with the mouthful. Colleen grabbed a couple of napkins. Mindy and Carrie came striding into the circle of light.

"Excuse me," Mindy said to Warren. "Is Luann around?"

Carrie and I gave each other a look. I couldn't read her.

"Luann? She's here somewhere. You don't have on a costume," Warren said to Mindy.

"Oh, I came as the girl next door," Mindy cooed. A hunk of half chewed mustard hotdog went flying out of Shelby's mouth and landed near the back of the barbeque pit. Mindy didn't notice, or pretended not to. Shelby coughed and laughed.

"Okay, you're gonna have to pick that up," Warren said. "That's disgusting, really, it is."

Shelby just kept laughing and coughing, her mouth ringed in mustard.

"There you are," Mindy pointed up at Luann, who had just come around the house with Mantis.

"What are you doing here?" Luann stopped and planted her hands on her hips. In her tight red dress I could see her little pot belly. Luann had a pot belly? God, it looked so good on her. How the fuck did she do that?

"I know what you've been doing," Mindy said to Luann.

"Girls, no fighting," Warren swung the long spatula out.

"And no farting!" A drunk cat lady said.

We watched her stumble away.

Shelby busted out laughing, again.

"You've been fucking Troy." Mindy pointed. Heads turned to look at her. I couldn't believe she just started going off, right there in front of Luann's parents. In front of everyone.

"Troy Mulligan?" Luann's head flew back and she just plain cackled. "Mom, did you hear that?"

Crystal sucked back her laugh, covering her face with her hand, but loud snorts were coming out anyway.

"Just laugh Crystal," Warren said. "You're going to get the hiccups."

Crystal laughed out loud.

Mindy was beside herself. She looked around at everyone. There was Luann and the rest of us. The tit and screw guys, not to mention a Ronald Reagan, a gorilla face, a sexy nurse, and Pinhead from *Hellraiser*.

"Are you here to kick my ass?" Luann stabbed her red-gloved hand in Mindy's direction.

The thing at Randy's house was supposed to be the hard part. This was supposed to be easy. Just a little thing. No big deal. But this was so much more complicated. There were people everywhere. Grown ups. And it looked as if Mindy and Luann were going to fight. This was the worst idea anyone ever had. I'm not Robyn. I can't do things like this.

"All right," Warren stepped in front of Mindy. "You and your friend can just go now."

"I just want to talk to her." Mindy appealed.

"I don't think that's true," Warren said easily.

"Let's go," Carrie took Mindy by the arm.

"No, Carrie." Mindy yanked her arm back.

"No, Carrie," Luann mimicked.

Robyn appeared beside me, "We can just follow them."

"What?"

"Fuck this. Get in the car."

I looked at Robyn for a second.

"Let's go." Robyn threw her hands up.

I didn't think. I just moved for the car door. I didn't know what was happening anymore. And I didn't care.

I rolled down the window and listened.

Crystal stood next to Warren. "This isn't the place for boyfriend fights."

"Who are you anyway?" Mindy asked, thrusting her chin out.

"We are Luann's parents, you snot-faced little bitch." Crystal said this with a perfect, pleasant smile on her face.

"Mindy," Carrie whispered.

"Fine, we'll go. But you and me are gonna talk, eventually," Mindy yelled over Warren's shoulder.

CHAPTER 29

Carrie backed down the driveway. Robyn did a full circle through the yard with her headlights out. She followed Carrie one car between.

We passed Rex's house and the headlights landed on Pike and Inez, walking along the shoulder. Inez was dragging a big pink panda. It was almost as big as she was.

"What are we doing now?" I asked Robyn.

"I dunno. But this ends tonight, one way or another."

Robyn followed Carrie into Stonehenge Estates, a cluster of huge new houses. Rambling and done with plenty of windows and fancy lighting. Still, there were only forty or fifty feet between them. When the place was being built, my mother said, Spend half a million and live right on top of each other. Money is wasted on the rich.

"Where are we?" Robyn asked.

"I dunno. This isn't Carrie's house."

There were only twelve houses in Stonehenge, so Robyn's car stood out like a flying saucer. One perfectly carved jack-o-lantern was on every porch in the exact same place with the exact same toothy grin.

Robyn pulled into a short driveway behind Carrie. I looked up at the house. It was huge. Three stories in some places. Lit up like a Christmas tree too.

"Overton. On the mail box," Robyn said.

"We're at Mindy's house?"

"Yep."

We got out of the car.

"WHAT the fuck is this?" Mindy asked.

"Just want to talk to your parents," Robyn said, walking across the lawn straight for the front door.

"You can't just . . ." Mindy called after her.

"I can't just ring the doorbell? Don't be stupid." Robyn was completely calm.

Carrie's head snapped my direction. I shrugged. I hadn't planned on this. I went for the porch, keeping my eyes on Carrie. The color went out of her face.

I ended up at the door with Robyn and Mindy. Carrie stood back in the yard just staring at the front of the house. I swallowed hard.

The door opened.

A tiny woman with short auburn hair, appeared with a bowl of candy cradled against her chest.

"Oh, I thought you might be a late trick-or-treater! What are you doing out here Mindy?" The woman's eyes flitted over Robyn and me. We were so totally out of place. We didn't belong with Mindy, we didn't belong in the neighborhood, and we certainly didn't belong inside.

"Carrie's just dropping me off," Mindy said and stepped into the house.

"Oh." The woman didn't know what to do with the door. Shut it, stand in it?

"We need to talk to you, and your husband, if he's around." Robyn said.

"Is something wrong?"

"Yep." Robyn gave one big nod.

A man appeared behind the woman.

"Hi, I'm Joe." He stuck his big hand out to Robyn and me.

"Robyn and Angie," Robyn spoke for me.

"Well, Robyn, what can we do for you?"

"It's about Mindy," Robyn said. "She helped her boyfriend force his dick into this girl's mouth." Robyn put her hands on her hips.

"What? That's not possible." The big man's brow wrinkled into a million tiny ravines.

"Carrie, tell them! Tell them I didn't do it!" Mindy's shout came over Joe's shoulder.

Carrie was standing right behind us. Robyn stepped back and made way for her, but Carrie just stood there, scratching at her palm.

"Dad, this girl was trying to steal Troy. They have been making up stuff all over school about Troy. But it never happened. She just likes him, that's all. You don't know what her and her friends are like." Mindy pointed at me.

"Carrie are you part of this rumor-spreading?" The woman asked.

Carrie glanced back at her mom's car for a second. I thought she might even run.

"I saw Mindy. Her and Troy. I was there," Carrie finally said, and I thought I might explode.

Joe Overton froze next to his wife who was white-knuckling the candy bowl.

"Dad," Mindy's voice was deep. "Let me tell you what happened. These people hate me."

It was true. I hated her.

Robyn folded and unfolded her arms. Her fake leather half-jacket squealed like tires on pavement.

"Let's go inside," Joe Overton said.

The group of us stepped over the threshold onto Planet Beige.

Robyn—in her squeaky jacket and tight jeans—settled on the arm of a big, overstuffed beige chair. I followed Carrie to the couch. Robyn fidgeted.

"Sit," Mr. Overton gently instructed Mindy and his wife. He tugged the candy bowl away and set it on the glass-top coffee table.

"Robyn." Joe directed his attention. He stood in the arch between the couch and the door. The passage was huge, but he filled it completely somehow. "Finish your story."

"It's not my story." Robyn looked at me.

Blood rushed to my head, I was so scared.

"She was following me around!" Mindy said. "From the bathrooms, I mean, in the bathrooms. At school."

"Why were you doing that?" Mindy's mom asked. She was sharp.

"I just, I wanted her to stop, I wanted her to leave me alone."

"Well, she can't very well leave you alone if you are following her around, can she?"

I didn't say anything. I just focused myself on not crying. I should have just knocked Mindy's teeth out back at Luann's party. It would have been much easier.

"Well, answer me. How can she leave you alone if you are following her?"

"She likes Troy, Mom. That's what it's all about," Mindy said.

"Mindy helped Troy trap Angie in a bathroom. He gave her a black eye. I saw it," Carrie said.

"Joe!" The woman turned to the man in the archway. "Do something!"

"What do you want from us?" Joe asked Robyn.

"For you to do something about your kid." Robyn shrugged in her squeaky jacket.

"Carrie, how can you say these things about Mindy? Are you on drugs?" Mindy's mother asked.

"She's the one that did it, anyway!" Mindy leaned forward.

"What did you just say?" Joe looked at Mindy. Her mother froze.

"Just that she's the one who, I mean she helped . . ." Mindy's words trailed off. Her arm sunk out of the air and back to her lap.

No one breathed.

"You can all go now. Thank you for bringing Mindy home, Carrie." Mindy's mother said.

Mindy sunk her head into her hands and we left.

Carrie staggered back to her car.

None of us said anything.

CHAPTER 30

Robyn dropped me off at home. I was exhausted. Everything in me was just spent.

Mom and Rudy were watching *Friday the 13th*, in the dark.

"Have fun?" Mom asked.

"Something like that. Anything leftover to eat?"

"Yeah, we ordered a pizza," Rudy said. "Your favorite: sausage and onion."

I grabbed the box and sat on the floor near the two of them.

"How'd you know this was my favorite?"

"From your birthday. I got you pizza, remember?"

"Oh my God!" My mother buried her face in Rudy's shoulder, turning away from blood dripping on the screen.

"Shit. It's like life-size on this thing." I leaned against the couch and watched the rest of the movie with them. Rudy could still have packed up and moved out right that minute and I wouldn't have lost any sleep over it, but, for the moment, it was fine.

I tucked Seth Thompson's business card into the drawer in my night table. What was I supposed to do with it? Call him? I wasn't even sure if he was my father, and how would I know if he knew he's my father? Besides, the guy was a cop. I'd never met anyone who trusted a cop.

I was really tired but my thoughts were going around and around. Mantis. I had a boyfriend for, like, one minute. Am I still a virgin? That sex thing didn't really work. Or did it? The cops are going to end up calling me for something. A witness or something. Rex is bloody and waiting for someone to find his dad so he can get out of jail. Mindy's parents know what happened. And Rudy is ordering my favorite pizza. None of my problems were solved.

The *Serial Killers* book was still on my nightstand. I picked it up and slid it under my bed. I'd had enough of all that. I stared at the ceiling for what must have been hours before I fell asleep. But once I did, I never moved until I heard Mom knocking.

"Yeah?" I looked around to make sure where I was.

"Carrie is here to see you," Mom called through the door.

"Just a minute." I looked at the clock: 12:47. I'd slept through the morning. My right arm was totally numb.

I poked my head out and motioned Carrie into my room. Her eyes were rimmed red and she didn't have make up on. Her hair was pulled back in a short ponytail and she was wearing blue jeans. I'd never seen that before.

"What is it?" I asked.

She sat down on my bed. I shook my sleeping arm out.

"Angie, the Overtons called my parents." Thin tears streamed out and she blew her nose on her sleeve.

"And?"

"And I'm in a lot of trouble and my mom is going to call your mom."

"No, no she can't," I said.

"I told her I didn't think you told your mom, so she brought me over to tell you to do it. She is calling tonight, and that is definitely going to happen."

"Shit. I didn't think the Overton's would want to talk about it."

"The Overtons don't. They called to tell my parents to talk some sense into me. It's my parents. They are really upset. My mom had a fight with Mindy's mom. Then my parents had a fight with each other. My mom's been crying all morning."

"What did you tell them?"

"The truth. I told them the truth."

"Even about you, you know?"

"Yes. I told them I was the lookout."

"You did? Why?"

"I have to tell the truth, don't I?" Carrie's eyes gave up more trails of water and she jerked her face toward the ceiling. That's what made Carrie so sexy—her absolute torture.

"I don't want my mom to know about it. Maybe I could talk to your mom. Maybe, I could talk her out of it," I said.

"Angie." Carrie turned to me. "You should tell your mom." Carrie sniffled and looked at me.

"There's no talking her out of it, huh?"

"No."

"Well, okay, then." My body was a rock. A rock with a rapid heart beat.

"I have to go. My mom's waiting for me outside," Carrie said.

"I met my dad last night."

"You never met your dad before?"

"He's a cop."

"Really? Did you, did he, I mean . . ."

"He gave me his card. I could call him, if I wanted to."

"Maybe you will."

"Maybe," I said, looking away as Carrie left.

I didn't bother waiting around. As soon as I heard the door shut behind Carrie, I strode straight into the living room. Rudy was there. But he was going to know anyway. Mom would tell him.

"I have to tell you guys something."

Both their heads snapped my direction.

"What is it?" Mom turned off the TV.

"Can we sit at the table?" I asked.

The table was official.

"I hope you aren't about to tell us your pregnant," Rudy said, holding my eyes.

"No. It's worse."

I told them the story. My mother patted my hand and listened.

Rudy sat so silent, I couldn't even hear him breathing.

"Why the hell did you wait so long to tell us?" Rudy asked when I finished.

"It's just a good thing you told us now," Mom said.

"Goddamnit!" Rudy's hand smacked the table top and everything on it rumbled.

"Don't be mad!" I said.

"I'm not mad at you, Angie. It's the one that did it. What was his name? I'm going to make him a hundred kinds of sorry!"

I'd started and I couldn't stop. I told them about the guns and Troy and Robyn and Randy and the cops. Everything except the Seth Thompson part.

My mother was gape mouthed.

"Angie, how could you get mixed up in all that? Police? GUNS?"

But Rudy was smiling. "You got him back."

"Rudy that's not the point!" Mom said.

"Yes, it is." Rudy was still smiling at me.

"Rudy, did you hear what she just said?"

"Yes, Rita. I heard every word. She got him back. Had him hanging out in the cold and everything. Damn, you women can be downright vicious." Rudy chuckled. He leaned his chair back and looked at me. He was nothing short of proud.

"Angie, that was really dangerous. What you did! You should have told me. We should have gone to the principal. This was the wrong way to handle things." Mom was pretty mad. Mad and just jangled. She was dropping ashes every where.

"Rita, don't worry. No one is gonna find out what happened. Those kids aren't gonna talk about something like that."

"It was still dangerous." Mom took her bottle of Seagram's out.

"We should go out today," Rudy said.

"Out? Out where?" Mom asked and made herself a drink.

"I don't know. Go relax some where."

"Wait, are we celebrating something?" Mom asked.

"Just relaxing. We could go to the Go-Kart track. There's a good one out on 44."

"Do you want to do that, Angie?" Mom asked.

"Sure. I've never done it before."

"You haven't?" My mother wrinkled her brow. "Well shit. Now I feel guilty. How'd I let you get this old and never been to a Go-Kart track before?"

CHAPTER 31

"You can't call the school," Aunt Jean told my mother.

"How is she supposed to go back if these two are still there?"

"You didn't think about this part, huh?" Aunt Jean said to me. She wasn't mad, but she was worried.

"I don't want to go back at all. Either way. I don't ever want to be there, ever again." I said.

"Angie, you are not dropping out of school. Just forget it," Mom said.

Mom and Aunt Jean sat at the table slowly sipping beers and smoking. My life had become one long series of people getting drunk and smoking while they figured out my problems.

"I think Rudy is right. I don't think they'll tell," I said.

"Finally!" Rudy called from the easy chair. "Somebody listened to something I said. Shit."

I left them to decide my fate and went to Shelby's. If they called the school I'd get busted for skipping. Maybe Troy would decide to tell his story. Everyone would be in trouble. I'd ask Robyn what to do. Maybe she'd help me one more time. It was weird. All of a sudden, loving Robyn. Like she was my sister. I'd never understood how Shelby could sometimes stand up for Robyn. Like the night she ran over and kicked Vince in the ribs. Now I'd do that. If I ever see it, that's exactly what I'll do.

"So, does Colleen have, like, a big fake dick?" I asked Shelby.

"You don't need a dick, Angie. It's not required."

"God, you are gonna be the best lesbian!"

"Shut up!"

"If you were Heather, would you get the tit?" I asked.

"Hell no. One is so hot! It's hotter than gaps in teeth," Shelby said. She poked her finger into her mouth.

"I would," I said. "I'd get it. My mistake would be not holding out for the car."

Shelby dunked a pretzel into a huge container of Rocky Road ice cream.

"You know Carrie has a plan to photosynthesize?" I said.

"That is seriously fucked up. Shit. She looks better when she's not so thin."

"I wonder if she's going to go back to school."

"I wonder if any of us are going back to school. We should all go to Hallsey! Get our own ashtrays in every desk. Wouldn't that be funny? Carrie Shuren at Hallsey?"

"Her parents were pretty okay. That's what my mom said. They're sending Carrie to a counselor. You know they offered to pay for a couple sessions for me? If I wanted to go?"

"That's fucking creepy!"

"Not the way they see it. They feel responsible. You should have seen Rudy! When my mom told him about the counseling, he laughed so hard he had to get stoned, and laugh some more."

"Are you liking Rudy all of the sudden?"

"No! But he hasn't been a total asshole lately." I shrugged. "Fuck photosynthesis." I jabbed a pretzel into the ice cream.

"I'm glad you broke up with Mantis, just so you know."

"Oh, I'll probably go back out with him. He just has to beg for a second. Shit. Everybody has to date a jerk sometime, right?"

"You don't have to start there."

"You gotta start somewhere, Shelby. Hey, I'm a manstealer, remember! And I'm the fat one!"

"You are not fat, Angie!"

"Yes I am. I'm fat and I'm a manstealer and I'm probably at least half gay and . . ."

"Oh, you are definitely at least half gay!" Shelby interrupted.

My eyes popped open. "How long have you been waiting to say that?"

"Since the first grade," Shelby said, stuffing an ice cream pretzel into her mouth.

THE END

Thousands of thanks to my BRILLIANT editors Ammi Emergency and Joshua Gass.

And many thanks to my other important readers: Shanna Owen, Casey Cottrell, D. Otis Cross, and Tennessee Jones.

Michelle Embree grew up in a working-class suburb of St. Louis. She dropped out of high school during the ninth grade and obtained her GED. Michelle Embree then worked for several years in sandwich shops and mall stores before moving on to small, classically oriented McKendree College where she earned her BA in sociology and philosophy. She has published articles on philosophy, media, and feminism, and currently writes the cult favorite fiction zine *A Zillion Chronicles of Near Love*. Michelle Embree now resides in New Orleans and is at work on her second novel, *Incinerated*. She lives with her beloved Chihuahua-Pomeranian mix, Mr. Pickles.